W.

For my brother

IF YOU'D BE SO KIND, AND YOU WOULDN'T
MIND, WOULD YOU REVIEW? DON'T WORRY
IF NOT, JUST THOUGHT I'D ASK.
HAPPY READING!

amazon.co.uk/dp/B0F7RVW3CY

1.

"I want her," Abel whined. "You hear me brother? I want my mama, right *now*!"

"If you want her then *here*!" said Tom, pulling out the heavy Colt Dragoon he kept in the holster on his hip and hurling it down at his elder brother's bare feet – the cool steel barrel bumping off his sibling's hot big toe. "Take that there fucking six gun and you go out and you find her! Get lost. Leave me be for Christ's sake!"

"You could have killed me doing that you know!" said Abel, rearing for a fight – or so it seemed to his brother – that Tom just wasn't interested in having.

"We'd both be better off if it had. Go on now and leave me be. Leave me be to mend this fence. Fucking sure you ain't gonna do it none. About all the use of a block ice in a fucking furnace."

"You swore!" said Abel, pointing out the plain facts as he always did.

"That so?" said Tom. "Hell, that's mighty perceptive of you Abel. Hey Frank?"

"Yes sir?" said Frank from down the fence a ways.

"Able Abel's gone and stated the obvious for us *again*."

"He always does Mister Liffey sir," said Frank.

Frank was about fifteen feet from the pair and though he didn't dare ever intrude on their fraternal conversations, he nonetheless interjected when Tom invited him to talk. Pretending not to listen, when actually listening quite closely, had become a skill he'd honed like a bowie blade on a whetstone. When he was invited in he always knew just what to say, which was why Tom took such a liking to him. He didn't speak out of turn though, for the fact was that he was black, meaning he was a man with limited options and fewer opportunities. In fact, Frank was wanted in another state, so speaking out of turn was not something one would catch him doing.

"Don't reckon we've much more light to go sir," said

Frank, using the back of his bare arm to mop up the sweat staining his forehead like a thick varnish on a freshly lacquered log table.

"Time for quitting? That what you reckon?" said Tom.

"Think so," said Frank, feeling like throwing the tools to the ground and leaving them there to rust, but not bothering to do so without first having obtained his employer's say so.

"Reckon you're right," said Tom. "Take the tools and gather them up while I fix us some food."

He threw the tools down for Frank to collect, then removed his handkerchief from the back pocket of his overalls.

"Of course maybe you've it prepared already Abel, am I right or am I wrong?" he said, dabbing at his own sweaty face.

"You're wrong," said Abel, swaying gently from side to side like a willow caught in a cool autumn breeze.

"By God Abel. Able to do nothing. Ain't that right?"

"Right," the elder brother grinned. "Goddamn nothing," he agreed.

Then the face melted into something sourer. Something forlorn and almost achy with angst.

"When's our mama coming home?" he asked all innocently. Sometimes Tom thought that he only asked such a question to rile him. If he'd understood his brother properly he'd have known that this wasn't the case. He liked a fight sometimes, but mostly just missed his mama.

"Go on out of my road will you!" said Tom, cocking his head back before making a mock head-butt in his brother's direction.

"Don't do that!" Abel scolded. "I'll tell pa."

"Our pa's dead. Many times I gotta tell you that? Honest to God brother, you're trodding all over my last nerves today. Tell you what? Why don't you go out and feed them there hogs? The bucket's just inside the shed. Surely you can do that."

"I don't want to. I want my mama."

"Mama's gone. Gone with the fucking wind. Woman up and left us years ago. Now leave be before I…"

"Before what? You gonna whup me? I'll tell. I'll tell mama what you done, then you'll get it. Tell her if you even think

6

about whupping me some."

Then the tears started. Once they got going in earnest then that meant an awful evening for the younger Liffey.

"Look," said Tom, taking his brother by the hand and guiding him into the shack they had for a home. "Listen to me closely. Your mama's gone. You understand me? *Gone*. She ain't coming back."

"But…"

"No buts. I mean it now, no buts. Be best you accept it once and for all and then we can get on with life as it is without her."

The elder brother's face contorted in confusion. "And…"

"Pa's gone too. There ain't no coming back for him none neither. Now you go and wash up while I cook us up some bacon."

"Can you burn it like mama does?" asked Abel. "Just the same way she does it?"

"I can do my best. But you just forget about seeing her again, you hear? Mama ain't coming back and neither is pa. Both of them ain't around no more. Alright?"

"Alright," Abel said, looking unsure but somewhat calmer. The tears weren't there anymore but he still wasn't fully settled. "Set the table for them anyway," he said, exacerbating his brother beyond all bounds of sanity.

"For fuck's sake, do you not *LISTEN*! They're gone! Gone, gone, *gone*. Goddamn it all to hell. I hate this hole. Hate this fucking life. Left us with nothing. Up and left me with a brother who has a brain the size of a fucking frog and a shithole shack that's so damn dusty I can hardly stand it," he said whilst, in his fury, picking up a chair and flinging it across the room, where it unfortunately collided with and cracked a dusty pane of glass that looked out onto the barren back yard where the pigs rooted around in that very same dust. "Do you see what you've done!" he screamed in Abel's face, with the elderly brother appearing to have shrunk in size considerably at his brother's bellowing.

7

"Everything alright sir?" said Frank from the front door.

"Does it look alright? Look what Abel made me do. *Look*!"

"Leave me be," Abel gurned. "Goddamn you who threw the chair. Not me."

"Well it was you that done the provoking. Pisses me off Frank."

Frank, being ever the diplomat, didn't disagree with a head shake and, likewise, showed his reticence to nod in agreement.

"Aggravating Frank. You better hope you don't have a brother out there somewheres. Because boy let me tell you this. They are sons of bitches. Break your back with whinging. Break your heart if they're dumber than a mule and keep crying for their *FUCKING MAMA*!"

Tom then picked up another chair, hurled it hard and this time struck Abel on the shin.

"Shouldn't have done that!" Abel cried. "When pa hears of this he'll be furious. You ought to know better."

"By God!" Tom said, seemingly talking to the roof. "He has the clairvoyance."

"What's that mean Mister Liffey?" said Frank, always eager to learn new words when they came his way.

"Why it means he can speak to the great beyond! Brother, you're a miracle."

"Shut up," said Abel as he massaged his already swollen leg. "Look what you done," he grumbled.

"God, it's a miracle. Think of it Frank. My own brother can communicate with those that have went into the great beyond. Brother! I want you to close your eyes. Close your eyes now and concentrate real hard. Picture pa. Picture him like as if he was right in front of you."

Abel looked to Frank for guidance. Getting nothing but a shrug instead, he shut his eyes and grinned along with his brother's command.

"Keep 'em closed now. Don't you open them peepers

for even a second. Picture pa. Now can you see him Abel? Tell me the truth now. Can you see him?"

"I can," said Abel, as his brother lifted a cup from the kitchen bench and dunked it in a full pale, making a shush signal with his forefinger for Frank to keep quiet.

"Can you call out to him now? Try Abel. Try it if you can."

Frank felt a giggle coming on that was soon dampened down by an overwhelming wave of pity for poor Abel Liffey. He wanted to tell Tom he was nothing but a big bully, but then thought better of it, for he'd been a bully many's a day in his younger years.

"You just call out now Abel," whispered Tom in mock awe.

"Alright," Abel nodded, eyes still squeezed shut tight. "Pa?" Eyes still closed he leaned forward. "He's looking at me brother. What you want I should say?"

"You tell him," Tom whispered with his hand on his brother's shoulder. "You tell him Tom says that he can go and *FUCK HIMSELF*!"

He then poured the cup of cold water right down Abel's back, the elder brother emitting a shriek so high it had only been replicated elsewhere in God's good kingdom when fruit bats get lost on their way home in the dead of night.

"Now set the table," Tom ordered, throwing the tin cup down on the dusty wooden floor of their shack. "Then sit down and wait for dinner."

Abel looked to Frank for guidance, getting another shrug instead. So Abel did as he was told and set the table. Then he sat down and waited patiently for his mama's black, burnt bacon.

2.

His mama always brushed his hair before bed, way back when he still had hair to speak of. When he got upset Abel tugged at his hair, and after so many years of temper tantrums there was little left. But back when his mother was still around, she'd come into the boys' bedroom and sit down on the edge of the straw mattress, her special brush in her hand.

She wasn't a particularly attractive woman. She possessed an extraordinarily bulbous nose, as well as a wart that sprouted several ugly hairs that for some inexplicable reason she never thought to trim. It would have been easy maintenance. A small pair of scissors would suffice for such a task, but strangely she never cut them. The nose was alright until about halfway down. At the midpoint it became a ball of cartilage, protruding in a way Abel thought charming; though Tom thought unpleasant. Tom was never fond of mother. Maybe because she never paid him the same amount of attention as she did Abel. Abel was the favourite, which was what softened him so, so Tom thought. The truth was that Abel was soft from the start. The boy'd been born differently. His mother knew that, though she was glad he was special. Poor Tom was just another baby boy, as common as the next and the next. Not Abel. Abel was the golden child upon whom his mother doted, as he would come to reciprocate when wise enough *to* dote.

Diligently, she would brush his hair nightly. She'd set her heavy haunches down lightly, so as not to disturb her son, sing a lullaby as she brushed with her ivory handled brush that Abel still clung to long after she'd run off and left them.

"Do you know?" she would say, which would get a grin from Abel, because he knew what was coming – it had happened every night, though never once failed to delight.

"Yes mama?" he would ask, playing his part.

"Do you know, that you are as sweet as a lady bug and as red and dotty as a strawberry flavoured bonbon?"

This got him giggling. It was as though this statement possessed a path that led directly to the simple boy's funny bone. Tom would feel queasy when such a statement was stated, feeling embarrassed by his brother for being so damn dumb -- though the real reason for his nausea was a blazing ball of hot envy eating away at him inside.

"Mama, will you get me a strawbry bonbon one day?" Abel asked almost every night.

"Now what would you want with a strawberry bonbon?" she would say.

"I don't know. Don't know what it is. Will you tell me what it is?"

"Maybe one day," she said, getting a kind of thrill from keeping this bit of information from the boy.

One day, when they were out playing in the backyard, Tom decided he'd had enough of this little interaction. He marched right up to his brother and said, "You wanna know what a bonbon is do you?"

"Oh yes!" said Abel, his little ruby cheeks ablaze with brotherly love.

"It's a big steamy pile of horse shit," snarled Tom. "So there, how do you like that?"

"It's not."

"It is. That's why mama won't never tell you what it is. Wants to keep calling you a pile of dung without you knowing about it none. You're an idiot. Bet you thought it was something nice. Well it ain't. So there."

"That's not…" Abel began blubbering.

"That's not what? Not nice? Well hell Abel, it's time you learned that that there lady lives in our house ain't nice none at all. Always tells me how much she really hates you. Tells me all the time."

"You're a liar!" Abel cried. "You're a big fat liar and I'm telling!"

"Go ahead. Reckon she'll just tell you more lies. Fill your head full of hope, then she'll just go right on back to calling you dung to your damn face."

"Fuck off!" said Abel.

"No *you* fuck off!" said Tom. He then shoved his brother to the ground, the elder getting a good scrape on his elbow for his trouble. "Tattletales get shot out in these here parts don't you know?" Tom said, pointing the gun he'd made with his finger and thumb directly at his sibling's head. "Hell, you'll be dead by

11

supper time if you tell. Ain't nothing as sure."

"Fuck you!" cried Abel as he got to his feet.

He then ran into the house screaming bloody murder for his mama, ranting about how his brother'd pushed him and hurt his arm. Tom just laughed, satisfied that he'd shattered the boy's dream of a mother who truly adored her eldest.

That night the same ritual occurred as it always did, though this time Tom had several welts from where his mama had whupped him with a belt, and Abel was lying still, this night not so eager to hear his mother call him a pile of dung.

"Do you know?" said the large woman with a kind smile plastered across her fat face.

"I don't wanna know mama," said little helpless Abel.

"Shush now and listen. Do you know that *you* are as sweet as a ladybug and as red and dotty as a strawberry bonbon?"

"I ain't mama," said Abel, looking around the woman's wide hips at his brother beaming a broad smile at him from his bed across the small space. Then Abel began to cry. Then he began to thrash around screaming. Then he started slapping himself in the face, and *hard*. He hit at himself and hit at himself, his screams loud enough to wake a corpse.

"Calm down!" said his mama. "Calm yourself at once Abel!"

Tom began to snicker, prompting a look from his mother that was so sharp it could cut solid steel.

"This your doing is it?" she asked the younger of the boys. "Because if it is I'll take the belt to you again." Tom shook his head, but when she turned away again, he stuck out his tongue at the woman. The mother of the boys grasped a hold of both of Abel's wrists and pinned him to the bed. "Stop now!" she boomed. "That's enough now Abel, alright? *Enough*!" But the boy was lost in a world of fury. Fury that didn't dwindle for some minutes, during all of which the woman who'd birthed him sat weighing him down waiting for the tantrum to cease. When he calmed, she blew her fringe away from her eyes and asked was he alright now? The boy blinked up at her, nodded, then rolled over, tired from the tears and in need of sleep. "Son of a bitch," she said as she stood, throwing the brush at her other boy's head, with the thing colliding with bone with an almighty crack. "You did this," she said softly. "You did it and I know you did. Get the fuck up out of that bed. Get *up*!" she said so sinisterly the child knew that there was trouble brewing for him.

He didn't want to get up, instead clinging tightly to the blanket, pulling it up round his chin as though the cloth were a shield she could not penetrate.

"When I say get up, you get up!" she said, tugging at the blanket. "By Christ, you're only making it worse. Now get... *UP*!"

With one almighty tug the blanket was torn from Tom's tiny hands. He thought quickly, thinking his chances of escaping another whupping would double the sooner he acted. So he bolted for the bedroom door.

His mother, though a fair size, was surprisingly nimble. She stooped and grabbed him by the bare ankle, making Tom fall face first toward that freshly brushed floor. The heels of his hands hurt from the collision, though he wasn't out of the woods yet.

"You're a wee bastard!" said his mother. But the boy was quick, and back on his feet again in a flash. He fled from the house out through the front door, slamming it so loud it woke their father from his drunken dozing.

"What in the hell?" he said, startled and confused by all the banging.

"Boy you get back in here," said his mother. "You get back here right now and you take your whupping."

"*NO!*" said Tom.

"No?" said his mother. "Did I hear you correctly there?"

"That's right," said Tom. "I said no."

"Son of a bitch," said his mama, a warm smile spreading across her plump lips. "I'll be damned."

Then Henry came to the door, his britches hanging down round his ass, his hair a tangle of messy curls, or what was left of them – he too was balding badly, as his firstborn child would someday come to be.

13

"What in the hell is going on?" he said, rubbing his eyes and squinting out into the darkness that his wife was looking at.

"Never you mind Henry. Go on back inside and nurse that there hangover. Don't concern you none."

"Damn coyotes I expect. Hope you have them there chickens in the coop."

"I have," said his wife. "Go on away on in there out of the road. Go on."

Henry grumbled something then returned to his bed. Tom Liffey's mama then told him that he could sleep out there that night. That it would do him some good to think over how he chose to speak to his elders. When Tom thought that sufficient time had passed, and that his mama'd gone to bed, he crept up to the house to try the doors. They were both locked, and poor Tom had no other recourse to remain outside, sleeping either with the pigs or lying on the cold hard earth. He had his pride, and chose the earth over the pigs.

He did not sleep well. Not well at all.

3.

Tom took great care not to make much noise as he crept out of bed once the world had gone dark. He didn't want to wake Abel, which wasn't a simple task to accomplish given how the elder brother was such a light sleeper. Any sound, no matter how slight, might cause him to stir and begin his whining for mama, which was always the worst at night. Not one night since she'd left did Tom not have to use that bloody brush on his brother's head. He hated how he'd had to replace his mother. Hated how he'd had to be both mother and father for Abel all day, every day. Sometimes he thought of running off like Abel's beloved mama had done. He nearly did some nights. Nearly vanished to leave Abel to his own devices, which would more than likely mean starvation, for he wouldn't know to go into town – he'd just stay at the house expecting both mama, pa and Tom to return sooner or later. No.

Leaving was not an option. But Tom did have one recourse.

He had his whiskey, which sat up on the top of the cupboard where Abel couldn't get at it, and, more than likely, didn't even know it was there to begin with. The younger brother was crafty enough to know to put it way up high, just like his pa before him. If the imbibing of alcohol were a profession, Henry Liffey would have left his family rich beyond measure after he'd croaked. But it wasn't a habit that paid, and the father of the family had fallen down drunk into a ditch one hard winter, lay there all night and froze to death right there. By the time someone happened upon him he'd begun to thaw, though many parts of his person had turned black with frostbite.

The feeling of fondness for the booze was as much a part of Tom as it was Henry, though if you asked him, Tom'd tell you that he had a handle on it, unlike his pa. But he didn't. Every night now he took to toting that jug out to the porch and letting it suck on him twice as fast as he could suck on the jug. It ate at him, though the young man let it. It oozed in like a poison, took more than it gave, leaving poor Tom Liffey grumpier than hell when the morning arrived.

The floorboard beneath the cupboard gave out quite a groan when stepped on, so Tom, being wily as a fox, trotted over the board with his chair, then – nimbler than a showgirl in one of the fancy shows he'd heard tell of from folks in town, but never managed to see for himself – he set the chair down really lightly, a few feet from that bad board and sprung up and down so quick it was quite a sight to see. Once the jug had been attained, the chair went back, and Tom Liffey went out onto the front porch to look out and see what he could see.

The night that the letter was en route to town, Tom took a stroll down the road a ways, well provisioned with plenty of fiery whiskey that burned in his belly and made his head lighter and lighter with every slug.

"Take it easy now Tom," he said to himself. "Not prudent for a fella to go wandering off a ways, when he's got folks that depend on him." But he felt something stirring in him that night. Like he knew what was coming but couldn't stop it.

He decided then that he'd head into town the next day, though it wasn't the day the money was wired.

Tom and Abel, as well as Frank – though the latter's association was unofficial – lived off a small supply of money wired in from Georgia each and every month. There was never a name. Just a wire saying that the money was for them. Tom took it but never asked any questions, for fear mostly that should he do so then the money might stop.

He worked like hell at the house, trying his damnedest to keep it neat and tidy. But the money they lived on was all because of this one mysterious benefactor. Tom thought it was his mama. Tom *knew* it was his mama, on some level. He was grateful for it – grateful for the whiskey it kept him in – but he wasn't about to question it for the fear of losing a tidy sum of income.

As he strolled, edging closer and closer to the stream, as well as that ditch that got his pa in the end, he thought more and more of mama. About whether or not she *was* out there. Living life large enough so as to be able to keep her two boys fed.

He assumed she'd started up a new life elsewhere. He knew Abel would lose what was left of the mind he had if he heard of mama's being alive, every bit as much as he knew of the torment that that news would mean if it came Tom's way.

He arrived at the stream, his feet bare and dusty. He hated the dust, decided that his feet could use a wash and, setting down his jug – though only temporarily – took a step in the water.

"Why it's cool," he sighed. "Water's cool."

He smiled to himself, though his was not a smile unburdened by crookedness. The drink didn't have a pleasant effect on Tom. He knew that the closer he came to that crooked, rickety shithole of a shack, the more the sourness would rise, requiring that he quell the animosity before daring to take a step into the same room with his brother Abel asleep in, snoring soundly.

"Hell," he said to the stream as he spat in the dust. "Don't need no feet washed," he said softly, still submerged up to his ankles.

He stood there a moment, waiting for whatever it was that did so to take hold of him and force him back to Abel. There was a breeze that blew over his naked shins, cooling him again.

"Take it easy now Tom," he said to no one, when somewhere far off in distance a lone coyote cried out. Tom felt for his gun, which was usually holstered to his hip, but was not there now. A panic surged through the young man. "Maybe it's alright," he said quietly. Then much louder he repeated himself, only to be greeted by a harsh silence.

Whatever coyote's out there, Tom thought, they're either racing right toward me or they're headed home. Either way, if it comes too close, I'll smash it to pieces with my bare hands.

He had no intention of doing so though. The young man was so drunk, a direct attack from a coyote, whether with friends or not, would inevitably result in Tom's demise and not the dumb animals'.

"Anyways," Tom sang to himself, returning to the minute riverbank to pick up his jug for another slug. "You take it easy out there," he told the coyote.

He walked up the stream for a time, hoping he'd come across the coyote, curious to see what it might do. Then he thought of home. He thought of the chickens. He thought of Frank and the wages he'd want when the money came through. He thought of the pigs, then he thought of Abel. Abel with that damn brush, beckoning his brother homeward with whining and complaints of parents either passed on out of stupidity, or long gone out of not wanting to be around as her boys became men.

He thought of Abel, spat in the dust and said "Well."

Then he took the path he'd etched out with dusty feet, heading back home.

4.

People came from all over to see Elsie and her girls, with some travelling many miles, having heard of her through other cowhands or travellers who'd roamed in and out of the town of

Taughrane Heights. Her manner was one that was built to be a whore, though she wasn't one any longer, instead leaving other, much younger girls than she to turn the tricks so she didn't have to. Her main attribute that the men roaming in and out of town were attracted to was her talk, with some boys paying just for a conversation with her and nothing else. Elsie and her words could do what most whores could only ever hope to accomplish with their bodies. Some cowboys claimed that a talk with Elsie was worth ten pokes of a lady, that she could get you there with words, meaning she was in very high demand. A talk with Elsie also didn't get you diseases, which made most men want that over a go on the others.

Her group of girls were well established to those who lived nearby as well, Tom Liffey being just such a one, albeit living way, way out on the very furthest outskirts of town. Tom didn't wish for anything from Elsie, except to ask if Sarah was free. Tom was in love with Sarah, and had high hopes of wedding her one day if she'd let him. She didn't dislike Tom. Matter of fact she was sweeter on him than she was all the others who used her service, because he was gentle and paid her handsomely for their time together, with most men paying the minimum rate for a rougher romp.

The day Tom came into town on a whim, the day of the letter, Sarah was sat upstairs in her room combing her mousy brown hair, her soft, porcelain white skin glowing bright like the moon on a clear, starry night. Elsie was downstairs sweeping as usual. The other whores had gone about their daily business in town, receiving more than a few nasty looks from the pious parishioners of the First Presbyterian church of Taughrane Heights, which wouldn't count for anything when the sun went down; and some of those same men came scurrying on into Elsie's while their fat wives waited at home with their knitting.

Sarah rarely if ever left the whorehouse. Her story was sad, and she only ever told it to Tom the once and, once, when Frank came into town to visit, and she was the only girl available that night. Tom did not know this, though if he did Frank would've been fired fast, as well as maybe being on the receiving

18

end of Tom's Colt Dragoon.

Sarah's father had been a drunkard, like Tom's. Though the way his end came about was a tad more dignified than freezing to death in a ditch. As well as an alcoholic he had been a gambler. Gambling and rambling all over the states, with his one and only daughter in tow, Buford Herron, Sarah's father, had landed in Taughrane Heights one night in the saloon directly across the street from Elsie's establishment. His daughter – after having dove down beneath a pillow to hide in the hotel room until her father arrived much later and, much more inebriated – did not know that her father had bet his daughter on a bad hand to an even badder man. The bad man's name was Benedito Solas, known to many by the handle of Snake-Eyes, given how he was so reptilian looking, as well his constantly munching on apples at every opportunity he got; the Garden of Eden, some said, was where Snake Eyes had been born.

A bad hand and bad luck befell Buford, for he'd bet away his child in drunkenness and Snake-Eyes had beaten him. Laughing loud enough to be heard down the street, Snake-Eyes bellowed at Buford to go and fetch his damn daughter, and to hurry the hell up about it. Buford told him he'd have to fight for her if he wanted her; that the repugnant reptilian – his smell of stale cigar butts and cheap whiskey greeted you long before he did – had better be prepared to shoot.

The reptile let out a holler, said that the gambler had better arm himself and that he'd see him in the street anon. His announcing to the whole saloon what had transpired at the table caught Elsie's attention. She didn't wait. While Buford Herron was being blown to kingdom come out in the street, kind Elsie McKinley busied herself with scurrying to the hotel, asking for the key to the room Buford Herron had booked into.

She ran like hell up the stairs, found the girl beneath the blankets, shivering and sweating up a fever, asking where her daddy was.

"Your daddy's dead sweetheart," said Elsie. "And if you want a life worth living, you'd best be coming with me now."

The little girl got little time to mourn, for she was

19

carried out through the back door to the hotel and discretely hidden away up in Elsie's room until Benedito's bad hangover hit him hard, the reptilian having forgotten all about the bet by morning.

Waiting for three or four days, Elsie didn't allow Sarah to come out of her room. Eventually Benedito saddled up and rode off, only to be hung in the next state over some time shortly after – for the crime of horse thieving, or so the folks of Taughrane Heights heard.

Elsie soon set Sarah to work with sweeping and emptying spittoons and such. It wasn't until she was eighteen when Elsie asked her if she'd like to earn a few dollars more by laying on her back for the boys that came through town, as well as those crafty few residents of Taughrane Heights.

Sarah'd known what the other girls did, and didn't think it that bad a thing to do for a living. Her father'd never touched her, even in his most drunken of stupors, though there were two or three men a month that had asked Elsie if that there little one was available. Elsie told them no, guiding them on to other girls, though she knew Sarah had a special charm to her from very early on.

This was Elsie's speciality. She knew women. More importantly than that she knew when one would make a good whore and went one wouldn't. Sarah was one that would, so she put her to work taking pokes.

Her establishment always had fresh sawdust on the floor, and she always made sure that the dust that blew in off the street stayed out, even when carried in by dusty boots. By the day Tom came into town just because he felt like it, Sarah was twenty and he nineteen. Not knowing where he was going, Tom Liffey lumbered on into Elsie's, whistling while he went, his hands the only things in his pockets, besides a nickel and a dime.

5.

"Looking fine ma'am," said Tom to Elsie as he always did.

"No change there then," she said as *she* always did.

She looked up from her broom, her back aching from being bent for so long without a break – she was quite a worker, with quite a work ethic. She took so much pride in her palace of pleasure that she forgot every so often to take it easy on herself. Relaxing did not come naturally to Elsie. Not naturally at all.

"All day long," she sighed, setting down the broom, resting it on a red velvet chaise lounge. "All day long I clean and sweep and still the damn dust keeps on breezing in. I can't cope Tom Liffey. I can't cope."

"Well hell, I don't want make it worse for you none," said Tom before lifting his left leg up and removing his boot, followed swiftly by the right one.

"Why you are kind," said Elsie. "You're very kind Tom Liffey, but I reckon it won't do much good anyways. I thank you all the same though. You want a drink? Dry out there today."

"Mighty dry. Damn winds won't stop blowing. Never ceased since last Friday. I'd take a drink, I surely would, only I ain't heeled with much money. Matter of fact I'm down to my last two bits."

"Well," Elsie grinned, "we won't bother none about payment. Parched as you are I don't think it's right to take your last two bits off of you. You can have a drink on the house."

"Here," said Tom, holding out his two coins, "take them anyway. I ain't one for charity."

"Who said anything about charity?" said Elsie. "I know you Tom. Regular customer ain't you?"

"Yes ma'am," he said.

"And you're aiming on returning as a customer again soon ain't you?"

Tom nodded. "Long as Sarah's here I'll always show up once my money comes in. Always."

"Mmmm," said Elsie. "I know that. Go you behind the bar there and pour us both a shot of whiskey. Parched myself what with all this darn sweeping. Sawdust just clumps the dirt together. You're kind for taking off your boots. Appreciate it Tom."

"I appreciate the drink. Ain't many madams would go and give a fella a free drink. Damn near have to roam the whole country to find a madam as kind as you."

"You stop now," she laughed. "Ought to make me blush blabbering compliments like that."

"Sorry ma'am."

"It's alright. Don't get none of that cheap stuff down below. Bottle at the end there's the good stuff. Don't need no swill that I give out to the swines that treat my ladies harsh. You grab the best bottle, right down at the end there."

"This one?" said Tom, holding up the bottle he'd found.

"That's the one. Make mine a double. You can have a double as well. Mighty few fellas get that stuff. Ain't liable to run out of it none in a hurry. Hombres and swine that saunter into my establishment are mostly meaner than rattlers. Why they even beat up some of my girls from time to time. Damn shame the way some of those cowhands handle a woman."

"Well hell, I hope none too much harm comes to my Sarah," said Tom, pulling the cork before gathering up two whiskey glasses and setting them the right way up on the bar.

"Well," said Elsie, "sometimes there's fellas she tells me about. Though I reckon the worst ones she never says nothing about. Always wears long sleeves, so as I can't see the bruises where the mean ones have dug in with their fingers. Afraid I can't always tell with my girls, Sarah included. Anyway, when you gonna marry her? Take that girl off my hands? Hell, I'll be sad to see her go, good whore as she is. But I tell you, ain't no one I'd rather see her run off with than you Tom Liffey. Girl dotes on you. I hope you know that. Dotes on you and then some I'd say."

"Sweet on her too ma'am."

"Don't keep ma'aming me. You can call me Elsie. Makes me feel as though I'm a hundred years old being called ma'am. It's Elsie, you hear?"

"Yes ma'am. I mean ma'am. I mean *Elsie*. Sorry ma'am."

"Can't say it's the brains she's sweet on. Fear there aren't none too many in that skull of yours."

"Oh I'm smart enough," Tom smiled, handing her her glass. Both she and he clinked their respective glasses together, then both flung their head backs, swallowing the superior whiskey with just one gulp.

"God that's good," said Tom. "You want another?"

"Not for me thanks," said Elsie. "Heard tell of a herd coming our way tonight. Means there's gonna be cowhands galore, and I need to be sharp for them coming in. You go ahead though."

Tom didn't need to be told twice. He poured himself another, though this time sipped slowly, savouring the fiery brown liquid like it was the last drop he'd ever have. It was good stuff. Really good stuff, and should be savoured, or so Tom thought. After he'd had a little sip or two, he set his glass down and asked Elsie as she flumped down on the chaise lounge if Sarah was in.

"She is," Elsie nodded, seemingly tired out and a little out of puff. "Making herself pretty I suppose. She knows when work's booming by instinct. Don't need to tell her none, though I don't know how she knows, for she nearly never leaves this here whorehouse."

"She's wise," said Tom sagely.

"Can't be none too wise if she's taken a liking to you Tom Liffey," she said, closing her eyes and fanning her face with her hand. Tom stayed quiet until at last she laughed and said she was only fooling around. "Reckon there ain't a fellow better suited to Sarah anywhere in the territory. Tell you this for free; there's few who I'd let take her from me. So count yourself lucky."

"I do ma'am. I mean Elsie. I do Elsie. Consider myself a very lucky man."

"Make no mistake though," Elsie continued, not really listening to Tom, but rather feeling just fine to continue talking

23

her thoughts out as though she were talking to herself. "Girl won't wait forever. No sir. She won't. Won't wait forever. Fella would have to hurry himself up a bit, if he were fixing for marrying. My Sarah's a peach. Plenty of fellas, though not many I'd approve of, would be happy to have her. She likes you though Tom Liffey. Yes, she does. Anytime she comes down them there stairs, it's always to that there door to stand and sigh and flutter those pretty lashes. I always ask. I always say, 'Sarah, just who in the hell is you looking for.' She'll turn to me and say no one, though I know that it's you she's after."

"Hell, soon as I'm able to buy a ring, why I'll ask her straight away."

"You got much money saved? You've come in today with what? A nickel and a dime. Damn it there ain't no ring you could by with that kind of cash."

"I've some saved up back at home."

"I reckon you ain't," said Elsie. "I reckon you ain't got more than that there in your pocket."

She scanned him for signs that she was wrong, then, satisfied she was correct, she spoke on before Tom could rebuff her remake.

"Pokes ain't free. That whiskey's on the house, though the pokes ain't. You aim on having a go with that there girl you're gonna have to pay. Full price. Hope you don't take no offence, but I ain't aiming to run a charity. Girls are worth a hell of a lot more than whiskey. Why a girl that you're in love with's worth even more I'd say."

"Reckon you're right," said Tom, taking his last sip for fear that she might just change her mind and take it back off him before he'd got it down his neck.

"I am right," said Elsie. "I am." She then started to tug at the front of her corset, grunting and groaning. "God damn man that made corsets ought to be taken out and shot. Why I'd riddle the bastard that thought that women ought to wear these things. Riddle him full of six holes, reload and riddle him again. Goddamn son of a bitch. Things are far too tight. Ain't fair on a woman."

24

"Why don't you wear pants?" Tom joked with a smile.

"Don't get smart with me Tom Liffey. Liable to stop you from seeing Sarah if you're fixing on giving me lip. Liable indeed."

"No, I ain't giving you lip Elsie. Just joking is all. I swear."

"Maybe it's ma'am Tom Liffey. Maybe it's ma'am."

Tom nodded and walked back around the bar, boots still in his hands. He didn't bother to wash the whiskey glasses, which would mean that Elsie would have to do it.

"You can wash them there glasses on your way out," she smiled at him. "After you've talked to Sarah." Tom's face lit up. "Up the stairs," Elsie said, flicking her head in the stairs' direction. "Don't take all day though. That girl's gotta work. With you not paying none that means she can't lay down for a fella who *has* got the money. Make it quick now you hear?"

Tom's earnest face filled Elsie with pity for the lad. Long ago she'd had men with that same look at the very mention of her name. Though not any longer. Elsie's time had come and gone, a fact that sometimes saddened her, but was quickly brushed aside once she remembered all the upkeep she had to perform on her person to keep herself presentable for customers. Now she'd let her appearance slide. Sure she could still talk, but her days of men lusting after her, hoping to lie down with the woman were well and truly over. Tom was still waiting, a little queasiness coming over his guts as it always did when just about to see Sarah.

"Go on," Elsie sighed as she stood. "Hurry on up there. The girl's got work to do soon."

Tom bolted up the stairs proclaiming his thanks. Then, once she heard him knock on her door, Elsie picked up the broom, beginning once more to sweep and sweep and sweep.

6.

Sarah's scream when she saw him was so loud it sent a jolt through the dog walking along in the street. The poor cur's head snapped and it tucked its tail, before hurrying on lest whatever made that sharp sound decide to come after it, meaning harm for all the dog knew.

"Cut that out!" Elsie shouted from downstairs. "Liable to wake the dead with that noise."

Sarah shook her head, dismissing Elsie, then grabbed and hugged her man.

"Now don't squeeze me too tight none," Tom laughed into her head of hair, breathing in her scent deeply. He loved the smell of her. It was a fresh smell; a far cry from the pig shit he'd had to become accustomed to at home. He loved her smell. Hell, he loved *her* more to the point.

"Come on in," she said, kissing his cheek and taking Tom by the hand, guiding him into her boudoir. Just as she was Tom's favourite person, this room was his favourite place.

"How you been keeping? Been a while since I last saw you," Tom said.

"It has, hasn't it? Naughty boy. Bet you was wishing you could come calling all this time."

"I was," Tom stated plainly. "Pining for you. You're all I ever pine *for*. Damn sure ain't got much else to have a longing for."

"How's Abel? How's Frank? Ain't giving you no trouble none?"

"Nah, Frank ain't. Abel's another story. Sometimes I just wanna grab a hold of his neck and squeeze, you know? Just squeeze and squeeze him like a lemon. Till all the life's left him. Hate how he makes me feel sometimes."

"He's your brother," Sarah said softly, her hand lightly landing on Tom's well weathered one, resting on his knee.

"Now come on," Tom pleaded. "Please don't remind me. I have plenty on my plate. Just plenty. Don't need no woman telling me my business. Don't matter if it's you's doing the telling or not."

Sarah gave him a look that said she meant business.

"*Really*? You're gonna scold me when you ain't been in to see me in almost a month. You know what, why don't you just get lost."

"Sorry Sarah, I didn't mean it none."

"No. No I'm serious. You go on out if that's the way you're gonna treat me. Many's a boy'd be glad of my advice. And I'd gladly give it. For free."

"Sarah stop. Now just stop now, alright? I didn't mean nothing by it. Brother just gets on my nerves is all. I ain't mad at you. You know I ain't."

He hung his head and scratched at his forehead, then let his hands dangle down between his legs. Sarah's stare softened somewhat.

"Sometimes I don't know about you Tom Liffey. If I had a brother why, why I'd love him all day long. I'd hug him and kiss him and damn near kill him with kindness."

"Wish someone would kill Abel. Leave me be in peace for the rest of my days. Damn mama of his has long since run off, and the darn fool still won't let up yapping about her. He's like a terrier that's mother forget to put in the quit when it comes to barking. Boy can moan for Texas. Takes some serious work settling him down again. Damn brushing and brushing at him every night. Like a goddamn horse that fella."

"It's a fine thing Tom Liffey. A fine thing to have a brother to love. You should be glad of it. I ain't got no one."

"You've got the other whores in here. Ain't they like a family?"

"They ain't," she bit back sharply. "They ain't one bit. Why they bitch and moan all the time to Elsie, 'bout how I steal all their customers from them. I can't help it if I'm popular. Ain't my fault."

"It's a fact that you're the prettiest. Prettiest by a mile I reckon."

"Yeah, well I reckon you ought to. Seeing as how

27

you're sweet on me and all."

The two young people sat in silence for a moment; Tom taking notice of a cockroach crawling out from underneath the gap between the sole of Sarah's shoe and her heel. He watched it walk forward a few fast steps, stop, then decide to take another route instead, before stopping and recommencing once more. Sarah just looked out the window.

"Warm day outside," she said softly.

"It is," Tom said without looking up, bringing his heel over the creepy-crawly so slowly and deliberately, before bringing his foot down and crushing the life out of the cockroach that had meant him no harm.

"Would you want to take a walk?" she asked him.

He lifted his head up from the cockroach killing business, a perplexed look plastered across his face.

"*You* wanna take a walk?" he asked, astounded by such an offer.

"Why not? Mighty fine day. Don't see why we shouldn't." She stood from her seat and flapped at her dress. "Might as well start to be seen in public together, seeing as how we're to be wed one day. Which is a day I hope is coming along quite soon Tom Liffey."

"It is," he said solemnly as he stood. "Soon as I can afford a ring it'll be put right there on this finger," he said as he grabbed the third finger on her left hand, raised her hand to his lips and very lightly kissed the back of it.

"Sure are a charmer, that's for sure," she said with a smile. "Come on now, let's go while the sun's shining. I need a new fan anyway. This one's all eaten up by moths. You can buy me it can't you?"

"Well actually I ain't got much money on me right now Sarah girl. Got a nickel and a dime, but that's it. Rest of it's at home hiding in a coffee can where Abel and Frank don't know about it none."

"You can owe me," she laughed.

"Like hell I will. Why I'm fixing on buying you a ring. Need every penny I can get. Got to save some first, 'fore I go and start forking out for fans and such."

"Such a miser," she sighed, before leading him out of the boudoir by the hand.

"Well I'll be damned," drawled Elsie. "Is that the princess out of her tower? Must be some charmer of a prince Tom Liffey, getting her to leave and all."

"Alright, alright," Sarah beamed. "I come down sometimes."

"Yeah, when the moon's blue and pigs are flying and horses leading the church choir you do. Must be damn near two whole weeks since you came out besides opening the door when Jasper brings you your supper and breakfast both."

"Yeah well," Sarah said, hooking her arm in the crook of Tom's and tugging him in tighter. "Where is Jasper anyways?"

"Gone to buy more cheap cigars from O'Grady's I'll wager. Where else he'd have gone I don't rightly know," said Elsie, hands akimbo as she surveyed the state of her floors, then, deciding that the dust had been dispersed sufficiently, she went round the back of the bar and began stacking the shot glasses in a neat row, ready for her bartender Jasper to serve with when the clientele would come in thick and fast later on that day. "Don't know where you're off to, when you could help me with these glasses. Goddamn Jasper's left this side of the bar in an awful state. Don't know why I don't fire him. Man's useless. Useless I tell you."

"We're just going for a walk in the sun. I'll help you some when I get back," said Sarah, trying to get Tom going, though the man on her arm was still a trifle parched, and half fancied asking Elsie if she wouldn't mind his imbibing of another drop.

"Don't suppose I could have some more whiskey Elsie?" he said, trying not to sound desperate, but failing helplessly. His lips were dry, and his eyes were pleading, but Elsie was not one to acquiesce this time, for she knew he had no funds for the purchase.

"You supposed right Tom Liffey, for you ain't having no more," she said, before spitting in a glass and giving it a good wipe with her half-soiled rag.

"Right," he nodded.

"What do you mean *more*?" asked Sarah. "Has he had some already?"

Tom said no at the same time as Elsie said yes.

"You didn't Tom!" Sarah scolded. "It's twelve o'clock in the day. Don't tell me you been at the whiskey already? Why it's midday!"

"My mouth was dry. And *she* was offering. Didn't want to be rude none now did I?"

"You could have said no," nagged Sarah. "What? Did she take the bottle and jam it in your mouth? That what you did Elsie?"

"I did not," said Elsie. Tom gave her a look like he was disappointed with her response, almost expecting her to cover for him.

"It was only a damn drop. Mouth was all dry and I didn't want to be rude. Oh hell! I don't need this. You can take your own walk in the sun. You can lumber along all on your lonesome. Don't need no damn escort. Sure wouldn't expect you to take to walking with a drunkard. Why it wouldn't be ladylike!" Tom said before stomping straight out of Elsie's pleasure palace.

"Please wait," Sarah cried. "I'm sorry Tom. Come on, wait up," she called after him as he made his way off down the street.

Sarah looked to Elsie as if for guidance, getting a shrug and nothing more. Then the mother in Elsie saw the sadness in Sarah at being spurned, so she said, "Well go get after him girl. Man won't wait around for you none."

So Sarah fled from Elsie's and chased after her man.

"Don't know what man might be worth the trouble," Elsie sighed. "But I'd bet good money that that Tom Liffey just ain't such a man after all," she said to herself, before spitting into a new glass, giving the thing a good wipe.

7.

"Wait up now!" Sarah yelled at her man. "Best not be making me run Tom. If you do I might just head right on up those stairs of Elsie's place, and it'll be the last time you ever hear from me."

"Alright," said Tom as he spun round in the street. "But we'll get this clear now. If I fancy a drink, then I'll have one. Woman or not, nagging or no nagging, nothing ain't gonna change that. There's little good comes my way in this world, and drink just happens to be the one good thing I got going for me."

"You got me," said Sarah, disappointed that she'd been outranked by whiskey.

"Well we ain't wed yet. You've charged me for every fuck we've ever had."

"Alright, one," Sarah said, puffing out her chest, "keep your voice *down*. And two, I only charge you 'cause Elsie says I got to. She'd get madder than hell if she knew I was giving out free ones. Why, when you wed me, maybe we won't have that problem no more."

"Oh we will," Tom scoffed. "Sure we will."

"How you figure?"

"First of all, you'll want new dresses. All women want good fresh dresses to wear. Why they go nuts with wanting fancy clothes fresh out of the box. Then there's the jewellery. Then there'll be other things that I can't quite think of right now, but I'm betting are out there waiting on my dumb ass to fork out hard earned cash for."

Of course he hadn't earned any money that came his way in life, but Sarah did not need to be privy to that piece of information.

"I don't need none of that," said Sarah. "All I need is you."

"Yeah right. Women are all the same. See some frock on a dummy in a shop window and they lose their minds. Reckon you ain't no different, that's what I reckon."

31

"You can reckon all you like, I'm telling you you're wrong. Just plain wrong. I don't require no frills or frocks. Just my man and a roof over my head."

"Yeah well, you'll have to get used to Abel if you're gonna shack up with me. Moans and moans all the damn time that boy."

"Well maybe you just don't treat him right. Maybe that's why he moans so much."

"Maybe. I brush him though, just like he asks. Ain't one night since mama up and left I ain't done that for him."

"He maybe thinks you do it rough."

"Right", said Tom, "you being the expert on brushing and all, you would know."

"I'm a woman ain't I? I have a head of hair I brush every day, don't I?"

"You do that," Tom said, scuffing the soles of his boots off the boardwalk that ran along Main Street. "Maybe we ought not to fight," he said softly, squeezing her hand. "I love you you know. Love you more than anything."

"Even more than whiskey?"

He felt like telling her then where she could go, giving him that remark, instead he just said yes and stuffed his hands down deep into his pockets.

"Take me for a walk Tom," she said.

"Where?"

"Anywhere. Anywhere you like, I don't mind."

"Might have to go to O'Grady's check on my mail, not that I ever get any."

"Why don't you write me some time?" she suggested. "I'd love that. We could write each other, lots and lots of letters."

"About what?" said Tom.

"Why about love of course! Our love. Why we could write all about our wedding. We could talk about the party we'd throw, and about everything you and Abel get up to around the house."

"Mmmm," Tom half agreed, though the young man would rather talk about anything else but his brother. Then Sarah

32

added a joke that got Tom's goat.

"We could write about my wedding dress. We could write about how you might pick out the prettiest one in town for me to wear."

"*See?*" Tom snapped. "Women are all the same. Go doolally for dresses."

"Tom…"

"Don't Tom me! Don't you Tom me one bit. I told you I ain't looking to buy you no fancy frocks. Fucking head's splitting open today. I thought hell, I'll pay a visit to my darling. Maybe brighten up my day as well as hers. And here you are, begging for a fucking dress like a dog would a bone. Well I say to hell with you. You ain't getting no dress. No damn dress nor cake nor nothing."

"I was joking you Tom," said Sarah, that playful smile on her lips dissolved by Tom's bluntness. "I was just joking around, but if that's how you really behave when I make a joke then maybe we ought not to go and get married at all. Seeing as how you've shown me just now how mighty short of a temper you have."

"Hell," said Tom, "how was I supposed to know you was joking? Ain't got no crystal ball you know."

"Well if you did you'd see your future inside of it without Sarah Herron, so how do you like that? And don't dare come crawling back into Elsie's place looking for me. Not at least until you've decided to tame that temper. I don't need no man that's angrier than a bull. So just you think on it Tom Liffey. You figure out how to speak to a lady proper, then maybe I'll consider wanting to be your wife again."

"Go on then," said Tom. He guessed she was bluffing, which happened to be correct.

"What?" she said, looking as though he'd just smacked her across the face.

"Fuck away off then. Who needs you anyway? There's plenty of gals out there'd like a man like me. Plenty of 'em. What? You think you're the only girl in town? Let me tell you sister, you ain't. There's many a woman would spread her legs

33

and *wouldn't* charge me for it. You go on now if you like. Leave at your own speed, I don't mind. Just don't let that swinging door to Elsie's place hit you on the ass when you walk in."

"You're a mean man Tom Liffey, let me be the one to tell you. You go on ahead and you get a poke from some other girl. I hope she gives you a gift you can't give back. Hope your pecker rots right off and falls to the ground. Hope a dog runs off with it and leaves you dickless the rest of your days."

"Deary me, you've quite an imagination."

"Yeah well you'll need one too, for you'll only be able to fuck me in your head from now on, for it won't be happening in real life ever again."

"Suits me just fine. I have a mighty memory, and I reckon I'll be able to remember us riding, though I won't. Why I wouldn't fantasise about fucking you if somebody paid me."

"Shut up," she said before turning to walk away.

"No you shut up," said Tom, trudging off in the opposite direction. He didn't turn until it was too late, and Sarah had sprinted off so fast she was back in Elsie's again in a matter of seconds. Tom wanted to run and chase after her and apologise but then thought it too soon.

"Leave her be a while," he said quietly to himself. "Leave her to cool off. Then tomorrow you can call round with flowers. Girls like flowers."

So Tom walked on through the town on his own, with no woman on his arm any longer.

"Let her go there," he said in an attempt to soothe himself, though the fretting had already begun. Boys came in from all over to Elsie's. If Tom wasn't in her mind to take for a husband, then another fella would fill his place quicker than lightning flashing. Fine fellas sometimes came along, and it would only take one to catch Sarah's eye and Tom'd be long forgotten about.

He thought of running straight to Elsie's. About getting on his knees and crawling across Sarah's bedroom begging. But he had his pride to think of. Even if he didn't have Sarah, he still had Abel. It was this thought that sent a shudder up his spine, scaring him back into his senses. He *needed* Sarah, just as he needed the drink. Abel alone was not reason enough to continue living. If anything, Abel made him want to give up and freeze in a ditch like his daddy'd done before him. He had to make things right. He had to.

"Best leave her be for a few minutes. Go back to her now and she'll still be hotter than hell. I'll bring her some flowers. That ought to cheer her up. Girls like flowers."

First though, for what reason he did not know, Tom thought that he should check the post office. Just to see if there *were* any letters.

The length of Main Street was littered here and there with life. Little old ladies tutting and scoffing to one another about something Samuel or John or whomever their husbands were had said in jest. Jubilant men wandered by, fresh from the barber's brushing at their hair in the glass shop windows, trying to make sure a single hair wasn't out of place, the other, more obedient hairs parted and pomaded down, glued firmly in place. Little kids fired finger pistols at one another in short trousers, with one being held by the ear and scolded by Al Montague the greengrocer for what Tom did not know. Maybe the kid had thrown a stone and the pebble had done a number on the glass pane in the shop's door. Whatever it was the scolding looked mighty severe, for the kid was crying, with two rivers of slimy slot trickling down from both nostrils, dribbling on into his mouth as he hitched in and out deep, deep sobs.

Tom wondered whether a hanging was happening today. Hangings were always worth a watch. Tom could read, but he never got much out of a book, be it a good or bad read, that didn't matter much. He had books. His mama'd left a large supply in an old trunk that Tom had long since forgotten, leaving it in the corner of his and Abel's room to gather up a large collection of mould. He never thought about it, but it was a real waste of good books. But hangings he liked. It wasn't anything to do with justice being done. What Tom liked was what the person getting hung had to say for themselves before that short drop that snapped their neck and left them twitching for a time until at last all life left them and the movements came to a halt.

He always wondered what he might say were he about to be hung. He thought of all sorts of clever things to say. Sometimes he thought he might promise to haunt some old hag who happened to be watching. He dreamed of standing on the gallows, scanning through the crowd to pick out his target, then with a wink, tell them he'd see her in about forty-five minutes back at her home; that *he* would see *her* though *she* wouldn't see *him*. Then he'd drop down and his existence here on earth would end, though maybe not as far as the lady was concerned.

"Yep," he said to himself as he marched in the direction of O'Grady's. "That'd be a good one alright."

When he came to the door to the post office, a woman was walking out, so Tom held the door open for her.

"Why you're a kind young man," she said, before turning back to Pat O'Grady in astonishment. "You see that Mr. O'Grady? Good kind man's as mannerly as they come."

"Maybe you could tell the woman I intend on marrying that," said Tom.

"I'd be glad to son," said the wisened woman, with a face as craggy as a cliff-face. "Where is she?"

"She's right on yonder. Up that there street, way on up at the end."

"You don't mean… You can't mean…" stammered the woman.

"Oh yes," Tom winked. "Why it'd curl your toes to hear tell of what we did when we first met missus. Curl your toes!"

"Hmph," said the woman. "And to think I thought you mannerly. Ought to be ashamed. Ought to hang your head in shame young man."

"Maybe I'll leave her granny. Get myself a more mature woman. One with some experience. What are you doing around supper time tomorrow?"

"Well I *never*!" said the woman, with her eyes wide with shock. "I've never heard the like of it in all my living life."

"You love it," said Tom, growing bored by this prude

36

10.

"Dear Abel and Tom," Tom began, dictating just as the parchment read in an elegant kind of handwriting. "Hettie here. You know, your auntie. Your mama, my sister, has fallen to an illness the doctor says means that she will not last much longer. Now she's told me she wanted me to write you, so that's what I'm doing. She supposed both of you boys'll be madder than a nest of hornets that's been poked at with a big stick. Says it's not likely you'll respond, though she still wants me to reach out, so that's what I'm doing like I said. Your mama says she regrets running off, but hopes that both of you can find some room in your hearts somewhere for forgiveness. She and I are inviting you both to come stay with us a time, until of course the inevitable comes to pass and your mother departs this world to enter into the good Lord's kingdom up above. We hope to see you soon. We're situated at your grandfather's place in Georgia. Please find the address on the back of the envelope this letter's contained in. Yours sincerely, Auntie Hettie, like I said. Hope to see you both soon. P. S. We'll wire you a substantial fee for the journey. We would encourage you both not to spend it on trivial things that aren't in any way necessary. If you do not wish to make the trip, you may both spend it as you wish. We won't begrudge you that luxury of living large for a time."

"Well hell Mr. Liffey sir," said Frank. "That's good news ain't it? I mean, not about your mother dying and all. I don't mean that. But about your mama wanting to see you two boys again. Ain't it good news?"

"Good news?" Tom said, flabbergasted at Frank's understatement. "Why you couldn't have given greater news if you came bearing the message that somebody'd up and died and left me a million dollars. Don't you *see*? Abel can get to see his mama again. You hear that Abel? You're gonna get to go and be with mama. Won't that be something?"

Abel looked a little disconcerted.

"Don't tell me," Tom said looking at his brother's

49

bothered face. "Fucking don't tell me. You don't wanna see mama now? Fucking Goddamn it all to hell. How in the hell don't you want to see her? For fuck's sake don't I ever get a break? Well I'll tell you boy, by God and all the angels up in heaven this I swear. You'll go to mama. You'll go to see her and you'll stay there with her for a change, for I'm tired. That old bag Hettie can have you from here on out. Then maybe I'll get some peace for a change. Maybe marry Sarah and settle down, without you whining all day long like a baby's that's hungrier than hell. *Shit*! She wants you. Didn't you hear that? The woman wants you, and there you sit with a face on you that'd turn buttermilk sour. *Shit*!"

"She ain't seen me in a time," said Abel. "What if she don't like me all growed up?"

"Oh she'll like you just fine brother. Better like you just fine, for you'll be put into her care once we hit Georgia."

"We going to Georgia then Mr. Liffey sir?"

"Sure are Frank. You, me and Abel. All three of us. Maybe even Sarah too, though I ain't figured that out none yet. Might have to turn on the charm to convince her some. But I want her along too. Maybe settle down in Georgia. Maybe get a ball of money off of Hettie. Set up a new home and live there the rest of our days. Might be able to buy big cigars, sit out on the porch smoking all damn day. Then when the sun goes down, darling Sarah can call us in Frank, for biscuits and gravy and the likes. Yes sir. Seems a mighty fine plan's forming in my mind. Mighty fine plan."

"I ain't never been to Georgia," said Frank, though the man was keenly aware that persons of his complexion were not dealt a fair hand in that state. "I think maybe," he said, mouth drier than a desert all of a sudden. "If it's alright with you sir, I might just stay here."

He didn't want to go to Georgia. That was a contributing factor to Frank's reluctance. But what was really the clincher was the fact that on several separate occasions, Frank, or more accurately, little Frank, had poked she who was his master's woman. Whatever else happened Frank found the thought of his employer finding that fact out was the catastrophe of all

50

catastrophes.

"'Fraid you won't be staying here Frank. I'll need a hand getting this boy here over to Georgia. You're the only fella I got that I can afford to help me. So you're going to Georgia too."

Frank tried to protest but the words got caught in his throat.

"There'll maybe be a beautiful black woman waiting for you there. Ain't no black women in town as far as I know. Now wouldn't it be nice to have a woman for a change? Surely you must be lonely loping about this place every day, with no woman to give you a poke."

Frank just nodded and looked down at his feet.

"Yes sir," Tom said triumphantly. "We'll all three go to Georgia. And Sarah. You Abel can stay with your mama forever, or at least until she croaks. Then maybe Hettie'll take over brushing duties. Don't reckon she's any rougher than I am with that brush of yours. You'd like that wouldn't you? A woman's touch? Hell, probably many miles more gentle than I am."

Abel just looked at his brother, head tilted to one side, processing the information he'd been given. Then, almost as though an actual penny had dropped, Abel's face lit up like a cowboy's campfire.

"I'm gonna get to see my mama!" he yelled. "You're gonna take me!"

"That's right brother. By God that's right. All the way to Georgia. Then I'll leave you there and you can moan all the live long day to her and Hettie. You'll be outta my hair for good. God almighty that thought sure is a sweet one."

"Wait. What do you mean?" Abel said, spirits suddenly dampened. "Don't you wanna stay with mama too?"

"Oh I'll sit for a while. Sure I will. Won't be staying with her overnight but I'll sit a while. Then I'll go and book into a hotel with Sarah. Stay there until we find us suitable lodgings where Frank can come and live too."

"Where do I go?"

"Where do you go? Why with mama you fool! Where

51

else would you go?"

"No. I wanna stay with you," said Abel.

"That ain't the plan brother. Be best you get this clear in your mind now. When we get to Georgia you'll stay with mama. You can come visit Sarah, Frank and me sometimes. Maybe for a half hour or so some days when I ain't got no hangover to contend with. Rest of the time you stay with mama. You understand?"

"You just want rid of me," Abel pouted.

"Hell, I reckon I earned it," Tom said turning to Frank for support. "Reckon I done my time with you, brushing and dressing and doing damn near everything for you but wiping your ass."

"Why can't I stay with you? I want to stay with you forever brother."

"Well then what are you always moaning about mama for? If you don't want her in your life then why've you given me such a helping of grief complaining about her being gone? Goddamn it, you're getting what you want Abel. You're gonna go be with mama."

"I want you too!" Abel said, tears beginning to trace out their little estuaries of sorrow slowly down his rosy cheeks.

"Well, we'll see when we get there," Tom said, wisely putting off worrying about cutting Abel loose until much later.

They still had to make the journey to Georgia. There was also the added complication of Hettie maybe taking a disliking to Abel. If she heard the way he whinged she mightn't take him. Then Tom would be bound to his brother for the rest of his days; a thoroughly sickening thought to the younger sibling.

"I'm gonna go into town to talk to Sarah some. You come along too Frank. You as well Abel. About time Sarah met the bane of my existence. Good for her to meet you too Frank, seeing as how you're gonna be travelling companions."

Frank waited until Tom had looked away before he gulped. Going to meet Sarah with Tom there too was the farthest thing from what he wanted, though the man would now have to

52

bite the bullet and be around both Sarah and Tom together at some stage, whether he liked the thought or not.

11.

"Oh no!" said Elsie. "You go on now. You're not wanted here. Sarah don't want to see you none, so on you go."

"Got to say sorry Elsie," said Tom. "Got something important to tell her too. So it'd be best you just stand aside and let me past. Man's got a right to see his woman when he wants."

"When I see a man I'll point him out to you, but you sure as hell ain't one yourself. What kind of a man behaves like that to a lady? No man does that. A bug might, but a man doesn't."

"I ain't no bug Elsie. We've got our flaws, every one of us. Don't mean it should stop us from getting what we want. Why I even brought my brother here to see her. That ought to say something about how serious I am about courting Sarah. See? That's him there, with thon whore yonder sat down in his lap."

"Looks like you," said Elsie. "Reckon he's just as rude too. And if he is he's about as welcome as you are, meaning not welcome none at all."

"Alright Elsie just move. My God, who made you the Marshal of morals. You've lain down with fellas from here to California. Fucked more than your share and then some I'm betting. Be best you leave taking the high ground to a woman with her legs kept shut. Instead of wide open like yours has been for most of your life."

"Listen you to me Tom Liffey. There's many a man's taken umbrage with what I say goes. Got more than my share of bruises in my time from all sorts of boys. But if you think that I'm just gonna hand over one of my girls to an ignoramus like you, well then you're about as simple as that there brother of yours looks."

"He ain't simple," said Tom. "He has his troubles, but I'd bet his brain twice the size as yours is woman. Why I bet he could count higher than you and all, no matter how dumb you think he is."

"Reckon you want to make that there bet?" said Elsie, eyeing up the brother behind Tom who didn't know just what to do with or where to put his hands.

His eyes bulged out of his skull with staring at the broad bosom presented by the low-cut dress on the woman sitting on him. Poor Abel had never been so aroused in all his life. Little did he understand his excitement either.

"Alright," said Tom. "I'll bet Abel can count higher. If he can you just leave me be to my business with Sarah. If he can't then you can kick us out. Sound fair enough?"

"Sounds alright," Elsie agreed.

"Well alright then. Let's see what he can do."

He ushered Elsie over in his brother's direction, which the proprietress of the property walked in, leaving Tom lagging behind so that he could make use of the distraction and hurry off up the stairs to Sarah.

"Say Mr. Liffey. Reckon you want to count for me?" Elsie asked Abel, who was perplexed by such a request though felt he should show off a little for the lady in his lap.

"I can count mighty high," he said with a smile, as his brother Tom rapped on Sarah's door.

"Don't strain yourself now. I don't want you hurting your brain none," Elsie laughed, causing the whore on Abel's knee to giggle.

"Gosh, it don't hurt me none to count. Why my mama's made me do it ever since I was young. Never could get the hang of reading and writing, but numbers came just fine."

"For fuck's sake Sarah," said Tom, trying to twist the door knob that was clearly locked from the other side. "I'm sorry Sarah. Swear to God I am. Why the good Lord can strike me down dead if I'm telling a lie. I mean it now. I'm sorrier than any man ever was. Why if I owned the world, why I'd give it all to you. You gotta believe me sweetheart. I was just riled earlier on is all. I swear. Come on sweetie, open up that there door for your beau. By God, I even left flowers for you earlier. Surely that should show you you mean *something* to me."

54

"Best you go on friend. This here girl's getting loving off of me at the moment. Might be a minute 'fore I'm finished," came the sound of another rooster in the henhouse on the other side of the door Tom was knocking on.

"Sorry friend," said Tom, though the anger'd begun to boil up like heated vinegar inside.

Tom accepted the fact that his girl was a whore, though that didn't make him any less mad when he heard tell of her being ridden right on the other side of the wood that separated him from her or him from them. The fact is he would have to propose. He'd have to propose, and she'd have to accept and then and only then would she give up the sporting life and settle into domesticated normality with just the one man, that one man, Tom hoped, being Tom Liffey and no one else.

Elsie meanwhile was almost bored to tears by Abel, who had reached one hundred and eleven. Elsie had lost the bet because even she could not get that high. Abel was grinning a great big goofy grin when a deflated Tom came slowly down the stairs.

"He can count," Elsie said once Tom was at his side. "Even if he can do nothing else, he can count. So you can stay if you please."

"Thank you Elsie. You're a real nice woman when you want to be you know."

"And you, I'll admit, are a man. Heir to all the flaws a fella can be. So I'll keep an eye on you mister. My girl Sarah means the world to me. I won't be handing her off to a fella don't treat her right. You understand? Ain't gonna give that girl to a fella fights and drinks and spits indoors all the time. Time to straighten up and prove yourself. And not just to Sarah, but to me. Maybe she's easy impressed. Sure she might be. But I ain't. I ain't aiming to give her to just any old Joe."

"How can I prove myself?" Tom asked, feeling frightened now for the first time that he might lose Sarah for good, if this whorehouse owner obstructed him in his business with the girl he truly adored more than anything else before he met her.

"You can make her laugh for one thing. Lady loves to laugh. Fella can't make that gal laugh and he ain't the fella for her. You get her giggling, and you keep her giggling all night and maybe then we'll see."

"Sounds fair enough," said Tom.

He would endeavour to keep things light. Keep her laughing with all of his might.

"Yeah," said Elsie. "I'll be watching. Even when you think I ain't, I am. I've eyes like a hawk. And I won't condone your coming together if I see one sign of upset on that gal's face friend. And I mean that."

"There, alright," said Tom, growing tireder and tireder of being told what to do by this woman who held no sway or any upstanding character in the eyes of John Q. Public. Proprietress of a whorehouse as she was, her opinion counted for a lot amongst the ladies in her employ, but not anywhere else. Tom felt a little slighted that he had to stoop so low as to have to try and impress the owner of a whorehouse. Though he settled down a touch once he realised he was in love with a whore himself, and that that meant he wasn't much better than Elsie.

"Can I have a whiskey?" he asked Elsie as she strolled around the back of the bar.

"Do you need one?" she said, picking up a rag to give the counter a wipe. Tom was about to answer when she did it for him. "Don't think you do. Don't think you need drink in you when you're trying to woo, do you?"

"Yeah I guess," Tom shrugged.

"No guessing about it. You don't need no drink. If you value that girl's heart you'll stave off the whiskey a while. 'Least until you've proved yourself."

"You're some gal Elsie," Tom grinned forcefully, feeling inside like he hoped she might trip at the top of the stairs, the result of this – though he didn't desire she break her neck – being bad bruises and a lesson learned to watch where she walked. Why he thought he'd even provide the shove she needed to tumble down the stairs from the first floor of her beloved pleasure palace. Though this was just a thought. Knowing Tom's luck, should he shove her she'd probably break her neck, and he likewise once the hangman pulled the lever and the wooden trap door dropped out from under him, with the rope straining and snapping his neck for all the townsfolk to get a good gawk at him swinging and swaying with his legs twitching for a time until eventually coming to a dead stop. He wouldn't push her. He could enjoy the thought though, which he did do as he walked over to Abel's table.

"You fancy a fuck Frank?" Tom asked.

"Ain't one of these women takes my fancy Mr. Liffey sir. Ain't a one."

"Why, I suppose you'd want one that's mahogany colored. Don't reckon Elsie has a girl of that variety."

Frank smiled, though the expression was a facade, for Frank knew, though Tom did not, that the object of his desire was as pale as milk. Maybe even paler. With mousy brown hair and a speckling of freckles across the bridge of her nose and the tops of her cheeks.

Choosing Sarah had happened whenever he first stepped foot in the pleasure palace. Poor Frank did not know then that she was the woman her employer adored. If he had he'd have stayed clear and avoided falling deeply in love with Sarah Herron. He had though, and the fact, however much it irked him, would not change any.

"Reckon so," Frank said softly.

"Still," said Tom, "take your pick and put it on my tab. Hell of a lot of money's coming my way. Why I don't see why you shouldn't get some fun out of it."

"Very kind of you Mr. Liffey sir. Expect I won't take the offer, generous as it is. Reckon I'm just fine by myself."

"You sure?" said Tom. "My treat. Don't got to worry none about paying me back from now until the judgement day. Don't you worry about it. Won't owe me one cent, I swear."

"It's alright Tom," Frank said, a look of sober sombreness washing over him, making the man paler, his face the color of ash.

"Hell, you must be serious. That there's the first time

you called me by the name of Tom. Take it you mean just what you say, so I'll leave it be. But at least let me buy you a drink damn it. You're a good hand, and an even better help. Hell, I'd be lost without you Frank. Honest to God I would. What do you say? Something to quench your thirst. I'm betting you're parched some."

"I am Mr. Liffey sir. Be just fine if you was to buy me a drink. Reckon I'd let you if that's what you want."

"It is. You wait here. Go get you a glass of beer. Best I can afford. Ain't gonna get stingy on you. I'll get the most expensive Elsie's got in the place. Don't move none now. You stay right there."

Tom then moved over by Abel and ruffled his brother's hair.

"Suppose you don't need no drink brother. Behave like a drunk half the time anyways, even when there's no whiskey pumping all through you."

"You this here boy's brother?" said the whore with her behind pressed up close to Abel's front.

"That I am miss. His only brother as a matter of fact. Why you asking?" Tom smiled.

"This here boy has a mighty big pecker on him. I can feel it through his pants. Pay good money to see it up there in my room. Reckon you'd pay for him to have some fun? I'd take him for free, only…"

"Elsie don't give no free ones," Tom finished for her. "Yeah I know that." He looked then at his brother beaming up at him. "Hell, he wouldn't know what to do miss. My brother can count some, but he ain't much use in the brain department."

"Don't matter if he don't know what to do. I know what to do," said the woman. Then, leaning back, her hand finding and caressing the left side of Abel's face, her lips right up close against Abel's right ear. "What do you say sugar? Fancy you and I have some fun upstairs."

"Uh-huh!" Abel agreed happily, made giddy with the excitement that was firing from his heart all the way down to below his belt.

"Boy you are one fool," said Tom. "I'm sorry miss, but that there fella ain't gonna satisfy you."

"Not from where I'm sitting honey," said the woman. "Why he could satisfy this here whole whorehouse. If he wanted to that is."

"He don't want to. He don't know why he's happy."

"I do too," Abel butted in.

"Why then?" said Tom. "Go on ahead brother. Why you happy?"

Abel looked up at his brother, sticking out his tongue in deep contemplation. He puzzled and puzzled. Then the nearest thing to an answer came to him.

"Pecker's grown some. Feels just fine. Reckon I like it," he said conclusively, as though this was the indisputable, definitive answer. "Like the feeling miss. Hope you don't mind," he told the woman wiggling every few moments, making that carrot of his feel as though it were about to go off like a firework on the Fourth of July.

"*Honey*," the girl purred. "Please. I think it's just fine. Natural for you to feel that way. Me being an attractive woman and all."

"No," said Tom, taking his brother's arm. "Just a woman. Being attractive ain't got nothing to do with it. Why it could be any warm body bumping up against his front and it would get him going. You ain't special. Sorry to disappoint darling, but you just ain't. You come with me now Abel. Come get some air and cool down a bit."

"But I don't want to," Abel said.

"Stay then sugar," said the whore. "Stay with Laura. She'll treat you just fine. Just the way you want." She then took hold of Abel's other arm and began to tug.

"You leave him be Laura. You go right on ahead and let go now, there's a good girl," Tom ordered.

"You fuck off," she snarled. "I don't like you. You're the fella was mean to Sarah. Treated her unkindly earlier today, didn't you? You're a bad one. Why this brother of yours is as far away from bad as anyone ever was. I can tell. You leave go of

59

him and let me show him a good time."

"Don't need no good time. Why he's probably liable to catch something off of your snatch. I'm betting you been with so many fellas your starting to go out of date down there."

"*Excuse* me?" said Laura.

"Alright that was harsh. And I apologise. Just leave my brother be and we'll forget about it, right?"

"No, *you* leave go. You leave go of him or else Elsie's gonna find out what you just said to me. You can kiss Sarah goodbye after that statement. I'll see to it that you never see her again, I swear it."

"By God girl, it's only a big pecker. What you going to all this trouble for?"

"Fella's kind. Always wanted a fella that's kind who's packing a big pistol downstairs. Don't get kind fellas that's hung. Hell, all the kind ones are tiny. Expect that's why they are kind, because they have to be, or no woman would go near them. That's what I reckon."

"That's what you reckon," Tom said quietly, resigning himself to the fact that Abel's first fuck was to be with a whore, and not a wife, which was what he wanted for his brother.

He looked into Abel's face. It was fraught with fear that he was about to be torn in two by Tom and this lioness that wouldn't leave him be. If Tom had asked he'd have told him he wanted to go home; go home and wait by the hot stove for mama's return. But Tom didn't ask. Instead, he let go of his brother's limb, letting go a sigh simultaneously.

"I'll pay," he said, shoulders slumped. "You just put it on my tab Laura. I'll allow it."

"Much obliged. Come on Abel. You come with me now. We gonna have us a mighty time together."

The whore then took Abel gently by the hand and guided him upstairs. In a matter of moments the door closed out the rest of the wicked world below, with Abel and Laura both bound for bed.

"Beer," said Tom, looking up at the door in disbelief. "Better get the beer for Frank."

He skulked moodily over by the bar, stopped and stood adjacent to the piano player that was punching ferociously at his keys like if he stopped for even a second the devil might catch him and haul the portly fellow all the way down to hell.

"Mighty fine piano player sir. If you don't mind my saying so," Tom said, though the man hunched over the ivories paid him no notice. He just kept on jabbing with fat fingers, looking up at the top of the music box occasionally, but mostly just staring down, studying his keys carefully. "Ain't a conversationalist," said Tom. He nodded and looked down the bar, assessing the quality of the clientele. He quickly came to the conclusion that if he had to play piano in a place like this, he too would refrain from talking to the people that breezed in and out of this seedy, smoky, sinful den of debauchery and hedonism.

He liked to come here to pay Sarah a visit whenever he could, but being employed here, he did not care for that notion. *Living* here was *completely* out of the question. He looked up at the door that now housed his brother, then his eyes flicked from there to the door belonging to his beloved. Boy was taking his time with her. Either that or Tom had missed him when he was leaving.

"Let me guess," came Elsie's voice from behind the bar. "Be a whiskey, won't it?"

Tom turned to find her blowing her fringe from her eyes, her skin sweating all over, which wasn't surprising, for the heat in the place was stifling.

It surprised Tom to see people puffing on cigars and cigarettes and the occasional pipe here and there, given how suffocating the atmosphere already was even without the smoke.

"Be a beer as a matter of fact Elsie. Hell, make it two. I'll imbibe myself."

"Don't know that that's wise. Why where is Sarah anyways? She still up there?"

"That's what I reckon. Reckon she ain't come down. Not unless she slipped by me."

"Maybe go up and knock. Fella she was with's probably long gone by now. You with that black fella? Frank is

61

it?"

"I am," said Tom.

"Right," said Elsie, "I'll take the beers over to him. You go on and check on your gal. But I'm telling you this Tom, you treat her right. I mean it now. I ain't fooling. Fucking treat her right or else I'll see to it she gets wise and kicks you out for good."

"Alright," said Tom, tucking in his shirt. After fixing his shirttails away tidily in his pants, he brushed his hair in the big mirror that hung behind the bar, but because the brushing brought Abel to mind, he cut it out quick.

He winked at Elsie, who smiled a small smile back before busying herself with the beers. Tom took the stairs to the first floor, every step forward growing heavier and heavier until at last he arrived on the first floor with an immense weight in his chest. His heart thumped and thumped like someone banging a drum in his chest. He was eager to see her, but he knew he had to play things just right, or it might mean losing the only girl he'd ever loved.

"Leave me be," Sarah's voice sounded from inside. She sounded as though she were crying. The thoughts of uncertainty in Tom were whisked away by the sound of Sarah's sobs, swapped out for feelings of determination. That fellow – the man who'd been paying for the privilege of time spent with the prettiest whore in Texas, according to Tom – was hurting her. Hurting her enough to make her cry. A fact that Tom would not, nor indeed could not abide. His hand groped for the handle and he pushed, only to find that the door was locked. He didn't hesitate. He took two small steps back and began to boot and boot. Down below all the chatter came to a halt. The only sound that persisted was the piano, played by the man fixed firmly in the opinion that the music would cease for neither love nor money.

"Leave me *be*!" Sarah wailed when Tom broke through the door, the heavy wooden thing falling to the floor with a loud bang.

Inside the sight was horrifying. It made Tom Liffey

loaded and cocked with crossness and hatred like a Henry rifle is a forty-four calibre bullet, the hammer drawn back and ready for firing.

He had a straight razor in one hand. In the other there was clutched a shred of torn fabric Tom took to have been ripped right off the dress Sarah was wearing. The sheets were stained with blood, and Sarah had a huge gash cut across her fine features, some of the blood dribbling down her chin and dripping down into a crimson pool on the floor. Her arms were cut up too. She even had a slice cut deep into her shin. She was sitting like a doll would, legs sprawled out in front of her, her arms up, both of them acting as shields to keep this fellow with the razor from working further on her face. Her face was a mess of tears and snot and blood. When she caught sight of Tom there appeared to be a glint of relief that flashed in her eyes. Tom hadn't noticed the man turn to face him. He only saw Sarah at first.

"Fuck off you," said the man. "Don't concern you friend."

"I ain't your friend sir," said Tom, taking no time to think and drawing the weighty Dragoon. "Drop the razor now, there's a good man. You just set it down there on the floor and you take two or three steps away from my woman."

"*Your* woman? Why you ain't too smart, is you? This here's a whore mister. Fella pays for a time with her, and I *have* paid. Means I can do as I please. So, like I said friend, fuck off and leave us be. Business ain't concluded yet."

The man then turned to Sarah and grabbed at her arm where a large cut was, causing the girl to groan loudly as he hauled her to her feet.

Tom didn't think again, just acted. He cocked his piece, paced two large steps in the man's direction and pressed the barrel of his big revolver right up against the back of his hateful head.

"You leave her be before I blow your damn head of *sir*. You might have called me friend but I ain't one to the likes of you. You told me to fuck off and I aim to disappoint. Drop that there razor and walk away, or I will shoot. Don't try me because I will. Woman's my gal. Ain't you Sarah?"

Her frightened eyes found Tom's, again a flicker of hope flitting through them. Sarah nodded, but still didn't dare speak. They weren't out of the woods yet. This man still had a hold on her. He still had that razor, and Tom had yet to fire.

"Friend, you best be leaving. If you don't, I'll kill you stone dead interfering in my *business*!" the man exclaimed.

"Ain't no kind of business cutting at a girl," said Tom, pressing the barrel of his pistol so hard against the man's head he had to hunch forward, slackening his grip on Sarah's arm.

"Alright," he said. "Alright."

The next thing Tom heard was the sound of the razor bouncing off the wood of the floor by the man's boots.

"Good," said Tom. "That's good. You get out now, you hear?"

Tom took a look at Sarah and directed with his head for her to make for the door. She didn't move, frozen with fear.

"Do as I bid Sarah. Everything's alright now. No one's gonna hurt you now none. Now go on girl."

Sarah tried to make a move but still this fellow held on. With his other hand he flicked down a derringer from his sleeve into his hand. He then let go of Sarah, tried to turn to face Tom, who had fired and hollowed the man's head in an instant.

The señorita pistol poked a whole through the floor, though that was all the damage done. Dropping down to the floor, the man left a mighty stain on both Tom's girl as he did on Sarah's good clean curtains. One would wash off easily, the other stain would not. Tom pointed the gun down at the man, afraid he'd not got the job done boring a hole right through the man's head. Sarah rushed right into his arms and held him so tightly. Her face pressed up against his collar bone. She thought for sure that she'd stay there forever and ever, from that day until the end of time.

12.

"Everybody out!" Elsie shouted over the crowd's murmurings and conversing about the shots that had just gone off on the first floor. "Everyone go on home. We're closing up for the night. Now on you go, you can come back tomorrow. There'll be a free drink in it for your troubles. Tonight though this here whorehouse is shut. So go on, *get*!"

The crowd mumbled and grumbled as they went reluctantly.

"Right you," Elsie puffed, "you let me have a look at them there cuts. Go get me a clean cloth Tom. A *clean* one now, not a dirty one. Wounds are liable to get infected if we take a dirty rag to them."

"This one?" said Tom from behind the bar.

"No no no. Not that one. That one's dirty. *Christ*! Here let me get it. You're useless Tom Liffey, do you know that? Useless. You'll make some sorry husband I can tell you that."

"There's no need for that. I'm only after saving her from that there fella. No need to get on my back about picking out the wrong rag."

"Yeah well," Elsie said as she retrieved a well washed rag, throwing the other one Tom had chosen back into the dirty bucket where it belonged. "Bastard," she said to herself when she walked around the side of the bar. "Bastard of a man," she repeated.

"Who me?" Tom asked.

"No not you. Fella that done the cutting. Had him figured for a mean one when he walked in. Knew to look at him that he was trouble, and I didn't say nothing. It's my fault Sarah. My fault, and I'm sorry. Should never have let him in. Didn't know he'd get up to this kind of caper. Knew he was bad, but I didn't know he was *that* bad. Boys come in here all the time for a poke and that's that. There ain't no need for mean men to take razors to my girls. No need at all. We provide a service, don't we Sarah?"

Sarah was shivering like she'd been left way up in Canada, sitting down dead smack in the middle of an icy river right in the middle of winter. She was sweating, something both Tom and even Frank found perplexing, given how she looked to be cold. A group of whores had assembled all around Sarah, some supportive, some giggling. Elsie tarred them all with the one brush, becoming angered all of a sudden by the gigglers.

"Get upstairs all of you! You go on now! No need for any of you girls to stand gawking at her. Ain't gonna make her feel better none."

"You want us to take the body out of the house?" asked one woman with fiery red hair and even more fetching freckles than Sarah had.

"That won't be necessary. We'll keep him out back until the Sheriff arrives in the morning. But one of you can go and get him tomorrow. Expect he'll be asleep at this hour."

The one with the red hair leaned in close and kissed Sarah on the cheek and gave her hand a squeeze. Sarah looked up and a small smile seem to blossom on her lips, leaving her face every bit as quickly as it had appeared. She was back shivering, hitching in and out shallow, unsteady breaths.

"Be best if you eat something," said Elsie. "Else that shock mightn't wear off until next week." Elsie looked over her shoulder at the last lady leaving and shouted, "You got any food in the kitchen?"

"There's some bread I think. There might be some butter," answered the whore whose hair looked as though someone had set a small stick of dynamite on her scalp and lit the fuse. Looked to Tom like her head had exploded, with all the hair shooting off in every direction. Mustn't take to combing that really regular, Tom thought, though she sure could use it.

"That'll be fine," said Elsie. "You go get it and bring it here. Then you get up them there stairs. Don't need no audience here."

The whore disappeared and Elsie dunked the cloth into a glass of water, wetting it before dabbing very gently at poor Sarah's cuts.

"Cut you deep," said Elsie. "That there razor must have been a sharp one."

Sarah hissed in through her teeth, wincing when Elsie touched a really raw part of her many cuts.

"Don't mean to hurt you none darling. Don't mean it at

66

all. But I gotta get them cuts clean. Maybe get some ointment on them and you'll be right as the mail. That sound alright?"

Sarah nodded. Tom stood helplessly and Frank sat quite close to Sarah, though the man didn't dare reach out and coil his arm around her shoulder, no matter how much he was dying to do so. Frank felt so sorry for Sarah. Tom felt bad, but Frank felt worse.

"Why do men do such things?" Frank asked as gently as he could, taking great care to make each syllable fall like a feather, not clang like a bell in the cut girl's ears.

"I don't know," Elsie answered. "Some men's just bad I suppose. Seems some come into town after leaving God knows what in their wake. Why I'll bet this ain't the first time that fella's done this. Reckon he had a habit of it."

"Yeah well," said Tom. "It might not be the first, but it sure as shit'll be the last. Made sure of it let me tell you. Brains is blowed to kingdom come. Don't reckon he'll wield a blade anymore after tonight. Won't even be able to take out his pecker for a piss. Man's dead." He then leaned down, took both of Sarah's hands in his and squeezed with all his might. "You hear that girl?" he said. "Son of a bitch won't hurt you none no more. Made sure of that. That fella's dead as a door nail. You ain't got nothing to worry about no more. Alright?"

Sarah kept her head bowed, but her eyes lifted to find Tom's. She nodded quickly, then, pushing poor Elsie aside – who was only trying to help – she wrapped both her arms around Tom and squeezed him so hard he thought he might pop like a pimple. She started to sob into his shirt, soaking the coarse, itchy fabric with her tears, though Tom didn't mind.

"Sit down Sarah girl. Go on. Let Elsie clean your cuts," he said.

Sarah nodded into his shoulder before letting go of Tom. She sat back down again, making minute sobbing sounds as Elsie continued cleaning. There came a clatter from behind as the whore who'd been sent to fetch food threw the tin plate down on the bar's countertop with an awfully loud clanging noise.

"There's your bread," the whore said. "I'm away

upstairs like you wanted Elsie. Else there's anything else you need."

"You got any ointment?" said Elsie. But the woman was already off up the stairs, and if she had heard Elsie's request, she didn't show it. Instead she slammed the door shut behind her. "Jealous," said Elsie. "Some girls get jealous," she explained to Tom. "Especially when it's me who gives another girl attention and not them. Though don't you worry Sarah girl. They'll get over it fast. 'Fore you know it they'll be back speaking to you again in no time. Go get the bread and butter Tom, would you?"

"Yes ma'am," said Tom, leaving Frank to sit and fret beside the girl he secretly hoped would someday be his. "Butter's a bit hard," said Tom from the bar. "Bread's a bit hard too."

"Don't matter none. It's all we got. Unless that girl went and hid all the other food, which I doubt. Don't dawdle now, bring it over Tom."

Tom lifted the plates and brought the bread and butter over by Sarah. He tore a piece off, tried to butter it but did a poor job, then handed her the bit of bread with a large lump of solid butter plonked down in the middle of it like a little yellow mountain.

"Maybe bite gentle first," Tom suggested. "It is a bit hard. Hell, I reckon even Abel would tell you that. The hell is that boy anyways?"

Frank scratched at his chin, then, with the same hand, he pointed upstairs to the door belonging to the only whore who hadn't appeared after the shots. She came out just then, giggling away at Abel, who lumbered out after her pulling at her dress to try and get her back to bed.

"Boy you got some appetite!" she said. "Some job you done on me."

"I didn't do no job," said Abel. "All I did was lie there and you made me feel funny. I liked it though. I did indeed."

"That there pecker did all the work," said the whore as she reached down and groped his groin, giving it a good hard squeeze. "Say Elsie," she shouted, leaning over the banister on her elbows. "What was that bang? Someone hammer a nail or something?"

"Somebody got shot," Tom shouted up. "You come on now and leave that there girl be Abel."

"He's alright," said Laura. "Why he don't mean no harm, do you honey?"

Abel stuck his thumb of one hand in his mouth and bit gently on it with his teeth, tugging at her skirt with his other hand.

"Who got shot?" she shouted down, before turning to look inside Sarah's room, which was adjacent to her own. "Christ!" she exclaimed. "Fella's dead anyway." Then, shouting back down to Elsie and Tom, "Why'd he get shot? What he do? He try to take a poke without paying?"

"He cut up Sarah," shouted Elsie. "And quit your hollering. She's scared enough without having to listen to you roar at us. You wanna talk you come down. Else you go back in your room like the rest of the girls and wait until I say you can come out."

"I'll come down Elsie," she said much quieter. "Come on big dick," she said to Abel. "You follow me mister man."

Abel giggled as she took him by the hand and led him down the stairs. He was like a puppy, and had taken to this woman in a way that Tom both saw and knew meant more moaning for him to have to listen to. Abel was already obsessed, meaning mama and pa wouldn't be the end of it. He had something new now to fixate on. Tom was not happy.

"Hell brother," he said once Laura and Abel were by his side. "You bothering that there lady?"

"I wasn't!" Abel declared. "Don't think I was, for I wasn't. Wasn't bothering her at all. Why we was making each other happy, wasn't we?"

"Uh-huh!" beamed Laura. "Happier than a couple of newlyweds walking out of a church on the sunniest day of the year. You couldn't charge for that. That there boy's able to ride a girl ragged. Real talent he has in them there pants of his. Hell, I'd pay *him* for the pleasure, not the other way around."

"Alright, alright," said Elsie. "Enough blue talk. This here girl's hurting. She don't need no talk about boys and girls

69

making love. Leave it be now Laura. Leave it alone."

"Alright Elsie," said Laura. "Didn't mean nothing by it."   "It's alright. You got ointment?"

"What for?"

"For Sarah's cuts damn it. You blind?"

"Yeah I reckon I do. It's in my cabinet upstairs."

"Well go get it," said Elsie. "And hurry up about it."

Laura turned to go, but Abel stopped her.

"I'll get it," he said. "You stay right there my love."

"My *love*?" Laura laughed. "Why you're quite the gentleman ain't you?"

"Yes miss," Abel grinned before bolting back up the stairs and disappearing into Laura's room once more.

"Mighty fine pecker, sure. That is a fact. But I reckon you was right Tom. Reckon he ain't been blessed with brains. But he sure knows how to please a woman. Boy's talented, let me tell you."

"*Enough*!" Elsie boomed. "Enough now, you hear? I mean it."

"Sorry Elsie," said Laura, linking her hands in front of her, her head bowed down like as though she were about to confess her sins before the Lord God almighty.

"Alright Sarah, stop pulling away. Got to get the cuts clean or else they're liable to get all infected."

"Sorry Elsie," Sarah said softly, before bursting into a downpour of hot tears.

"Oh there now. There now sweetie. It's alright. Ain't gonna get you again. Your man made sure of that, didn't he? Didn't you Tom?"

"Did indeed," Tom nodded. "Knocked him right out of the land of the living when I squeezed this here trigger. Sent him heading for hell as fast as bullets can fly. Fucker's brains didn't stand a chance. Why I reckon them there curtains is ruined from here to Christmas, even if you was to wash them every damn day. Yes ma'am, that's what I reckon."

"Right," said Elsie. "Put a little indelicately but there you have it Sarah. Fella's spirit has flown. Forever. Won't be

70

hurting you none no more. Won't be hurting *any*one no more. His hurting days is over."

"That's right," Tom nodded, planting his paw on Sarah's shoulder. She was still crying, though her right hand found its way up to Tom's and grabbed the first finger and clung on like a helpless baby would grab at a man with her tiny fist. Then Sarah looked up at the first floor, her brow furrowed, for Abel had appeared again in the doorway to Laura's room, his arms full with the entire medicine cabinet, having ripped the thing right off the wall.

"I wasn't sure which ointment you wanted, so I thought that I'd be smart and bring you them all."

Tom looked on in horror, as did Frank, for Abel was well hidden coming waddling down the stairs, the colossal cabinet concealing the sillier of the two brothers behind it.

"Reckon you'll have a choice. Better that way. Better than me having to go to trouble running up and down again."

Everyone looked like they were almost offended by how stupid Abel was. Sarah was the first to smile, as well as the first to get giggling. By the time Abel had thunked the cabinet down on the table in front of her and Elsie, Sarah was laughing loud and clear. Pretty soon she was doubled over in a kind of hiccupping hysteria. Then Tom too began to laugh. Then Elsie, then even Frank cracked a smile. The only one who wasn't smiling was Laura, now feeling a little uneasy about having taken this imbecile to bed.

"Boy, have you lost your mind?" she said. "Take that there cabinet back up to my room now."

"Now hold on," said Elsie. "Give me the ointment first. Fella's gone to the trouble of delivering us the medicine. Might as well get it before he carts it off again."

Elsie opened the cabinet containing all kinds of elixirs and creams. She found one with antiseptic qualities, removed that one then shut the cabinet door again once more.

"Very kind of you, isn't it Laura?" Elsie said in such a stern manner her employee got the message.

"Mighty kind Abel," Laura replied reluctantly.

"Thank you, my love," said Abel, standing there looking about as dumb as a fence post.

"Please would you take that back upstairs now Abel?" said Elsie. "You're very kind."

"No problem, ma'am. Why I'd be happy to," said Abel, before lifting it and letting out a good groan – the thing was right and heavy – then carting it off back up the stairs.

"What's wrong with him?" Laura said to Tom in hushed tones.

"Your guess is as good as mine," he answered. "You get to forget there's something wrong, until he does something that reminds you again. But I'll tell you this, you've done me no favour by fucking him. He'll go on and on and on about you now. Never let up. It'll be Laura this and Laura that, all the live long day. Don't reckon we can turn the clock back now though, can we?"

"Well I ain't taking him for my own. Might be blessed with a mighty tree trunk of a pecker, but he's dim. Dimmer than any fella I've ever taken to my bed. Boy's not right in the head."

"Hush now the pair of you," Elsie interrupted. "There's more important things to worry about. Sarah for one."

"Sorry Elsie," Tom and Laura said in unison.

"Don't go saying sorry to me. It's Sarah you ought to say it to. Standing there bickering while she's shivering and shaking."

"Sorry my love," said Tom.

Laura just said "Sorry."

Sarah had a strange smile on her face. It wasn't a warm smile; it was almost mean. Made mean maybe by what had been done to her, as though the man doing the cutting had simultaneously bitten her and delivered a spoonful of venom, that was now just about ready to pour out of her.

"He's so dumb," she said quietly. Then she lifted her hand to her mouth and howled into the back of it. "He's so Goddamn dumb I can hardly believe it," she said, now doubled over again, though this time it seemed to Tom she'd never stop laughing. "Look at him!" she pointed as Abel came down the stairs with that gormless, glazed look in his eyes and that stupid grin. "God almighty!" Sarah cried. "I'm gonna bust open!"

"Calm yourself girl. You'll make the fool feel bad if you carry on laughing like that at him," Elsie instructed.

"But Elsie! Look at him! He's so simple!" she howled. "He's so damn dumb!"

"Don't keep *on*," Elsie instructed. "Stop now before you hurt his feelings. He was kind enough to go get you this here ointment. Now *stop*."

"I can't!" cried Sarah. "I can't!"

Then Abel was with them again, still smiling, still brainless.

"What we laughing at?" he asked. This got Sarah going even more, which in turn started Abel to laughing. Pretty soon Sarah and Abel were laughing together, the sound filling the whole whorehouse to the brim with cheer.

"I don't even…" Abel tried to get out round his guffaws, "I don't even know… what we're laughing at!"

"You, you dummy!" Sarah said heartlessly. "*You*! I'm laughing at you! Jesus Christ you're the dumbest boy I ever seen walk into this here establishment, and believe me I've seen plenty."

The laughter had stopped on Abel's part. The boy's brow was well furrowed, his eyes filled full of confusion and hurt.

"You're laughing at me?" he said in a helpless voice.

"Yes!" Sarah confirmed. "That's right!"

"Go you on out Abel," said Elsie. "She don't mean nothing by it. She's just in shock. She don't mean it. Tom'll take you outside won't you Tom?"

"Hah?" said Tom. He'd been studying Sarah hard, trying to decipher where she'd been broken on the inside to make her mean, which she never was before.

"You'll take him out for air, won't you Tom?"

"Yeah, right," said Tom, taking his brother by the arm and leading him outside.

"She's laughing at *me*?" Abel asked as he went.

73

"Wasn't laughing at you," Tom told him. "She just ain't feeling right right now. That's all. Ain't laughing at you. You did a good job bringing down that there medicine."

"Maybe I shouldn't have brought down the medicine box. Was that a silly thing to do?"

Tom wanted to say yes. That that was a dumb thing to do. But he sensed his brother was hurting having been made a mockery of, so he said something else instead.

"You did fine Abel. You got what we was looking. You did right by Sarah. Okay? So don't go feeling bad none."

"What about Laura? Did I do right by her?" he asked.

Tom scanned his brother's face, finding no lively intelligence lingering behind his eyes.

"Yes," Tom said, "you showed her a good time. Real good time I reckon. But listen, Laura, that girl, she ain't yours Abel. Ain't like mama. She don't belong to you and she ain't family. Fancied a fuck, but that's all. Alright? Now I need you to understand this. It's very important that you do. Don't take her being all affectionate to mean she wants you in the way you do. She doesn't. It's her job to do what she did with you Abel. It's her work. We won't be bringing her to Georgia, so don't ask. You understand? This is important now, and I need to know you understand."

"It's her job?" Abel asked trepidatiously, the hurt in his face more than apparent to Tom.

"Jesus Christ," Tom sighed. "Look. Laura was nice to you, yes?"

Abel nodded.

"She showed you a good time?"

Abel nodded again.

"Well she did that 'cause I paid her to. If I hadn't she wouldn't have done it. It's like buying a bag of candy in a store. You don't get no treat unless you pay for it. You see?"

"So Laura's the candy?" said Abel.

"That's right," Tom said, planting his mitts on both of Abel's shoulders. "She's the candy. And I've paid for it the once, but I won't be doing so again."

"Why not?"

"Because she don't want to go again."

"Why not?"

Tom thought then that his only recourse was to hurt his message into Abel, and though it brought him no enjoyment whatsoever to do so in this instance, he was compelled to hurt him nonetheless.

"She thinks your dumb Abel."

"I'm not dumb," Abel argued. "Why I can count higher than you or Frank can."

"Can't read though, can you? You can't take care of yourself. Shit brother, you can't even brush your own Goddamn hair."

"I can," Abel pouted. "I can too. I just like it when other people does it for me. If you don't know that then maybe you're the dumb one."

With that Abel turned on his heels and went stomping off into the night. Tom ran his hand through his hair, with the other hand on his hip.

"Jesus Christ brother," he whispered at the darkness, before turning to go back into the whorehouse, where Sarah, the girl he loved, was waiting.

13.

"Go out and get him Frank, would you?" Tom asked. Frank stood and put on his battered hat.

"Where's he off to?" he said.

"Don't know. But when you find him take him home. I'll be back shortly."

"Right," Frank nodded. But before he went, he had one last little look at Sarah, who didn't lift her head to acknowledge the man, though he didn't mind. She was in shock. She'd been hurt bad and wasn't for noticing men much at that moment. He left the whorehouse and dissolved into the blackness shrouding the entire town of Taughrane Heights.

Elsie had a tiny white mountain of cream on her finger, and though she did not know what it was or what it was supposed to be for, she nevertheless applied it to Sarah's cuts carefully and with the maximum amount of gentleness she could.

"That's you now," she said once the white mountain had been reduced to a smudge, the cream coating every cut visible. "You feel a bit better now?"

"Yes ma'am. Yes Elsie."

"Alright then. Now Tom, before you go, I want you to take that fella's body down them stairs and out through the back door. Coal shed out the back's where we'll store him. Wolves won't get him there. He's to stay there until the morning, when it's a decent hour to wake the Sheriff. If he was wakened now why then he might be inclined to have a feeling for framing you to be the murderer. We wouldn't want that. We'll go get him in the morning, then you can explain yourself thoroughly. That sound fair enough?"

"That all sounds fine. Except I want to know what you intend on doing with her," said Tom.

"She'll be going back up to sleep in that there room. Once I've washed all the blood and bits of brain away."

Sarah's eyes flooded with wet, salty tears, though she didn't blubber. Instead, she sniffed back some snot, then very quietly asked if she could stay somewhere else instead.

"Why of course! Jesus! Not being very sensitive am I Sarah girl?" said Elsie. "You can stay in my room. I'll sleep in yours. That sound fair enough?"

Sarah didn't nod or shake her head. She looked up at Tom with a pleading expression on her face, that he knew meant she wanted far, far away from this wicked place.

"Elsie, I think…" Tom began, but was interrupted by the establishment's owner.

"You think *what* Tom Liffey? You figuring on leaving with this here girl? Hell, I'd sooner send her off with a pack of rabid wolves than let her leave here with you tonight. You don't treat her right. I can, and you can't. Ain't leaving with you. Out

76

of the question. Girl's staying here and that's final. No more talk about it."

"Elsie, she don't want to stay here," said Laura.

"Laura girl you just keep that there nose of yours out of it. Don't know what the hell you're still doing here anyway. Why you've fucked his brother for him. Did that boy a favour some. Maybe rode some sense into him for a change. But don't you dare start in on me too. Don't need no ganging up on me."

"I wouldn't want to stay here," Laura offered. "If something like that was to happen to me I sure would want away. All's I'm saying."

"Yeah well don't just say. You can keep your thoughts to yourself. You can go ahead on up them stairs right about now. No need for your interjecting. Didn't ask none at all for your opinion, and far less do I want it."

"She's not staying here," Tom said, bringing a smile to Sarah's face. "She's coming home with me."

"Over my dead body. Bitch is the best whore I have, and I ain't giving her up. So you can stick that in your pipe and smoke it. She stays and that's that."

"I don't…" Sarah began before coughing out the choked tears in her throat. "I don't want to stay here Elsie. If it's all the same to you, I'd like to go with Tom. I ain't gonna be sporting none no more anyways."

"Why sure you are sweetheart. He was just one man. Don't let him put you off. Why he's just one fella in a hundred. Hell, one in a thousand maybe. You ain't liable to run into none of his kind ever again. And I won't let you. If I see a fella I think's bad, I'll just tell them to get lost and leave fast 'fore I go get the Sheriff for pestering my girls. You'll be safe enough, so you'll stay. Now no more talk about it. You go on into my room and rest now. You sleep it off and I reckon you'll feel far different come the morning. I'd bet my life on it."

Sarah stood unsteadily, taking two tiny steps toward Tom.

"I'm heading out with Tom Elsie. That's what I want and that's the way it's gonna be. Be best you get that in your head now and settle the fact down. Don't want to stay here anymore. I'm through with this here whorehouse. Through with sporting. Gonna settle down with my man. Maybe have babies and raise them with him, if he'll let me."

She looked up into Tom's face with those large, blue doe eyes that had charmed so many men before him, but would only cast their spell from then on on him and him alone.

"I will. Why if I had a ring on me, I'd put it on your finger and wed you first thing tomorrow morning. If you'd let *me*, that is."

"I would," Sarah smiled.

"So that's it?" Elsie said, throwing up her hands despondently. "After all I've done for you, you're just gonna up and leave me for some fucking fella ain't got no money, ain't got no prospects, except maybe a burgeoning problem with whiskey that he can keep in check no more than that fella up there's gonna get up and walk and talk again!"

"Don't take it thick Elsie," Sarah cooed. "This here man might have no money, but he's *my* man, and that counts for far more than any amount of dollars."

"Doesn't," said Elsie. "What are you gonna live on? *Air*? Money don't grow on trees, in case you didn't know that already."

"Elsie, stop!" said Laura. "Leave it alone," she said, letting her hand land on Elsie's. "You shouldn't scold them like that. If I were Sarah I wouldn't stay."

"Oh shut up," said Elsie. "What would you know? You been whoring so long and so hard you don't know nothing else just like Sarah. Both of you girls owe me for letting you live here, and you'd best be remembering that. Now both of you go to bed before I really lose my temper."

"Go on Sarah," said Laura. "Leave now and don't you dare look back."

"Bitch you'd better be shutting up some time soon, else I'm liable to show you a thing or two about behaving."

"Go on now," said Laura. "Forget about this witch."

"Why you little…" said Elsie, somewhat struck but this

display of insolence, knowing of nothing better to do than to slap the girl hard, which she did do.

"Fuck you Elsie!" Laura cried as her palm pressed up against her hot cheek. "You can be a real bitch sometimes, you know that?"

Elsie took a tuft of Laura's hair, hurting her badly by tugging at it.

"You listen Laura. And you listen good. Long as you're under my roof you'll speak to me with a civil tongue. Don't need no whore who doesn't know how to speak to her boss. Be best you consider up and leaving if you're gonna continue to talk to me like that."

Elsie then released her hold on Laura, leaving her to massage her tender scalp as she looked down at the floor.

"You're fucking staying missy. Make no mistake about that. This Tom fella's no good. Get up them stairs now and get to bed, before I lose the rag with you too. Don't want to have to hurt you more than you already have been, but I will if you don't see some sense. You understand?"

Sarah studied Elsie hard. Her employer's face was not displaying the slightest smidge of pity. It was cross and determined looking, and Sarah knew she had no hope of convincing Elsie that her leaving was a nice notion.

"I'm going now Elsie. I'm going," she said matter-of-factly, before hooking her arm around the crook of Tom's elbow and tugging at him until he got going.

"Good *girl*!" Laura cheered. "Nice one Sarah!" she boomed before her employer took a tuft of her hair and began dragging the poor girl up those stairs to her bedroom.

"You shut your mouth and stay out of it!" Elsie shouted as she turned the key to lock Laura's room from the outside. "You're staying even if Sarah ain't. Not losing two girls in the one night. No fucking way!"

Elsie then came down puffing and panting in an enraged way. She searched through the pleasure palace's front door, but, only finding darkness, decided to go behind the bar and pour herself a stiff drink while she lamented losing probably the best – or at least the sweetest – whore in the whole territory.

Sarah looked back just the once, but didn't dare to a second time for fear that her resolve to leave might shake or quake and she should race back and run right up those stairs and stay working for Elsie. It wasn't easy for her to leave the woman after having been with her for so long. But now that that mean man had done what he'd done to her, her leaving was quite, quite necessary. By the time she reached Tom's house however, she wasn't thinking about anything else but her man, that warm arm of his that she clung tightly to, and the day that would be coming sooner or later when Tom Liffey would make her his wife.

14.

Sarah's eyes opened, blinking in the thick, heavy rays of light landing on eyeball then eyelid, then eyeball then eyelid and so on. It took her a few moments to see that there was a shape standing by her bed. Then again a few more moments to discover that, in the dingy room that had appeared much larger during the darkness she'd entered into it, Tom's feeble-minded brother was watching her, just a few feet from her face.

"You come home with Tom," he said plainly – stating the obvious as Tom called it so very many, many times.

"You're right there," she said sleepily. "Where is he?"

Abel shrugged. She rubbed at her bleary eyes, then her hand went out to the side of the mattress she'd known Tom to be on when she'd drifted off. When she found it vacant a flutter of panic flitted all through her. She was suddenly alone with a man again, and Tom wasn't there with her. She started and jumped up out of bed in the nightie she always wore under her dress. The thin fabric flowed behind her, accentuating her bodily bumps like a shallow brook shows off each and every stone that it rolls over while the river runs. Abel liked the look of her. He couldn't help it. But that wasn't the reason he was staring so hard. He hadn't had his head brushed for the first time in a long, long time, and he supposed Sarah might be kind enough to do it for him, which he requested of her right away.

He was clutching the brush, brandishing it like a blade – or indeed a razor – as he chased after her as she fled from the little cramped shack, on out into the dazzling sunshine. She stepped in pig excrement in her bare feet but couldn't have cared less. She wanted, no, *needed* to see Tom that very instant, and she felt as if nothing might stop her until she did.

"*Tom*?" she shouted. "*Tom*! Where are you?"

There was no answer. Had he gone? Had he left her all alone with his simpleton brother and the pigs for company? Rage flooded through her. Hating him, she scanned all about her but still could not find the man she sought. Then she felt hands cover her eyes from behind her.

"Guess who?" he said.

It was Tom's voice alright, though the man's choice of how he greeted the girl couldn't have been poorer. She elbowed him in the belly as he stood close behind her, though the blow wasn't too hard, so the wind wasn't knocked out of him.

"Don't 'guess who' me Tom Liffey. Don't you know I been cut up? Don't you know I'd be scared when you don't answer me calling you? You're a real jackass you know. Have as much brains as that idiot brother of yours."

"I was only funning you. No need to get cross. Anyways, I'm glad you're up. You can fix us breakfast. Frank and I are starving. Haven't eaten anything yet, and you're just the woman to remedy that fact for us both."

"Better not do that again," said Sarah. "You best be answering me when I call. You hear? Don't need no man sneaking up behind me and scaring me like that. Not after that fella last night."

"Sorry," said Tom, scratching at his itchy nose.

"Abel's talking about being brushed or something," she said after a moment.

"Shit! Don't tell me he's started in already with that?"

"With what?" said Sarah.

"He'll plague you now. Now he knows a woman's about he won't want me doing it no more."

81

"What? Brushing his hair?"

"Yeah. You might think a thing like that wouldn't grate on your nerves, but after a time it does. Doesn't let up every night until you do it for him. I'm sick of hearing him moan to me about it. You may do it now."

"It's only brushing his hair," she said.

"That's what you think, though after a month's worth of moaning you'll see what I mean. Anyway, will you fix us some breakfast? Bacon and eggs maybe? Mighty hungry girl. Got to see what you're like as a cook, if I'm aiming to marry you. Don't want no woman can't hardly cook worth a damn."

Sarah's eyebrows lifted so high they nearly flew all the way up off her head.

"Excuse me?" she said, astonished at this remark made by her husband-to-be.

"I'm only kidding. If you can't cook I won't give a damn. I love you Sarah, that's all there is to it."

"Better," she said, eyebrows beginning to lower.

"But you might as well give it a go. Just to see if you *can* cook. Hell, Frank and I'll eat anything. Abel too. But before you do cook us up something, would you run a brush through my brother's hair?"

"Sure," she shrugged, "but I want you to come in with me."

"Why?"

"*Why*? Because I don't want to be alone with a man right now, that's why!"

"What harm's Abel gonna do? Fella's as harmless as a bluebottle. Gets on your nerves like one, but he don't do no harm."

"I don't care. I don't feel like being alone with men right now."

"Now's the time *to* be alone with a man then. Got to get over that. I know you been hurt, but you gotta get over that right and quick if you're gonna live here. He won't harm you, I promise. And if he does you just holler your damn head off. It'll make me come running, and it'll scare Abel something serious.

But I tell you, he's a house fly. Makes a noise that'd step on your last nerve, but there's no harm in him. No harm at all."

Sarah stared hard at Tom. He just smiled back. So she scoffed and turned to go back inside the rickety shack she now had to call her home.

"And get the bacon on!" Tom called with a cupped hand to his face. Frank then sidled up beside Tom, taking a liberty by telling him he ought not to treat his woman that way. "Who made you the expert?" Tom said, somewhat floored by Frank's boldness.

"Best not antagonise a woman when she's got the fear of men in her. Liable to take to hating you. Sure she'll stick around, but that hatred of hers'll grow and grow, getting bigger and bigger until she's just about ready to bust open. Then there'll be hell to pay Mr. Liffey sir."

"She'll be fine. Just you collect a couple of eggs from the coop. Don't need no advice from you Frank. Why, have you ever even been with a woman?"

Frank felt like telling him that yes, he had. His woman as a matter of fact. Instead, he just shrugged and skulked off in the direction of the henhouse to go get those eggs.

Inside the shack, she'd begun brushing.

Abel hummed a tune to himself, then, when she stopped and said, "There. That's you now. Looking mighty fine Mr. Abel. Mighty fine indeed."

Abel giggled to himself, tickled by her calling him Mr. Abel. He liked that. Thought that he should return with the same joke himself.

"You're looking mighty fine too Mrs. Sarah."

She didn't laugh. She didn't feel like being the object of any man's desire at that point. Abel sensed her reticence to find amusement in his calling her Mrs. Sarah, so he apologised quite contritely.

"I'm sorry for calling you Mrs. Sarah ma'am. Awful sorry. Please keep brushing. *Please*. I don't want you to stop."

"No," she said. "It's alright you calling me that. I don't mind. But that's enough brushing for today."

"It's not!" Abel said, his voice climbing higher in volume. "It's not enough! I want you to keep brushing. I say when to stop. *Please*! Please ma'am!"

"Alright!" she said, lifting the brush again. "Alright, calm down. Don't get mad mister."

Abel giggled again.

"Mister," he said to himself. "I'm Mr. Abel."

This brought a smile to Sarah's face, though the girl couldn't help feeling as though this was just the beginning of the rest of her life – brushing an idiot's hair and putting up with her husband's commands for fixing him and his farmhand food. She wondered if she'd made a mistake leaving Elsie's. If Elsie would take her back if she showed up there that very morning. But then she thought of that man and his razor, ruling out the option of returning to her old place of work. Brushing Abel's hair might've put some strain in her wrist and elbow – he had very thin hair, but it still took a lot of effort to get the brush through it – but it was way better than running the risk of being carved up like a steak dinner every evening by some strange man. While she brushed, Abel came out with another corker of a statement.

"Do you think that Laura lady would like to be Mrs. Abel?" he asked his hairdresser, who in turn rolled her eyes, tutted and sighed, saying she didn't know, and that he'd have to ask her himself.

He nodded, stood straight up and said he'd do just that and that she should tell Tom he'd gone into town if his brother asked.

"Now wait," said Sarah. "Hold on. You don't want to appear too keen. You've only just met her last night. Now's not the time to go running your mouth with talk of marrying. Maybe leave it a few days darling. Don't want to come off as desperate. Girls don't like a man that's pining too hard. Puts them right off."

"Oh I wouldn't want that!" Abel said, his face washing white with fear, for he didn't wish to lose Laura, not after having had such a tremendous time with her the evening before.

"No you wouldn't. So why don't you just sit down there like a good boy. Be bacon and eggs for you in a minute if

84

you're good. You gonna be good Mr. Abel?"

Abel nodded, then let out a loud peal of laughter.

"Let's see if we can get Tom to call me that!" he boomed. "Bet you anything my brother won't."

"We can try, can't we?" said Sarah, getting out the pan from the cupboard and beginning to busy herself with the frying. "*Tom!*" she called.

"*Tom!*" Abel cried out straight after in an impersonation so close to Sarah's voice it frightened her a little.

"What is it?" Tom yelled from the yard. "You burn the bacon?"

"No, come here," said Sarah, as did Abel, again imitating his newfound friend.

"Fuck's sake. Here hold this a minute would you Frank? Fucking start of it now. Nag, nag, nag," Tom said before appearing at the back door. "What is it?" he said testily.

"Mr. Abel and I were wondering where the bacon is," Sarah said.

"He knows. Wait, what did you just call him?"

"What? Oh you mean Mr. Abel? Why he's that fellow right there," she said, pointing in the direction of the dunce who had a smarmy smile smeared across his face, amused beyond all bounds of reason at Sarah's being complicit in fooling his brother Tom.

"*What?*" Tom said, scrunching up his face.

"Mr. Abel," said Sarah. "Don't tell me you don't know Mr. Abel now Tom Liffey. Look, he's right there."

"I know my own damn brother. Been looking after him all these years."

"You mustn't know him, because he tells me that you don't call him by his proper name."

"Name's Abel. At least so our mama named him, 'fore fucking off to Georgia."

"Don't swear," she said firmly. "And that's not his name. Name's not just Abel."

"Well what is it then?"

"It's Mr. Abel," Abel interjected, unable to keep that

85

excitement simmering, instead allowing it to bubble up and over his happy pot's rim.

"Oh," said Tom. "Beg your pardon. Pardon me *Mister* Abel. Forgive me Mister Abel. Should have told me that that was your proper title. Why I been calling you the wrong name for oh, I don't know how many years. You two are clowns, you know that. That bacon ain't gonna fry itself up. Did Abel… sorry, *Mr.* Abel tell you the way he likes it?"

"No," said Sarah.

"Likes it burnt black. Burnt to a crisp so as it stinks up the house something serious. But being my brother, and being the biggest moaner in Texas, he gets his way whether we like it or not."

"I ain't having it stink up the place. Mr. Abel sweetie, would you be so kind as to take your bacon the way I make it?"

"I don't know," Abel said uncertainly. "I like it burnt black. But maybe, if it was tasty, I could maybe try it your way."

"*What*!" Tom squeaked. "Did my ears just deceive me, or did my own brother change his mind on something? Sweet sunny Jesus! *Hallelujah*! Is the apocalypse nigh? Has the good Lord given us as sign that he is come again? Oh Jesus! Sweet Jesus, Mary and Saint Joseph! It's a fucking miracle! Frank! *Frank*! You hear?"

"Hear what Mr. Liffey sir?" said Frank from where he was perched on the porch.

"Abel changed his mind."

"No sir!" said Frank, flabbergasted beyond belief. "Ain't Abel who changes his mind some. Why it's always been us that has to change for him Mr. Liffey sir. That's the way it is," said Frank, though curiosity took ahold of him. "What he change his mind about?"

"He's gonna try bacon a new way."

"Well I'll be Goddamned. I never thought I'd see the day."

"Nor did I Frank. Nor did I," said Tom, before bounding across the room, reaching out to take Sarah's face in both hands, before planting a kiss on both cheeks, her forehead and, lastly, lips. "I love you Sarah Herron. I love you more now than you can possibly know. Next step's getting rid of that brush."

"Be a while before that happens," Frank said cheekily, choosing to ignore every kiss Tom planted on his future fiancé, though the ignoring was akin to disregarding a man who's taken to digging his blade into poor Frank's loving, yet unrequited, heart, back and ribs. Really hurt the man to see him kiss her, and it hurt twice as much to watch her just let Tom do it. Though there was nothing to be done. Dumb Abel came to serve retribution for these quick kisses by dampening down the flames of Tom's joy like rain lashing down on a bonfire.

"Brush is going nowhere," Abel said authoritatively, in a way that meant he meant business. "Brush is going nowhere," he repeated again, softly the second time, fiddling with his beloved brush as though it had been bequeathed to him by a princess.

"Come on Frank," said Tom, patting his employee on the back. "Best get back at it." He then turned towards her and blew a kiss to Sarah, but her back was already to him. He looked at the back of her head and thought he'd never seen such a pretty back of a head in his whole life. Then, turning to Frank once more, said, "Can you imagine it Frank? Bacon you can actually eat! You believe that?"

There were more than a few things that Frank couldn't believe, number one on that list being that Sarah'd chosen him for a partner. Frank didn't think much of Tom looks-wise. He was lanky, like something you'd pull through the barrel of a gun. He had a high forehead but, admittedly, very blue eyes. His character wasn't up to Frank's high standards, though he'd given him a job and taken him in, so Frank owed Tom his loyalty for that. Though he wanted to tell Tom: "I can't believe it. Can't believe she'd pick you too. I mean what does she see in you anyways?" But this would go unsaid, even if it meant it'd eat Frank up inside every time he saw the two together. Instead, he just forced a smile, shrugged and said, "No I can't. Can't hardly believe it at all." Then the two men went back to work, waiting until their breakfast was ready.

15.

"I'm stuffed," said Tom as he sat back in his seat and unbuttoned the two dungaree straps to let his front bib fall down to his waist. "Why I ain't eaten so good in quite some time girl. Goddamn marvel in the kitchen."

"Click that there bib back in place. 'Least while you're at the damn dinner table," Sarah scolded. "Didn't your mama never teach you manners?"

"She tried to, but they never stuck," Tom said, winking at Frank. Frank didn't laugh. Frank had decided to play the long game; meaning maybe biding his time to see if maybe Sarah saw some sense and cut the bond between Tom and her. He would wait, as a spider does for the fly, then Frank the farmhand'd scurry on over to that fly and keep it there in his web and never let it go. Or so he hoped he would anyway.

Abel burped abruptly very violently, saying, "Excuse *me*!" just as swiftly after the wind did when it came up. "I'm so sorry. Shouldn't burp in front of a lady."

"That's alright mister. Mighty kind of you to offer your apologies. This animal on the other hand…" said Sarah, standing and reaching out to ruffle Tom's hair, before collecting the crockery.

Frank wanted to wait. Wanted more than anything for God to grant him the patience he needed. But he couldn't. He reckoned he'd have to start labouring after her sooner or later. He figured, why not sooner?

"Say miss, where in the hell did you learn to cook like that?" he said, standing and lifting his hat from the back of his chair before bringing it up to his chest in a kind of humble looking stance.

"Oh I've always been able in the kitchen," she said, dunking the crockery in the cold sink water.

"I'm in the kitchen," said Abel.

"No not you honey," she said, flicking her fringe out of

88

her eyes with a jerk of her head that Frank found to make her look like the prettiest of mares he'd *ever* seen. "Able's a word darling. Not just a name."

"Able Abel," Tom said sagely, nodding at his brother once he saw that his older sibling had gotten the picture.

"Have we any hot water on the boil anywhere?" she said.

"Are you asking me?" said Tom.

"Well who the hell else would I be asking dummy?" she said before hopping over to her man, giggling all the way, then tilting her husband-to-be's head backward and kissing him in a kind of upside-down way.

"Do you need me to go get you some water?" said Frank, ready to tear Tom apart at the seams should he continue in his unabashed exhibition of caresses and kisses and all the rest towards she who he hoped would take to him instead of Tom Goddamn Liffey. "Like me to get you some?" he said, crumpling up his good, if badly battered, hat. He was ready to rip his own skin off, just so as the act might stop her fawning all over Tom.

"That'd be fine Frank. Thank you. You see Tom? Now that there's a gentleman."

"No," said Tom. "He ain't just that."

He then swung his arm over the back of the chair, studying Frank for a moment before saying,

"He's a *good* man. The very best of them. That's our Frank. Gentleman too though I suppose."

"I'll get you that water now," Frank said to Sarah, before placing the crumpled hat on his head then heading on out, grabbing the bucket by the porch on the way.

The windy weather outside did nothing for his spirits, as did the pigs, who came up snuffling and snorting around his boots, begging for food. Frank normally treated them kindly, when they weren't chewing on his only pair of boots. But today he was in no mood for fun of any kind, and certainly not for fun with those damn pigs.

"You pigs get! You hear? You go on now and leave me be. I ain't joshing."

The pigs weren't to be deterred however. They followed close behind Frank and dug into his heels with their snouts. Then one made the mistake of nipping at the back of his leg and the poor farmhand lost it altogether.

"Leave me be Goddamn it!" he roared.

He turned to kick at them, causing the animal he'd booted to squeal in pain and run for cover over by the porch step. His friend was less afraid, and even attacked Frank for having hurt his buddy.

"Best you don't try it now," Frank warned the filthy animal. But it was too late. The large beast charged him, bumping into his knee and subsequently knocking him on his ass. As he tried to get up, another annoying animal snorted and charged too, though this one Frank got with the bucket. The blow dazed the pig, giving Frank just enough time to get to his feet, flee from the yard and hop the fence. He was panting as he walked wearily over to the well.

"What a shit life," lamented the farmhand. "Fucking raw deal all my damn life. Liffey boy has everything, and here's me with nothing. Got to change. Got to. Tide's gonna turn Tom. Just wait and see if it don't."

He lowered the well bucket down into the hollow hole in the earth, then tugged at the rope until it came back up full. Frank then had an awful idea. A truly nasty idea. He thought then that, if the opportunity presented itself, he might poison poor Tom. Though it would only come to that if Sarah showed some kind of sign that she was swaying in Frank's favour. No point, he thought. No point killing another man if the woman we're fighting for ain't gonna go with me none once he's dead and buried. But it was a nice notion. It gave him hope. It wasn't much, but it was something, and that was all that mattered to the man then.

The plains all around were dry, save for this one little well, and the river running down the road a ways. The sun scorched the earth, leaving it a hellish place for a fellow to get lost in. It had been here that Tom had happened upon Frank in the first place, with Frank having been chased out of Louisiana for some bad business by badder men.

As Frank poured the water from one bucket into the other, he though back to the bad bastards that had made him a killer. And it *had* been that way. Frank was not naturally a man to take a life. He'd been forced into it. Teased and prodded at by too many people and far, far too often for any sane, rational man to put up with.

The day he'd become a killer; he'd actually been handed the weapon to do the deed. Those damn Donard brothers just wouldn't leave well enough alone. Bob and Marv Donard didn't treat the slaves they put to work with much sympathy, and Frank even less so, for no other reason than they sensed that underneath there was a rage brewing, that they just couldn't wait to uncover, whatever the cost of the poor black man's wrath might mean for them.

Bob bulged in the gut, with a big belly bursting behind the buttons of his grease smeared shirt, the underarms of which reeked to high heaven. His brother Marv didn't smell much better, though that brother's shirt always *looked* clean, even if the smell said it most certainly was not.

They'd been working Frank outside their shack on the plantation, not dissimilar to what the shack of Frank's future employers looked like, though again, the future employer's place – the one belonging to Tom and Abel Liffey – did not stink something serious. Frank puzzled and puzzled what the smell had been before they'd started ragging on him. He couldn't quite place it, though the thoughts of wondering what it was kept his mind busy while he worked with his little rusty handsaw. He'd been set to cutting up a tree that the brothers had chopped down, though Frank did not know why, when he'd seen with his own two eyes the stack of logs, presumably for the fire, lying out the back of the shack. He supposed they needed to give him something to do since he'd been banished from the big house. He'd been put to work mainly with the laundry in the big house belonging to Nathaniel Jones, a man widely considered to be a gentleman, though to Frank and his fellow slaves was more of a pompous, overinflated fellow with a penchant for poking at his slaves with his silver-handled walking cane.

"Come on now," Nathaniel would goad. "Go on to work now. Not paying you for doing nothing now am I?"

This remark would often provoke much laughter from his fellow family members, though one day Frank had had enough.

"You ain't paying us nothing," he said, sounding soft, though there was a hidden fury lurking beneath this very bold but blatant statement. He was not being paid. None of them were. Their lives were unenviable neither by the highest aristocracy or the dirtiest dog with only one leg left.

Nathanial Jones's jab didn't sit well with Frank, but more than that, Frank had himself a girl to impress. *She'd* impressed him, though the trouble was she was white, which was a no go in the state of Louisiana. Frank had about as much of a chance courting her as the fellow did sprouting wings from his back before taking off into the air like a blackbird seeking some seeds elsewhere in a more enlightened part of the United States of America.

She was pretty, there was no denying that. And though the other slaves seldom expressed any interest in white folk, Frannie Jones was one exception to that unspoken rule. Matter of fact it had become a running joke that the first thing that the slaves would do if they were ever made free, would be to come-a-courting at Frannie's door, asking her if she fancied a fuck out in the barn by the stables.

Now Frank was not so vulgar, with his lusts lying more in the realm of love-making rather than a quick fuck in the hay. He was head over heels, and what was worse, she'd shown a keen interest in him as well, wanting her daddy Nathaniel to set Frank far more tasks relating to the catering of her needs about the house than any other slave.

She probably would've taken him to her bed, for the girl was frivolous and, knowing the trouble it'd land her in – as well as the very real possibility of causing Frank to lose his life – still persisted in getting her daddy to promise her he'd put Frank to work with helping her with her various needs.

Now Frank was not stupid. Sure he'd had his thoughts of taking her in the barn. He even supposed that she wouldn't object. But Frank, unlike Frannie, who was a silly girl in her nature, knew that that kind of action could only spell trouble. Frank found that the more kindly she behaved to him the more he felt compelled to act out in unnoticeable displays of rebellion towards his owners.

Once, when he'd finished all of Frannie's numerous demands for the day, he was put to the mind-numbing task of folding away the handkerchiefs in the drawers of Nathaniel Jones. Just before he popped them in said drawers though, Frank found a great deal of joy could be had in taking said handkerchiefs and placing them down the back of his baggy britches, leaving them a moment in the sweaty crack of his ass, *then* popping them in their place in the drawer.

Once, on another occasion, Nathaniel had asked him to go fetch him a nice cool glass of lemonade from the kitchen, when Frank was laden with a horrific head cold. Frank found the lemonade jug alright, but before pouring the glass for his master, Frank's finger pressed over one nostril, then the slave's slimy snot was propelled by a pressurised blast of air out the other nostril on down into the bottom of Nathaniel's soon-to-be drinking glass. God, how Frank found so much amusement watching with a small smile as Nathaniel drank down a mouthful, before letting out an "Ah, refreshing!" in approval. The idiot even went so far as to thank Frank for such a zesty, thirst-quenching drink, to which Frank bowed before scurrying off back to the kitchen for a good healthy cackling session. Doubled over, howling at the imbecile with the snot-laced lemonade, Laverne, a black giant of a woman, with an ass the size of a planet, puffed out an exasperated exhalation of air and said, "I don't know what you is laughing at mister. But I'm betting that that ain't only lemonade Mr. Jones is gulping down. Am I right?" Frank didn't trust Laverne, for she was an awful sycophant who smooched the white folks' asses at every opportunity that presented itself. Sure, she maybe just wanted to survive, same as Frank and every other slave in the state, but Frank knew better than to let her in on his little joke.

"I heard something funny," he said. "That's only lemonade Mr. Jones has."

"Well what's the joke then?" Laverne said, folding her fat arms across her huge chest, bunching up her bosom and in doing so making her tits look even more massive than they already seemed to be.

"You wouldn't get it," Frank said, staring hard at Laverne.

She wasn't going to get it out of him. Should she stare all damn day she wouldn't. So instead she tutted and went on about her business busying in the kitchen.

But yes, "You ain't paying us nothing," was what Frank had said in front of his master as well as his pretty southern bell of a daughter.

"Did I just hear you correctly? Did you, a *nigger*, just speak back to *me*?"

Frank shrugged.

"Sure did," he said.

"Did I hear correctly?" said Nathaniel Jones, just about ready to burst, but still so very discombobulated by this unexpected insolence. His slaves were always obedient, a fact he took some measure of pride in whenever relating his tales of kindness towards his black chappies as he called them.

"There daddy," said Frannie, "he didn't mean nothing by it, did you Frank?"

Frank shrugged again, as if to say I sure fucking did mean something by it. Bastard don't give us no wages, he thought. That there bastard's in charge of the men that work us ragged and whip us raw. About time someone said something true to him.

"He's really sorry daddy," Frannie said fretfully. "Don't take him away from me. Please. I like Frank. If you want to whup someone, whup me."

"*Quiet now Frannie*!" Nathaniel snapped. "Now just you be still you hear? Won't have no daughter of mine defending darkies."

He then studied Frank very carefully, before a thought came to him.

"Hell, I ain't gonna whup you boy. But I tell you what I is gonna do. Gonna put you to work. *Real* work. Work that'll break that black back of yours and have you begging for a bullet by breakfast time tomorrow. You're gonna go work for the Donard boys. But I'll give you some advice. And though this advice is for free, I'd take it to heart. Them there Donard boys is mean. Mighty mean. They're nastier than hell to the boys that I put to work with them, and that's just the white ones. The black fellas don't last, like you won't. Why they'll work you to the bone, then, when you do drop down exhausted, they'll slap themselves on the knee and say, 'Well, that's another one done. Sure been nice knowing you blacky.' Then they'll take their guns off their belts, pop you in the head and that'll be that. And I ain't sorry to see you go son. Don't think I didn't notice you sniffing round my gal here. You think a keen tongue'll take you far with my Frannie and you are fucking mistaken my friend. You go on now. Billy Japser'll take you to them boys. Ta-ta now Frank."

The last Frank saw of Frannie was when he looked over his shoulder as Billy Jasper led him away from the big house. She was waving at him when her father grabbed her by the wrists and took her back inside.

Frank felt foolish for making only such a small transgression. He'd much rather have killed the man. Killed him and the rest of his kind save Frannie, then rode off into the sunset with Frannie's arms wrapped around his middle, their horse snorting and sweating as they pushed the animal faster and faster; as fast as the beast would go.

Frank had been granted the opportunity to get one full night's sleep before the Donard boys put their new toy to work. This was what they thought of black people; toys to be played with until they'd been broken, then a new one would be supplied to stop them crying, then the process would restart all over again, going through slave after slave ceaselessly.

Frank sawed at the tree, while Bob brandished his shotgun, which had been given to him brand new by Billy Jasper, who was both Bob and Marv's boss in a way. Why, it'd almost made Bob cry when Billy handed him the weapon. It glinted in the sun, a blue finish on the barrels, with hammers that made a supremely pleasing clicking sound when cocked back. But he was careless with this weapon. What he did was his own fault. Frank could not be blamed, but it is a fact that Bob did not get to enjoy the shotgun he so cherished. He didn't even get one shot off when Frank removed him and his brother from the land of the living, putting them on a train with a one-way ticket to hell.

Frank was working, Bob caressing his gun like a man might a lady, and Marv chomping down on an apple that, had he been allowed to continue, would be munched down to the core, then seeds, stem and all would go down Marv's throat – the man was not one to waste fruit, or any foodstuffs for that matter.

"You know what I reckon Marv?" said Bob.

"What do you reckon Bob?" Marv said in between chomps.

"I reckon I got me a theory as to why we don't get overrun by slaves."

"If you're gonna speak on speak up. I can hardly hear you brother, not least of all when you mumble."

"Sorry brother," Bob said much louder. "Like I was saying, there's enough niggers around to overpower us. We white men are in the minorty. So to speak."

"Don't know that word."

"Well allow me to explain. A minorty is a small amount of something. In my meaning it means white folk. We white folk are in a small amount. Now the niggers ain't. They is in the majorty."

Marv went to ask but Bob was way ahead of him, holding up his hand so that his brother wouldn't interrupt his flow.

"Majorty means a big number. Niggers is in the big number, we whites is in the small. You with me so far?"

"Mmhmm," said Marv, still munching, with apple juices running down his grubby beard, then landing in light little droplets on his shirt. "I'm with you," he said around apple.

"So," Bob deliberated. "If they is in the majorty, and we is in the minorty, would that not mean maybe that they would be able to get the best of *us*?"

"Seems to make sense," said Marv.

"So why don't they?" said Bob.

Marv's eyes glazed over, fraught with thought. This look meant that some serious thinking was in progress.

"Shall I tell you?" said Bob at last, after giving his brother sufficient time to puzzle.

Marv nodded, watching Frank's bent back as the poor slave tried his best not to listen to the trash these two men were talking.

"It's because they're bred that way. We've whipped it out of them. They don't know no better than to serve now. No more backbones left." Then, much louder so as Frank couldn't miss it, "Ain't that right you black bastard? Been beaten out of your ma and your pa and your sisters and your brothers," said Bob before giving Frank the opportunity to answer.

He didn't. He grumbled that the man was a prick, but the brothers didn't hear him say it he'd done it so quietly.

"Yes sir," said Bob. "Been beaten out of the generations."

"Or beaten in," said Marv.

"Care to elabrate brother?"

"Well, maybe it's not that it's been beaten out of them. The fight I mean. Maybe the fight's still there, but buried beneath the fear that's been beaten in."

Bob studied Frank's back a moment, before turning to Marv.

"Now that *is* interesting brother. Beaten *in* you say?"

Marv nodded, the apple halfway done.

"Hmmm," Bob pondered.

"Pity we can't test it," said Marv. "Might never know."

"No," Bob said, not listening to Marv's last remark. "No I think that you're wrong. Reckon you're wrong brother, no offence meant."

"None taken," said Marv.

97

"Maybe we could put it to the test," said Bob. "Be willing to make a bet?"

"That depends on the bet brother. All depends on the bet."

"Well," said Bob, gently removing his shotgun from his lap, then putting the thing butt down on the porch both men were sitting on. "Say I was to give this here negro my shotgun. Should he have it beaten into him, then the anger underneath might show. Should he have it beaten out of him, then the dogs have barked and the anger's flown."

"Mmmm," Marv hummed, only half listening really.

"Now I'm so sure it's been beaten *out*, that I'd be willing to hand this here boy my shotgun," said Bob before standing up, lifting the gun and breaking it, before sliding two shells neatly, one after the other, into both barrels. "Black boy!" Bob boomed. "You wanna hold this here gun?"

Frank didn't stop sawing. He didn't shake his head. He didn't nod. He just sawed.

"Say," said Bob, "I'm talking to you. You answer me when I speak to you nigger. Now I'll ask again, and I won't ask one more time. You want to hold this here gun of mine?"

"No sir," said Frank, "no sir I do not."

"Now I have a wager to win boy. So you're gonna hold this here gun whether you like it or not. Now turn around and face me, 'fore I let both barrels fly and fuck you up big time."

Frank gently laid down his handsaw, setting it on the tree trunk he'd been working on. When he turned the brothers saw the fruits of his labour, as lots of beads of perspiration were dripping down his forehead, some stinging his eyes, some trickling into his lips. He could have used a ladle of water right then, though he didn't think that this was the time to ask.

"Come and take it off me now nigger. Go on now, I'm allowing it."

"I don't know if that there's a good idea Bob," Marv said, munching postponed temporarily.

"Shut up," Bob snapped. "Won't ask again nigger," he said, so Frank reached out and took a hold of Bob's gun.

It was heavy. Far heavier than Frank had imagined. He being so slight, the thing made him have to strain to keep himself upright. He held it like the thing were a deadly, dangerous, very venomous snake, to be kept at arm's length at all costs.

"See?" said Bob. "Boy won't do anything with it. You know why brother?"

"Because he's black?"

"Because he's *black*," said Bob.

"But that don't prove nothing," said Marv.

"How so?" said Bob.

"Because he ain't been provoked. He ain't got no reason to shoot us up."

"No *reason*?" Bob said, floored by his brother's stupidity. "No reason? Why we're white. We work blacks to the bone and never give a one a kind word, nor water sometimes. He ain't got a reason and I'm Abraham Lincoln himself."

Bob chortled at this thought, then stared hard at Frank.

"But if you want proof," he said. "If I'm to win this wager, well then we'd need to provoke him, wouldn't we?"

"Not when he's holding a shotgun brother. You take that there gun off him if you fancy having a bit of fun at that nigger's expense."

"Hell brother, that's the point. My argument's that it's been beaten out of him. Yours is that it's been beaten in. Now how in the hell am I gonna prove my point when he ain't got no gun."

"Just think it's a bad idea is all."

"Ah shut up," said Bob before disappearing inside the shack.

Marv munched at his apple again; a good big bite that made talking practically impossible. Though the apple was soon spat out when he saw his brother come trudging out with the whip in his hand.

"No brother," said Marv. "No, take that there gun off the nigger first, 'fore that there boy gets wise and lets *us* have both barrels."

Marv went to stand but Bob pushed him back down in

his rocker again.

"I'm telling you I'm right, and I aim to prove it. Now just you stay sat down brother. Be alright, I swear."

Marv looked up with big pleading eyes. He wasn't above begging his brother to see sense, but he didn't think it would do any good. Bob had got it in his mind and that was that. There'd be no impeding him on what he intended to do, so Marv took comfort in chomping at his apple like a horse in a field, watching his brother go about his trying to prove he was right.

"Now nigger, you turn your back to me boy. Go on now, turn around."

Frank stared at the Donard brother with the whip. He looked down at the gun and thought very hard about whether or not to use it for the purpose it was intended.

"This ain't a good idea," Marv said from the porch. "Please brother, be careful."

"Will you be *quiet*! Quit telling me what to do. Turn around nigger. You'll do as your told or I'll take that there gun back off you and blow your toes off for the trouble. Don't think I won't, for I will."

Frank felt the weapon's weight weighing him down. He knew such an object could inflict a great deal of pain when pointed at a man and the trigger pulled.

Pointing it at the Donard brothers brought a small smile to his face, though Frank was yet to be completely convinced that doing so was a wise idea.

"I'm telling you brother," Marv moaned. "I'm telling you he'll kill you. You don't take that there gun off him then I will."

"You won't," said Bob, turning to his brother before cracking the whip at the ground by Marv's boots. "Be best for you if I don't have to use this whip on you. Which I will brother, no questions asked."

Marv looked at his brother, fear filling his eyes because deep down he knew that this slave was not above letting both brothers have both barrels.

Bob lunged at Frank, grabbing him by the shoulders.

"I said turn around," he said as he twisted Frank's frame so that he was facing away from the brother wanting desperately to do the whipping and, in doing so, proving he was right – which to him was the most important thing in the world at that moment. "Now we'll see," said Bob, beaming a big fat smile at Frank's back.

He took three paces back, then let Frank have a good crack of the whip, which was such a mighty lashing it immediately got him down on his knees.

"How you like that *nigger*?" Bob grinned gleefully. "You like that do you? You wanna use that there shotgun?"

Three simultaneous cracks followed thereafter, the third of which breaking the skin and drawing blood.

"Brother," said Marv, "you best stop now. That there boy'll blast you with that there gun. I'm sure of it."

"Will you…" *Crack*! "Keep…" *Crack*! "Quiet!" *Bang*!

The brother called Bob's back spat a spray of blood all over Marv's good clean shirt, staining the garment with a misty stain of dark red. His face too was covered in blood, which he attempted wipe off before the next barrel found his head, making mush out of nose cartilage, breaking teeth, shattering skull bone and blowing brain clean out the back of said skull. Both brothers dropped down to the ground at the same time. Marv's apple was still in his hand – he hadn't the time to drop it and go for the gun on his hip. Frank couldn't believe it. He stood staring at the brothers' bodies, shaking like a leaf. It is a hell of a thing to kill a man, and these two were Frank's first. The gun felt twenty times heavier in his shaky hands. He let it drop down to the ground, then approached Bob's body.

"Mr. Donard?" he said, not quite knowing whether he expected a reply or not. He could see that the body wasn't breathing in and out, which was when the fear kicked in. He, a black slave, had killed two slavers – he'd looked over at Marv and seen that he too was remaining recumbent and completely lifeless, not drawing breath like his brother. But Frank, for all his faults, was not a stupid man. He knew there were horses that came through the road running adjacent to the Donard brothers' shack. He knew too that those horses had riders on them, cowhands and such, who had eyes in their heads that could see. He knew that should they see the bodies of two men lying face forward in the dirty, leafy earth, that there'd be an alarm raised, meaning that he'd be promptly chased by a pack of men and a pack of bloodhounds on leads, threatening to rip those men's arms right out of their sockets with tugging so hard. So he did what any sensible person would do.

Dragging them in was an arduous task to accomplish, given how heavy Bob and Marv were. But he did it. He got them into their bunks, pulled the blankets up round their ears and, after surveying the scene, and deciding that the ruse looked sufficient enough for him to make good his escape, he did just that and ran.

Running through the bracken and barbs that bit at his shins, he did not know where he was going, just that he was going to go as far as he possibly could. He didn't stop to sleep, staying on the move during the night as much as his body would allow.

Only when the sun came up did his body fail him, and Frank dropped down to the ground. With his face pressed to the earth, consciousness threatening to leave in a moment, he wondered whether that noise was the wind; if it wasn't hounds, and that the ears on either side of his head were deceiving him.

He slept for an hour before pressing on out of the state to the west. Walking and walking for many, many miles, over the course of a great deal of days he passed over the planes until he hit Texas, eventually finding Tom and Abel's shack, whereupon he collapsed.

It was Abel who spotted him, though it was Tom who carried him to their bedroom. He watered and fed Frank, getting him back to health in a surprisingly short spell of time. Tom offered Frank to work with him, helping out about the place where he could. Frank decided that he was destined to spend the rest of his days working for two brothers, but that these pair were far from mean, and, he suspected, would treat him fairly. He'd been right. Tom was kind to Frank, as was Abel, which was why Frank had to struggle with his conscience for having hated Tom so badly as he stood with that bucketful of well water.

He supposed he should go back. Bringing the bucket back to the house his feet felt heavy. He didn't know why exactly, though he suspected it was all Sarah's doing.

16.

Frank and Tom took turns puffing on their pipes, inhaling then ejecting the thick white clouds out into the air all around them, either out through their mouths again, or, in Frank's case, nostrils. Tom didn't like it when he breathed his smoke out through his nose, though Frank found a great deal of pleasure in smoking that way. It hurt the black man's pride that he only possessed a simple corn cob pipe, and that Tom's was made out of a magnificent mahogany colored briar. He'd often thought of stealing it, though thought thereafter that there would be nowhere for him to smoke it where Tom mightn't see, save in town. But it was nice to be in a kind of comfortable company with a white man, even if he harboured a secret kind of hatred for this one in particular.

Frank felt as though he didn't want the sun to go down, desiring for it to stay put in its place peeking out just above the horizon, never disappearing totally, with a little light lingering all night long. But it would go eventually, and there was nothing Frank or Tom could do about it.

Their heads were almost invisible in their respective clouds of smoke when Sarah came out of the shack tutting. She didn't like smokers. Didn't like the smell. Probably because some of her clients came in with the stench clinging to their clothes from having smoked cigarettes and cigars galore downstairs before Elsie'd sent them up to see her.

"Tom, I'm going to bed," she said. "You planning on joining me or what?"

"Why woman, you don't need to ask me that. That there's the biggest favor any fella could get, getting asked by a lady like you to take her to bed. But I'm smoking here. You go on in and get yourself ready girl. I'll be in in a moment."

"Maybe wash your neck with water from the well," she

suggested. "Smell of smoke on you's is enough to make me gag."

"Got it sweetie," said Tom before she went to lean in for a kiss, then thought better of it and stood straight up again all because of the smell.

"Stinking!" she gurned. "Smell of you! My *God*!"

"Go on in the house," he said. "Be in in a moment or two."

"Fine. Goodnight Frank," she said to the man whose eyes were fixed firmly on her face – those same eyes shielding the thoughts of longing behind them like soldiers being busily manoeuvred and ordered about by captains behind the walls of Fort Frank. He stood up and took off his hat, and though Sarah didn't pass comment, he sensed she was touched by the gesture.

Just leave this here Tom fella, he thought. Then you run off with me and *I'll* love you. Love you a hell of a lot better than this Liffey boy. Bet your spurs I will woman.

Tom took out his pipe tool then and began scraping the remnants of black tar and ash out of the bowl. He'd finished scraping for a few moments before he decided to speak.

"Want you with me Frank. Want you to come along, although I can't say it'll be easy on you, going where we're going and all. Want you to know I'm aware of the risks, but we'll go get you some papers proving you're a free man. Maybe we'll get by just fine."

Frank stared hard at the sunset, supposing somewhere inside that if he stared just hard enough the sun mightn't make a move to leave them be. When the last few rays of light landed on his brown skin, the sun setting on yet another peaceful evening on the Texas plains, Frank replied to what his boss'd said.

"Suppose I wasn't to come, you reckon you'd be fine on your own?" he said, not shocking Tom at all to hear this his first hint at refusal of making the journey.

"Don't know. Been so long since we *haven't* had you around, I don't know how well I'd cope with the work. Hell, Abel sure as shit ain't gonna do much good. Boy's my brother, but that boy's head just ain't right. Work, or the drive *to* work doesn't abide within him."

Tom flicked a bug off his knee, then the sounds of grasshoppers chirping started like they always did. Frank and Tom relied on the noisy bastards to help lull the both of them to sleep. Abel too. They neither one knew a night's sleep without the sound, it had been with them that long. Frank had lived during a time and in a place where there were no grasshoppers, though the man didn't like to think on that time too much. Mulling over the Donards' demises brought a smile to his face, but as far as remembering his past, that was as far as he usually dared venture. As far as Sarah's taking to the grasshoppers chirping, neither man knew. Though Frank supposed his boss would find out soon enough.

The employer stretched out his long legs in front of him. Frank watched the horizon, hoping the sun might return.

"I need you Frank," Tom said.

"You don't need me," said Frank, before holding out his hand and asking Tom for the loan of his pipe tool. Tom almost placed in his hand, then a strange sly look appeared on the employer's face, causing the employee's bowels to take a turn for the worse.

"What you make of Sarah?" he asked.

"She's nice," said Frank, forgetting all about every inch of her body he'd paid to possess back when she was a sporting woman, fixating instead on Tom's knowing eyes.

"That what you reckon?" Tom said, the look vanishing as though it had never been, before he deposited his tool into the well-worn hands that that employee of his possessed.

"Yes sir," said Frank. "Reckon she's real nice."

Too nice for you, he thought, though dared not say – not yet anyway.

"She is. Too nice for me anyways. Don't know what she's doing with me," said Tom.

Frank couldn't help himself from having a chuckle at this. Tom turned to him and snickered himself. The two men's laughter rose and died, crashing on the shore like a wave in the ocean.

"You ever had a woman?" Tom said after a moment or

two of staring out into the evening sky.

"Did once," said Frank. "White gal, so as you'd expect it wasn't a fruitful relationship."

"I'd've thought you'd like the ladies of well… you know…" said Tom.

"Of my own kind?" Frank smiled.

"Well yeah," said Tom. "Meaning no offence."

"None taken," said Frank.

He fiddled with his cheap pipe, scraping out the gunk with Tom's tool, then handed it over to his boss again.

"Frannie," he said so softly, as though the name might crack with being so delicate; as though the name *needed* to be handled with care.

"Hah?" Tom said indelicately.

"That was her name," said Frank. "Frannie."

"German girl?" said Tom.

Frank snorted.

"No. Not German."

Tom looked at Frank and saw the pain etching itself deep into his features at the mention of this woman. Then he thought to himself he'd be better treading carefully on this subject matter, so he made it easier for Frank to talk.

"Nice name that," he said, though he wasn't particularly partial to the sound of it. Then the connection came to him. "Frank and Frannie!" he exclaimed. "Why hell! It was meant to be!"

"'Fraid it wasn't. White women in Louisiana don't take to courting black men. Maybe if it were here in Texas I'd've had a chance. But in Louisiana? No sir. No way."

"What happened?" said Tom.

"Tell you one day maybe," Frank said. "You got any more of that cherry and vanilla tobacco?" he asked.

"Sure do," said Tom, reaching into his front pocket on the bib of his overalls to produce a cowhide tobacco pouch. "Thing's near empty," he said. "If you're fixing to smoke you might as well smoke the lot. I'll be heading into town tomorrow to get more anyways."

106

"Kind of you," said Frank, wondering then how he could ever have come to hate this man, though seemingly helpless to change the fact, all because of Sarah Herron, whom he hoped would never be forced to take the name of Liffey. Then, as if Tom could read minds, he brought up this unappealing topic like a dog brings up its dinner after eating too many blades of lush green grass.

"Yeah," he began. "Be heading into town tomorrow, see if my money's come through. Then I'll maybe mosey on down to the jewellers. You can come with if you like. I'll need help picking out a couple of horses. Reckon you're the man for the job, because I sure as shit ain't."

Frank sat silently, fidgeting with the long leather straps dangling from the tobacco pouch.

"You really fixing to marry her?" he asked.

"Sure am. Soon as that money comes through then I'm buying that ring. Why I've waited long enough already. Got to tie her down. Women are apt to get flighty unless a fella shows he's committed. And I *am* committed. Don't think I've ever loved a thing more than I do Sarah."

"What about Abel?" said Frank, trying subtly to poke his boss's bubble full of holes.

"Aw well hell, that there's a different kind of love Frank. Sometimes…" he said, leaning in close to Frank. "Sometimes I wish I never had no brother to begin with. Is that bad to think? I mean Abel ain't got much of a life. Sometimes I think he'd be better off six feet under. *Sometimes*. Not all the time, but sometimes."

"He's happy I reckon," said Frank, trying to make Tom feel as bad as he could without giving away that this was his true intention. "He's happy getting his hair brushed," Frank said, hammering in a guilty nail, then removing another from his lips, then taking it and hammering it down too: "He's happy fantasising about seeing your mama." Another nail: "He's happy with Sarah too I reckon."

"Alright Frank, alright!" said Tom, scratching at his chin. "Jesus Christ, I said sometimes, not all times. No need to

107

rub it in."

"Sorry Mr. Liffey sir," said Frank, before opening up the pouch then raising the thing to his nostrils to get a good whiff of the fine smelling tobacco housed inside. "This here sure does smell nice," he said, before pinching some in his long fingers then depositing the brown shredded matter into his corn cob pipe bowl.

"I'll get you some tomorrow. Pouch for you very own," said Tom, taking the hint – though this wasn't the first time Tom had made this promise, and Frank did not hold any high hopes that he'd follow through on his vow this time either.

The two sat, Frank fiddling with pouch and pipe, Tom regretting handing out the thoughts of his having occasionally wished that his only brother wasn't around anymore.

"You happy with Sarah being around?" Tom asked.

The question was jagged like a cactus to Frank, and wouldn't have been so loaded if it weren't for that look of Tom's from a few moments before.

"Why yes sir," said Frank. "I am indeed. If you're aiming to keep her around, well then you do that."

"Good enough," said Tom, yawning a big, tired yawn before scratching at his belly. "I'll be heading on in. You can keep the pouch until morning. I won't be smoking no more tonight."

"Thank you sir," said Frank, before Tom planted his paw on Frank's broad shoulder, then retreated into the shack to go get some shut eye.

Frank was studying his boots like as though he were taking a test in school on the subject of shoes. Then, realising that he had a hang dog look, suspecting that the boss might be watching, began busying himself with the pipe. He removed the match from its home in the little cardboard box, scratched the head of this little wooden arsonist, then, once it was lit, brought it over the bowl of the pipe. With Frank drawing breath in and out, the burning flame bobbed up and down until the tobacco was lit. The little match, now useless to its owner, had the life shaken out of it, before being flicked down to the dusty earth just beyond the porch step. Frank sat back and puffed until the tobacco'd been burnt to the bowl. Then the man stood, stretched, and promptly went to bed. He did all this pretending that Sarah was not on his mind, though she was. The girl even entered his dreams that night, as it had done many nights before.

17.

"We ain't all going into town! Christ I'm only gonna be gone an afternoon!" Tom roared.

"Why not?" Abel demanded. "My mama might be there!"

"The woman will most assuredly not be there brother. You can go ahead and bet your life on it, for she fucking won't."

"Don't cuss like that in the house Tom!" Sarah barked. "Be best you keep a civil tongue under my roof."

"*Your* roof!" Tom squeaked. "Christ almighty, *your* roof already? Why good golly gosh, you hear that Frank? Her roof now!" said Tom, turning to find Frank now absent from the room.

Frank had disappeared because he'd sensed a row coming and craftily figured to himself that if Sarah didn't see him when a row was blowing, she wouldn't associate rowing with him when the winds were down. So he just made himself scarce, leaving Tom to deal with her foul mood all alone. Frank could have kissed him for riling her. As he walked over to feed the chickens, he felt like doing a jig, though didn't for fear of being seen. Still smiled though, because his face was pointed in the other direction. Such a grin he had on him. He looked like the cat that had got the cream.

"Don't you try and bring Frank into this," said Sarah. "Man won't laugh at me like you. Won't make fun. Reckon if he was to come in to me at night, he'd have made a considerable effort to get the smell of pipe smoke from off of his person. Pong off you was mighty when you came in to have some fun on top of me. Made me sick! Just plain sick."

"So maybe I won't no more," said Tom.

"What?" said she.

"Maybe I won't lay down with you. How do you like that?"

"That's just fine with me," she said, scraping back her seat and lifting all four plates stained with smears of runny egg yolk and bits of black bacon – just the way Abel liked it – which was the cause of the aggression from Tom to begin with. He didn't see why Abel should have his way in every little particular. Probably it was because he was simple that Sarah took pity on him. He didn't mind that one bit. But burning bacon that *he* had to eat was where the man drew the line.

"Yeah," said Tom, wiping some spittle that had been dribbling from his face in fury. "Yeah, I bet you won't. Reckon you're so used to men being with you you can't cope without getting poked near every night in life. You ain't fooling me."

"Mr. Liffey," she said, getting a giggled out of Abel, who repeated his name quietly, preceded of course by that new favourite word of his; mister. "If you think that you have a tongue as honed as a razor, well you're dead wrong. If you think that that there brain of yours is as quick as a pistolero, you're wrong still. I do not *need* men to lay down with me. It brings me no pleasure. In your case, I think I can say quite safely, that the enjoyment level obtained on my part is poor. Pretty darn poor."

"You calling me a lousy lay?" said Tom, feeling as though the jug on top of the cupboard was crying out, begging him to reach up, uncork his good friend and take a mighty big swig for his troubles.

"I am," she said, becoming the straw that broke the camel's back.

"Well then," Tom said as he rose from the table, "if I'm so damn lousy in bed, maybe you'd be better off in Elsie's again?"

"*Excuse* me?" said Sarah, stunned at the suggestion.

"No I don't think I will," said Tom. "You can take off. You can take off and go fuck for five dollars at a time, maybe even three. Reckon Elsie'll have lowered the price now, given that you've run off and left her in the lurch. But you get this into your head woman, like a hammer hitting a nail you let this drive in. I wouldn't pay one dollar. Not one. Wouldn't pay fifty cents for a fuck with you."

"That so?" she said. "Well how about a nickel?"

Tom smiled at this, though Sarah did not. He laughed long and hard.

"Hell girl, you are a good one. Come on out and sit a while on the porch. Pet the pigs if you like, but don't feed them none. They keep the snakes away 'cause they eat them. They won't if they've been fed."

"Ain't finished," said Sarah quietly.

"Beg your pardon?" said Tom.

"You fucking heard me," she said.

"Girl I wish you'd make up your mind. First you say there's no swearing under your roof, then you come off with language like that. Make up your mind, would you?"

"It ain't my roof. It's yours. You can have it to cuss in all you like, for I'm leaving Tom Liffey."

"Oh come on darling, I was only funning. I didn't mean nothing by it. Why women and men were made for fighting. It's what we do. You go anywhere in the world and you'll find it's like that. Now come on out and sit in the shade a while. We won't bicker again for another week. I swear."

"Swear nothing," said Sarah. "You've shown me your colors Tom, and I ain't too keen none. No sir, I am not. Why Elsie'd be happier than a bee flying from flower to flower all day to see me walk through those swinging doors of hers. And as for me, well, I sure would be happy to lie down for strange fellas once more. Might get a decent fuck again."

"I don't," said Tom, trying to get at some bacon stuck between his teeth. "I don't believe you."

"Yeah, well you best believe it boy, because it's happening."

Tom tried for a moment to get out the bit of bacon but couldn't. The frustration of this and not Sarah caused him to snap at her.

"Fine! Go on. See if I care. You'll be begging for me to

111

come back for you in a week. I'd bet my wages on it."

"What wages? What money do *you* make? Elsie told me you hadn't any money at all just the other day. Said you was flat broke. *Bum*! That's what you are, a bum. And I sure as shit don't intend on sticking with you when you shout at me at every goddamn opportunity presents itself. I'm gone, get out of my way."

Sarah trod across the room, ready to shove Tom down should he come between her and the door. Tom did step aside, allowing her to pass with quick, hate filled steps on out through the yard and onto the beaten path between the Liffey boys' humble home and the town of Taughrane Heights. Then Abel started to whine in Tom's ear about his mama.

"I wanna go to town," he moaned. "I want my mama."

"Mama ain't in town Abel! Fuck *me*."

"Who's gonna brush my hair now that the nice lady's gone?"

"Goddamn it, I don't *care* Abel. I couldn't give a good fuck about you *or* your hair. You've hands, don't you? You can damn well do it yourself if it's so fucking important."

Abel started to cry and ran right out after Sarah, his heavy haunches wobbling while he went, his great gut swinging side to side as though the man were filled to the brim with too many glasses of water weighing him down at the front. He caught up with her, even though she sure was moving mighty fast. He was well and truly out of puff as he came up behind her. She didn't turn. She just kept on marching.

"Lady," he panted. "Nice lady."

She didn't turn.

"*Sarah*!" he shouted.

She stopped then, though did not turn to face him.

"You go home Abel, you hear? You go right on home now, for I can't take you with me."

"You have to. I ain't got no one to brush me. My brother don't do it the way you do. He don't do it soft. Brother's real rough with the brush."

Abel wiped some snot with the back of his hand, then

kicked about in the dust while Sarah thought how best to get rid of the feeble-minded Liffey.

"I'll tell you what," she said, turning at last to face the man, if one could call him that. "You can come up to see me. Tom can't, but you can. You bring your brush into town. Right on into Elsie's pleasure palace. You tell her your name and she'll see to it that you go up to the right room. I'll brush your hair for you. I will. Every night if you like. You might have to wait when I'm with other fellas some nights, but if you can keep patient, I'll see you eventually. Alright?"

Abel only blinked at her.

"You were real nice with the brush," he said helplessly. "Better than mama I reckon. Though I can't really remember her brushing it, it's been so long. Can't I come stay with you?"

Sarah felt a lump developing in her throat, as well as an admittedly small splinter in her heart. He was truly helpless. She despised the fact that he only had Tom to comfort him, for Tom wasn't much comfort to anyone she'd learned.

"Honey," she said, planting a hand gently on his cheek and wiping away a tear with her thumb. "There's no way you can come with me."

"Maybe Elsie'd let me lay for fellas. I sure wouldn't mind it," he said, causing Sarah to laugh a little.

"Do you even know what that means Mr. Abel?"

"No I don't," he admitted. "But I'd be happy to learn. Tom ain't so kind you see. You are. I like that. Truth be told I like you a lot Sarah."

"I know you do sweetie. But I don't reckon there'd be many fellas'd want to take you to bed."

Abel let out a sigh with a hitch in the middle, breaking it into two sighs for the price of one.

"You go on now. You go on home and you come into town tonight. You bring your brush Mr. Abel, and I'll brush your hair so, so carefully. Alright?"

Abel just looked at her like a dog seeking food.

"Go *on*," she said, not wishing to stand in the sun any longer, wishing instead to keep on marching so as to quickly quell the doubt inside as to whether or not Elsie *would* take her or, conversely, wouldn't, meaning she'd have to make other arrangements. She looked at him for a moment. Then, because the boy showed no signs of ever moving from that spot on the dry plains, she turned and recommenced her heavy-footed plodding off in the direction of the town.

Abel took one step forward in her direction, then, thinking that if he did continue to pester her she might rescind her kind offer to continue brushing, decided that he wasn't able to keep her from leaving, so should do as he was told and head back to Tom. He turned his back on Sarah after one last look at her and, feeling fine about the arrangement, practically skipped all the way home, as happy as he'd been in quite some time.

Tom meanwhile was drinking down more than his fair share of whiskey when Frank spoke through the front door, the very sound of the man causing Tom to start and clumsily get to his feet and hide his precious provisions contained within his jug back where he'd found it in the first place.

"Don't come in," he shouted. "Don't come in Frank."

"Yes sir," said Frank, figuring his boss must have been abusing himself and almost been caught in the act.

After the jug was safely stashed away again by Tom, he strolled over to the door a little unsteadily and opened it to find Frank standing, hat in hand, with big sad eyes.

"She gone Mr. Liffey sir?" he asked, though the man knew the answer.

"Yeah, she's gone. Though not for very long I expect. She'll be back once she realises it's no life lying down for strangers breezing in after being with who knows what whore, with who knows not down between their legs. Liable to catch something or other. That'll teach her."

Tom then spat on the ground.

"Might save me some money anyhow," he said quietly, more to himself thank Frank, before taking a seat on the rocker the porch to watch as his brother Abel ambled towards him.

Sarah had receded further and further into the distance, in the direction of town. So much so that she was now a tiny black

114

dot, though a dot that Tom still very much loved. Tom decided then that all four of them would go to Georgia, himself, Frank and Abel and Sarah. That they'd give it a day or two for Sarah to come back after coming to her senses, then the bunch would make for Galverstone to get the train. After he'd outlined his scheme Frank replaced his hat on his head, compressing the thick fuzzy blackness of his hair down really hard so as the hat stayed in place properly.

"You reckon she'll come?" he asked his employer as he took a seat right beside him.

"She will," said Tom, eyes fixed firmly on the dot that was his lady love, doing a damn good job of ignoring Abel's approach. He tried to spit on the earth just beyond the porch, but failed, the spittle instead splashing on the wood. He leaned back and tried to find his dot but could not. "She will," he repeated to himself more than to Frank. "She's got to."

18.

Tom traipsed into town the next day with the waft of leftover liquor on his breath, body and even rising up from the feet inside his boots. He was sweating the stuff out of his system, plodding with the persistence of a man who knows if he doesn't do something then the hangover'll have him bent over a barrel all day and evening, and maybe even the next day if he's that unfortunate.

He wouldn't go to see Sarah. He didn't feel like giving her the satisfaction. And besides, being that hungover'd put him at a serious disadvantage in his ability to try and woo the woman. He found he could hardly walk in a straight line, let alone converse with complex, witty statements provided on his part that might make her think taking him back to be a good idea. His tongue was not keen. It was dull, as a blade is that's been used to whittle way too many birch branches and come away useless and in need of some serious sharpening up again.

No, Tom would not be seeing Sarah if he could help it.

Though maybe a cup of coffee'll do the trick, he thought, the first smile of the day threatening to take hold of his lips. Ladies like a sober man, and coffee sure does make a drunkard sober. Maybe I will, he thought. That's right, maybe I will do just that. A cup of coffee. Yeah, sure, that'll do, he thought. Though for him to have the funds for coffee he'd first have to pay a visit to the post office, to see if his auntie's wire'd come through.

The man was praying for the sun – which was harsh beyond measure that blistering afternoon – to go away and stop trying to burn him to a crisp like his brother's bacon. Belching out a particularly putrid burp, he stepped through the door of the post office to find that same old granny he'd offended before scowling at him for having been so rude as to burp as loudly as that in a lady's company.

"Control yourself young man," she said. "There's no need for that kind of behaviour in public. Maybe in your own home it'd be fine. But in the company of a lady, that's unacceptable."

"And when I see a lady, I'll make sure not to burp around her," said Tom, before burping again, though this time into the back of his hand.

"You're disgusting," said the granny. "God didn't grant you a great deal of manners mister."

"He certainly did not. Though thank fuck for His having blessed me with a big prick. Thank God almighty for that."

That made the woman scoff, turn and pick up her parcel before trotting by Tom and on out of the shop. She muttered something to Tom about a grandson, but Tom couldn't care less.

"Lot of money coming my way Pat. Plenty I reckon," Tom said to the man trying his upmost to stifle his laughter.

"Leave that lady be. She has a boy who'll box your ears for being too rude to her if you aren't careful," Pat said.

"Oh hell, it's only a bit of fun. Don't do no harm, does it?"

"I know it doesn't, but she don't. And I expect with the way she tells it to her grandson, *he* won't take it to be harmless banter neither."

"Well, whatever," Tom shrugged, sticking his hands in the front pockets of his overalls.

"There was a wire came for you. You won't believe how much," Pat said, a sort of sly grin on his cheeky face.

"Reckon it's around four hundred. Am I close?"

"Five," said Pat. "Five hundred dollars."

"I'll be damned," said Tom. "I was sure it'd be four."

"You ain't complaining are you?" Pat pouted as he squinted at Tom. "That sure is an awful lot of money. Man might be grateful to receive such a tidy sum as that. You ain't grumbling now, are you? Might not give it to you if you grumble."

"God damn Pat, you know me better than that. Why hell, sure I'm glad of the money. Just because I didn't guess right, don't mean I ain't grateful."

"Good," said Pat. "Fella ain't got no right to grumble about receiving no five hundred dollars. Damn well won't hear of such a thing."

"Then I won't grumble no more."

"Good," said Pat, picking up a wad of bills before licking his thumb, then counting out the correct amount.

"A man," he muttered, "a man with five hundred dollars ain't got no right complaining."

"And I ain't complaining no more. Just you do the counting, and I'll get out of your hair. Or what's left of it anyway. Look like a boiled egg Pat O'Grady."

"A boiled egg with *your* money. A boiled egg that's your only chance of getting this sum, without getting strung up by the neck."

"What you saying Pat?" Tom asked the badly balding man behind the counter.

"Saying, if I was inclined to take offence at your remark of my resembling an egg, if I was inclined of course, I might just take a walk on down to the Sheriff's office. Might tell him you took the money. If I was inclined of course."

"It's my money," said Tom, totally knocked for a loop.

"Well, if I was to say you took more than the share was

wired to you, you might wind up in a world of trouble. But I might not be so inclined, if…"

"If what? What you want? You want me to apologise for having hurt your pride by calling you an egg? If that's the case then Pat, I sure am sorry, and I would be very grateful if you was to kindly accept my apologies."

"You ain't sorry," said Pat.

"I am. I am indeed sorry."

"Ain't one bit, but…"

"Cut the crap. I've said sorry and that's that, now please, pretty please, give me my money and let me get out of here and get a drop of coffee down me. My head's hurting and you ain't doing it no favours."

"But," Pat continued as though the man in front of him hadn't said a word. "I would not feel the need to take a trip down to the Sheriff's should you be so kind as to donate a portion of cash to your postmaster's pockets."

"*What*!" cried Tom.

"Keep it down Tom. Just a fraction you understand. Not much. Maybe a hundred. If that's too much then the lowest I'll accept is seventy-five, but that's the least I can go to I'm afraid."

"I never heard the like of it," Tom said in astonishment.

"That may be, but one way or the other I'm gonna get paid."

"Won't get paid if I hang," said Tom, thinking he'd caught Pat out, though not really warming to the notion of his neck snapping so as he might best this thieving son of a bitch.

"That's where you're wrong," said Pat. "Because if you hang, he'll reimburse me. The Sheriff that is. So I win either way Tom. Now I'm sorry, but I need the money. And either you give it to me straightforward like, or that neck of yours snaps for the trouble and I walk away with my money either way. So, what's it gonna be?" said Pat, interlacing his fingers in front of him, his composure cool, calm and collected as though the man were merely asking for the loan of a handkerchief. Hardly believing his ears Tom told him he could have seventy-five, snatched his four hundred and twenty-five and stomped out as Pat O'Grady called after him not to take it so thick, that it was only money.

"Only money," Tom grumbled. "Goddamn seventy-five dollars you stung me for. Fucking *bastard*!"

The thought of coffee quickly evaporated, as the steam of the stuff does after climbing up and up out of a fresh cup into the air above, just as soon as Tom saw the bar. Buying a glass of beer sounded like just the ticket. And why wouldn't it? His pockets being pretty heavy with a wad of cash meant he could buy beer. Pat had put him such a sour mood that he saw no other option than to imbibe, in an effort to soothe the postmaster's, or rather, scorpion's stinger sticking out of his ass as he walked down the street.

The bar was empty, which wasn't surprising given that it was eleven o'clock in the morning. The bartender, a fastidious fellow with hair neatly parted right down the centre, with little spectacles perched upon the very tip of his nose was not a man one would expect to run a saloon. Though this was not the case, for he was quite capable of running his business, all thanks to the shotgun, whom he had named Bessie, behind the bar, kept loaded and cocked at all times should some man become too rowdy, or start waving his pistol around. Old Bessie'd ensure that such a man would become quiet in an instant, or hand his pistol over the bar before he got a shot off inside Michael Carmichael's establishment. His last name was on the sign above the door, but everybody who knew of the bar just called it Car's, Carmichael being too much of a mouthful.

Tom Liffey had always thought it strange for parents to call their kid a name that had two Michaels in it, but never did state his finding it strange.

"Don't suppose you'd be so kind as to furnish my fist with a glass of beer. Been nursing a headache only a beer can cure Michael. Mighty kind of you if you was to pour me a glass. Got plenty of money. Plenty."

"Bar's not open yet," said Michael Carmichael in his signature high-pitched voice that brought a smirk to the faces of every cowhand who ever breezed by Taughrane Heights and fancied wetting their whistle.

119

"I've got ten bucks here that says it is Michael Carmichael. And if that don't do the trick you can take twenty."

"Price stays the same and the bar ain't open. You can come back in an hour. Be happy to serve you then."

"Now hold on here a minute," said Tom, slowly starting to become bothered by just how bad his day was going so far. "You're telling me, that *you*, a business owner, won't take twenty damn dollars for a drink ain't worth but ten cents?"

"That's the way it is. If I was to charge you twenty dollars a drink you'd be cussing me out to every cowboy in the territory. Ain't got no reputation as a thief yet, and I aim to keep it that way."

"Well how's about you charge me ten cents, I drink it down faster than as if I'd crossed a damn desert, then I mosey on out and don't say a word to no one about it. How'd that be?"

"Be fine if it was twelve o'clock," said Michael. "But by my watch," he said, as he took out an ornate shiny silver pocket watch, popped the cover, regarded the time with one eye shut so as he could see properly – on account of the poor lighting – then with a click closed the precious trinket and popped it back in his waistcoat pocket. "By my watch it's seven past eleven. Meaning…"

"Meaning what Michael Carmichael? Meaning you're scared to give a fella a drink in case them there folks you attend the Presbyterian church with will look down on you?"

"*Exactly!*" said Michael. "Exactly sir. That's precisely why I won't, and why *you* will have to *wait* another…" Again the watch was out, again the cover was popped, again that one eye shut tight and again it disappeared just as quickly as it had appeared. "Fifty-four minutes now. By my watch that is. Though I fear that if I haven't wound it right then that time is incorrect. Either way we'll have to wait for the clock in town to chime the hour. Then you can have your drink. Matter of fact you can have several. Several drinks, as many as you like while you behave decently. Once you stop behaving decently, I'll take old Bessie, stick both barrels of her up against your chin, and we'll walk out of my saloon and you'll never enter it again, unless of course you wish to be shot. Which you will when I see you step through those swinging doors. Now, I can offer you a cigar. I can even offer you a cup of coffee, which would do you much more good than a drink. But alcohol shall not be consumed in my establishment before that there town clock has struck twelve, which will be in…"

"You get that watch out again and I'm gonna take this here Colt Dragoon and blow your damn hand off," said Tom, with a look in his eyes that didn't scare Michael Carmichael any, but did convince him that Tom Liffey was not above following through on such a promise. It was due to this quick assessment that Michael Carmichael closed the watch before his hand had had a chance to remove it from its home in his pocket, then placed his hands on the countertop.

"Coffee then? You can take it or leave it. I'm not dying for your custom. I'll have plenty of custom coming through today. Don't need yours, but I'll be happy to serve some coffee."

"You do that," Tom said, removing his hand from the grips of his pistol then lifting it to scratch at his stubble – which was fast becoming beard more than it was staying stubble.

"Fine," said Michael, the first sign of a smile starting to appear on his little ferrety face, though the man, Tom thought, was the sourest apple of the whole damn bushel. Be better off in the company of that robber Pat O'Grady, Tom said to himself. Be better having my pockets pilfered than being here in this bar with this gnome of a bartender, with his oily hair and those silver specs of his just begging to be broken by a boot heel coming down hard with a very pleasing, very noisy crunch.

"Coffee's already been brewed," said Michael.

"Oooh," Tom said mockingly, "lucky me!"

The fastidious bartender ignored the remark, remembering it as the first instance of insolence as a paying customer – his rule was that everyone got three strikes, three strikes then they were out. Tom's remark about the Dragoon could be ignored because he was not a customer yet then, he was however, now on strike one.

The bartender set a tin cup down on the countertop with

a small hollow clinking noise. Then Tom watched Michael Carmichael hoist his faded blue tin kettle up, fascinated at how slowly the man was operating as the thick black liquid landed in the base of the cup with a splashing sound, followed by the familiar noise of liquid colliding with liquid as it trickled down from the kettle, making the cup less and less empty until it looked as though the muddy coffee might just about spill over the tin cup's rim.

"Right and hot, is it?" Tom asked.

"Try it and see," said Michael.

"I will," said Tom, reaching out to take the cup, though not making it due to the fist flying fast through the air to his left, making that crunching sound he'd imagined Michael's glasses might make, only this crunch being due to the bridge of his own nose busting.

Blood was gushing out of both nostrils as soon as the contact was made. It dribbled down his chin, some becoming clotted in beard hair, some dribbling on down and landing on his undershirt. He toppled over off the barstool and landed with a thump that hurt his elbow something serious.

"You gonna be rude to my grandma now you skinny bag of puss? Hah? You gonna talk to her like that again? *ARE YOU?*"

Tom didn't know where this voice was coming from, or even to whom it belonged. But he didn't have time to figure for very long because that was when the booting began. The toe of some enraged entity became lodged at an alarming speed, hitting him fast and digging deep into Tom's belly.

"Be best you stay down mister. You come up and I'll break your jaw, then we'll see how you get on trying to talk to my grandma like she's dirt. Like she's nothing."

Tom tasted blood when he realised who his assailant was.

"Why you're the grandson," he said, spitting some hot blood from where it had dribbled down into his open mouth. "Goddamn, got some stones to come in here and start trouble."

"Shut…" Kick! "Your…" Kick! "Fucking…" Click

122

went both of old Bessie's hammers, a sound that brought Tom more joy than the moans that came from Sarah when he did right by her in bed.

Tom looked up and saw the straight steel barrels pointed directly into the cheekbone of this granny's boy. Tom got a look at him. He was tall, and broad in the shoulders. He was well fed, though far from fat. If Tom hadn't deduced it already from that powerful punch, he'd have guessed he was a boxer by trade, which just so happened to be the case.

"You just take two steps back sir," said Michael Carmichael. "That's you. You too Esther."

"Esther!" cried Tom as he got up on his feet as though he were a newborn foal finding them for the very first time. "That your name?"

He was still hunched over when he saw her standing, pinch-faced and every bit as humourless as she'd been when she last saw him.

"Hell, that is a mighty pretty name for such an old bag. Name like that don't belong on a gal as ugly as you. I know a name'd be better. It's an Indian name, but it sure would suit the look on your face."

"Tom, that's enough now," said Michael.

"Chews On Dung. That's what I'd've named you. Face on you like that one and you deserve such a title. Yes. I reckon so. Chews On Dung does just fine."

"You better be quiet you," said Esther. "Else this here grandson of mine'll send you to an early grave. He will, won't you Ryan?"

"I surely will. I'll thump a hole in his skull for him. Rearrange those teeth too," said Ryan.

"Well I'll admit, I ain't been to a dentist in quite some time. You'd know about that Esther, wouldn't you? Hell, I can smell your breath from *here*!" said Tom.

"Enough Tom," said Michael. "You two want to fight you can take it outside. Not happening in here. You boys better take heed else one barrel's blowing you open Tom, just as it is you Ryan."

"Reckon I'll wait outside then," said Ryan. "Reckon…"

But Tom was too quick. He didn't want to wait all day in the bar because he might just spend every cent of that four hundred and twenty-five threatening to burn a hole right through the pocket of his overalls. He'd lose it gambling, or end up so drunk he'd eventually think it a grand notion to buy the whole bar a round, then maybe three of four subsequently. He wasn't for staying, so he took that tin cup and threw the contents of said cup in Ryan's square face, scalding the man severely so as he doubled over screaming in agony.

Tom shoved Esther out of the road as though she were a dummy in a shop window, which to Tom wasn't far off the mark, then made his way swiftly out of the saloon, heading straight for home.

His belly was aching, and his nose was throbbing, but he knew if he stuck around too long, that boxer fellow would soon stand up straight – albeit with a face redder than beetroot – then come chasing after Tom to hurt him seriously, maybe even kill him. Tom took no chances and ran as swiftly as his long, lean legs could carry him. He sure was shifting when at last that shitty shack came into view. He'd never been happier to be home than he was then. Then Abel started to cry, and Tom's happiness washed away with those noisy, noisy tears.

19.

"You need mama! You need her Tom! You're hurt real bad."

"Brother," said Tom, taking a hold of his brother's face, cheeks damp from sobbing so much. "Listen to me. Mama's in Georgia. Now that's far away. That's far, *far* away, alright? So if mama's far away, you tell me how she's supposed to help me with my busted nose. You tell me brother, because I sure do love it when someone explains the impossible."

"But she'll help."

"Fuck's sake!" Tom said, throwing up his hands. "Hit him a smack for me Frank. Brothers ain't supposed to hurt one another. You'd be doing me a big favour."

"Don't hit me Frank," said Abel. "Please don't hit me. I'll brush your hair."

"I ain't aiming to hit you. You hold still Mr. Liffey sir, need to wash that nose. Think the bone busted right through the skin," said Frank.

"Son of a bitch. Bet I'd have wound up in jail you know, if I'd have seen him coming that is. Why I'd have taken my Colt Dragoon and driven a hole right through that there fella's head. Hell, it might even have been worth time in jail, just to see him drop. Would've made some noise, big as he was."

"Well," was all Frank said.

"You need that lady. You need the lady does the brushing. She'll make things right, I just know it," Abel whined.

"You go get her Abel. You tell her from me that she's wanted. Tell her she'd be best coming right on back to us, if she knew what was good for her," said Tom.

"Maybe give her a bit of time to cool off," said Frank, feeling deeply that if enough time lapsed between their final row and the next time they both laid eyes on each other, she'd be about as interested in him as a cat is a very large, very rabid dog that's foaming and frothing at the mouth, barking bloody murder.

"Who made you the expert?" Tom said. "You go get her Abel. Tell her she's wanted here and that this is where she belongs. Bitch'd better behave herself too, once she does come crawling back."

Frank pressed a little harder on the split skin, just enough to inflict some pain, though not enough to cause Tom to deduce that this pain was the product of having called Frank's love a bitch.

"Be careful will you!" Tom said. "Don't it look sore enough without you pushing down on it?"

"Yes it do sir. Sorry Mr. Liffey sir. Ain't got delicate fingers. Got big brown ones to work with, and while they're good for working with animals and driving fence posts down into the ground, they ain't made for fixing faces."

"You reckon I need a doctor?" Tom said, seething at the notion of losing any more money to another asshole in town, taken for a ride as he had been by Pat O'Grady, a man Tom took to despising with a passion, and hoped that he'd never see again. This would have been true if Tom was bound for Georgia. But as bad luck or fate or whatever other force makes things happen the way they do in people's lives, Tom was not headed directly to Georgia. God, or whomever, had other plans for that Liffey brother. Bad times lay ahead for Tom. Getting his nose fixed by the town doctor was the least of his worries.

"Don't know," Frank said before sighing a deep, tired out kind of sigh.

"Something on your mind?" said Tom, trying to touch at the red raw flesh exposed from beneath the flap of skin on the bridge of his nose. He *could* feel bone. "Face is fucked," he muttered.

"Maybe you didn't treat her right," said Frank, taking great care to speak each syllable with a kind of soft sound and a gentle touch. Tom was cross, and though Frank did not intend to make him any madder, he could no longer hold his tongue.

"Didn't hear you," said Tom, looking into the silver sheet of tin the three men used for a mirror when shaving. "What'd you say?"

"Said maybe you should have treated that lady right. You treat a woman all kind like and she ain't apt to take off on you. You didn't treat her right, and I mean no offence by that."

"There's no other way to take it other than to be offended. I'd be bothered if you weren't right, but you are. I know I didn't treat her right. Ain't got the gift of patience. Patience and a kind of cool temperament ain't in me. Maybe if I was like you she'd have stuck around," Tom said, arching his eyebrow up suggestively, eager to hear Frank's response to that.

The farmhand fought the urge to say something he'd regret, and subdued the fight in him to say, "Well if I did have her, I'd treat her like a Goddamn queen. Then the girl'd stick around. Then *you* could abuse yourself at nights to the thought of

126

her, and I'd get to make her moan!"

All this remained unspoken, sitting in Frank's heart as it knotted the organ up like a bit of gnarled old rope that could be found lying around out the back of the shack. Instead, Frank merely said, "Yeah well." And that was it.

"Yeah well nothing. Go on out and get after Abel. He's apt to get lost. Don't matter if he can see the town in front of him. I wager he'll still make a wrong turn."

"Ain't too kind on him none neither," Frank said as he lifted his badly battered hat off the seat next to where Tom was sat. "Wouldn't surprise me none if he didn't up and leave one of these days too."

"Yeah? Well maybe you could disappear too. You're more than welcome to take off any time you feel like it. Nothing keeping you here."

Tom was wrong. Dead wrong about that. The thing that kept Frank in the employ of the Liffey boys was that girl. That gorgeous girl who Frank found to be such a delightful creature he could just about put up with most of Tom's horseshit, though the rope tethering him to the Liffey's was frayed and in very poor condition. Should he see a window of opportunity appear he would leap at it like a lion does a deer for its dinner.

"Yeah well," was all Frank had to say again, so he said it and left, taking care not to bang the door behind him. He might have hated Tom Liffey, but without him he'd have no place to live so close to Sarah Herron, and that though was much worse than anything Tom Liffey could throw at him.

Frank walked out towards the end of the path in the front yard, flicked the latch on the gate and made his way off the property. He would take his time, trying to think while he walked of all the things he hoped he could summon the courage to say to Sarah. He hoped they'd come out. He hoped he could bring them out. He did not want to be tongue-tied, only able to offer another, "Yeah well."

Abel was walking at a brisk pace, armed for any combat that might have come his way with only a brush, which he had no holster for, therefore forcing him to carry it like an

127

amateur gunfighter totes his Colt.

He was worried about Tom. He was worried that his face might just keep on leaking blood, and that his brother'd drop down dead before he managed to get Sarah. Then the thought of his mama entered his mind.

"What if mama's in town?" he whispered into the thick, hot air around him. "Jeepers! What if!"

All the thoughts of Sarah soon cleared, making way for thoughts of mama and mama alone. All the way to town he built up the presumption that he might find her upon arrival. That she'd be waiting with open arms somewhere, and that they'd meet if he looked just hard enough. The thing was was that he didn't know where to start. He'd heard of Elsie's Pleasure Palace. His brother'd talked about it enough, though Abel didn't realise he'd already been there.

Then this new thought appeared: what if Tom had been secretly seeing mama all this time? And what if he and her had just said to each other, "We won't bother telling Abel?" This thought made him mad. Made him grip that brush handle so hard his knuckles went white and the bit at the end – where he'd chewed some nights – dug into the heel of his hand, leaving a deep red mark.

"Maybe," he said softly, before sauntering slowly through the town, seeking out this Pleasure Palace. "Pity I can't read none," he said as he walked by a fantastically dressed fellow with a brushed, black derby hat, with tufts of silver white hair sprouting out from underneath both the man's hat and, Abel noticed, nostrils. He didn't know how to speak to strangers so well, so thought that it might be best to talk to them on their level – or at least the level he thought they were on.

"Excuse me," he said, raising his trigger finger with that badly gnawed brush still squeezed in the other three fingers. "Excuse me my good man. But would you be so kind as to tell me where the Pleasure Palace is?"

"What makes you think I know friend? You calling me a lech?"

"But of course not my good man. For the thing is, I

don't know *what* that word means, my good fellow."

"Bah!" said the man with a dismissive wave of his wrinkled hand. He walked on, leaving Abel standing with his nose in the air all snooty like. "Lech," he said quietly.

Then another man, a man who had on a moleskin shirt and a very severe combover which was fooling no one, came along. This time Abel was armed with the correct vernacular.

"Excuse me," he said in his normal voice.

"Yes sir?" said the man with the dire do.

"I'm so sorry, but you wouldn't happen to be a lech, would you?"

"A lech!" said the stunned passerby. "Piss on you. You calling me a lech friend?"

"No," Abel said as though this man was simpler than he, "I'm *asking*, not calling. I need to find a lech who knows where the Pleasure Palace is."

"Well I ain't no lech, but the Pleasure Palace is right down there at the end of this here street."

"Thank you!" Abel said, so glad he'd found someone to help. "I'm so glad I found a lech. To tell you the truth though," he said, taking hold of this man's arm and leaning in for a conspiratorial whisper. "I actually don't know what it is."

"What? A lech?"

"Yeah. Haven't a notion."

"Well I ain't one," said the man, before leaving this seemingly strange fellow, whose vocabulary was questionable, to tend to his business.

Brush in hand, Abel marched right down where he'd been told to go, giddy with anticipation as he swung open those doors to Elsie's. He didn't know where to look. Ladies were everywhere. All kinds too. Ones with big behinds, ones with big bosoms. Ones with plenty of meat on their bones and ones with hardly any at all. Abel couldn't believe his eyes. Then the thought of mama came to him and, not knowing where else to go, hurried to the bar through the throng of men howling at what must have been some very funny jokes.

Some of these men, when they titled their heads back

to bellow a big hearty cackle, gave Abel a good look at where either the teeth were sat rotting in their heads or, in most other cases, had disappeared from their heads altogether.

They weren't handsome men, for the most part. Some were young and vibrant, and Abel could tell that the ladies on *their* knees looked like ladies who were enjoying themselves. But the ugly men. The girls that sat on them didn't look too happy to Abel. Though Abel had sense enough not to go and ask one if she was happy, for most men in this large, sweat-smelling room were well armed, each having at least one gun on their hip, if not two.

He didn't see his mama amongst this herd of women, and he didn't see Sarah, though the fellow couldn't remember that that was her name. So Abel pottered over to the bar, behind which a woman was serving glasses filled with what didn't seem like soda water to Abel.

"I'm so sorry to bother you but…"

"No need to say sorry Abel son. All men are welcome. Why we cater to the needs of every cowhand roams into this town. You after another girl or a glass of beer? We've whiskey too, though that's not handed out too liberally. Lots of fellas get too drunk too fast on the stuff, and if you don't like that there rule then there's other establishments in this here town'll be happy to get you drunker than hell."

"I'm after my mama," said Abel.

"Your *mama*?" said the woman. "Well hell, I don't think I've got a girl that sports under my roof's old enough to be your mama. She got a name?"

"No," Abel shrugged after thinking for a moment. "Just mama," he said, supposing that such a label should suffice in identifying the one woman he sought after so vehemently.

"Don't know no woman goes by mama. Got one girl has a child, but by God, it's just a baby. Any brothers that child has couldn't be your age, her mama's too young. You want a girl instead?"

"What about the lady?" said Abel, referring of course to Sarah.

"Gonna have to be more specific son. As you can see I

130

got lots of ladies. She got a name you could give me? Maybe then I could help out."

"Her name?" Abel asked as though by quizzing this woman, that she'd be able to supply the name.

"Yes son, a name. Name's are what people are called by. We ain't all mamas and ladies. I'm Elsie."

She didn't stick out her hand, but he did, introducing himself as Abel Liffey.

"I know that. You're Tom's brother."

"Yeah," Abel beamed. "That's right. Tom's my brother. He loves the lady I'm looking for. Though I figure he wants her for a wife, which I don't."

"What *you* want her for?"

"For brushing," Abel said before fishing out the brush from where he'd hidden it when stepping into this place – pilfering pockets was something his mama'd once warned him about, and Abel figured that if he lost that darn brush he'd commence to crying and probably never, ever stop.

Elsie started to laugh, quietly at first, then gradually getting louder and louder until her head was tilted back and the bare bit of her bosom which showing started jiggling in a way which almost hypnotised poor Abel.

"I'll be damned," she said, wiping the tears from her eyes. "I ain't never had no man step through that there door demanding that one of my girls brush him."

"Oh I don't want her to brush *me*," said Abel. "That would be silly. I just mean my hair."

Elsie hiccupped up a giggle, then fixed her eyes firmly on Abel.

"You want Sarah to brush your hair then you'll have to head to Mexico. Girl's gone."

"Mexico," Abel whispered.

"That's right," said Elsie. "Run off with a Mexican fella last night. Your brother Tom's to blame. Girl kept on saying she'd show him. Said she'd get back at him for barking at her. My girls may be whores, but they're girls first, whores second, meaning they got feelings. Fuck with them once too often and they'll run off, and I sure as shit ain't one to blame them for it."

Abel puzzled, his tongue poking out of the corner of his mouth.

"Maybe…" he began. "Maybe you could brush me. Maybe if you did it soft, like the lady."

"Lady's got a name son. Name's Sarah. Not lady. And I'm sorry, but brushing I ain't got time for. You see all these folks, these folks fancy fucking and drinking, and tonight I'm in charge of handing out the drinks. Ain't got time to brush no nincompoop."

"I ain't a nincompoop!" Abel insisted, though if truth be told, Abel found the word so funny he had to force himself to keep his laughter back. "I ain't," he said, the smallest hint of a grin on his face.

"Well," said Elsie, "you've come into a pleasure palace, and not just any palace, but the finest in the territory. You've come in, toting a brush, wanting one of my girls to brush your hair, when instead you could have a fuck and maybe a drop to drink. If that don't spell nincompoop to you then you're a fool Abel Liffey. Just a plain old fool."

"You're the old fool!" Abel snapped, though now smiling broadly. "What are you? A *hundred*?"

"Get out!" Elsie barked.

"But I'm only funning."

"You just called me old. You don't never call no lady old. On you go now," she said, lifting the brush off the bar then throwing it across the room. "And take your fucking brush with you!"

"No!" Abel cried as his head followed the path the brush made through the air. "No, no, no, no," he said, starting to slap at his head. He turned back to the lady that'd thrown it, as angry and as simultaneously scary a look on his face as Elsie had ever seen in her life.

"Leave now honey. You can come back for your brush in the morning. My girls'll find it for you. I'm sorry I threw it away on you. Okay? I'm sorry. But you shouldn't call a lady old. Now you know I suppose."

132

"Give me a drop of whiskey and a look at them there tits," growled a very grimy looking man with a big bushy beard and sweat glistening on the forehead poking out from under his hat.

"You can have one but not the other sweetie," said Elsie.

"Make it a double then. Two tits and no whiskey," said the man, but Abel wasn't listening any longer. He was now down on his hands and knees searching hurriedly, hitching sobs in and out of his breast, more panicked than he'd ever been before. At home he'd *always* known where the brush was. If it wasn't in his hand, then it was in his other hand. And if it wasn't there then it would be hiding under his pillow, the only other place it could possibly be. And he made sure it was there maybe a hundred times a day, not daring to go very long without checking. Now it was gone.

"Bitch," he said quietly as he manoeuvred between thick legs and thin legs alike, trying not to get his fingers stomped on, though failing more than a few times. It was then that Frank sauntered in through the door.

"Damn, here's another one now," said Elsie, peeved by the fact that another member of the Liffey household – albeit not a relation – had now come in to presumably bother her some more. "Frank!" she called out, flapping her hand about in the air above her head. "*Frank!*" she repeated.

Frank saw her waving, walked over and hunched over the bar as Abel had done moments before, so as she could hear him properly over the din of this den dedicated solely to debauchery and not much else.

"Elsie," Frank said to her. "Is Sarah up in her room tonight?"

"No," said Elsie. "No she ain't."

"Well where is she then?" said Frank, frankly flabbergasted that the girl was not to be found where she could almost always be found.

"She's on her way to Mexico," said Elsie. "*What!*" said Frank.

133

"I said she's on her way to Mexico."

"No I heard," said Frank. "What's she on her way to Mexico for?"

"Fella came in. Told her he'd take her along with him if she wanted. Man pointed a gun at me when I told him he couldn't have her. She said to wire her wages for the month to the town they was headed to."

"Where's that?" Frank said, feeling sick to his stomach worse than he ever had in his whole life, and the man had lived the majority of his life on a plantation, and sure as hell had seen some sickening things in his time.

"Now where was it again?" she said, lifting her finger to her chin and digging it in in a mock puzzling manner.

Frank took out a very crumpled, very distressed looking dollar bill, flattened it out and slid it across the bar toward Elsie. The woman's eyebrow lifted like a fishing hook had caught a hold of it, with the fisherman tugging and tugging at the rod in his hands.

"That all she's worth?" she teased.

Frank didn't sigh, he didn't show any sign of having been bothered because Sarah was the woman he loved, and Elsie was right. Though the woman standing before him with that arched eyebrow didn't know that there was no fee in the world Frank wouldn't pay for that piece of information. That the man was desperate beyond compare. That he craved Sarah Herron's company more than an opium fiend fancies a drop or two of laudanum in his morning coffee.

He counted out ten dollars, flattening every one as he did so. When they were all laid out, the man with the beard came over, belching and unsteady on his feet, sticking said beard up in Frank's grill.

"Got you a little blacky," said the man.

"Leave it be Elmer. He ain't a dog. He's welcome."

"*Welcome*?" squeaked Elmer. "Hell, when a black man's welcome in a whites only pleasure place, must surely mean that the Lord's second coming is imminent," he said before spitting on the sawdust coated floorboards, a small droplet

134

splashing against Frank's boots, though the black man did not notice it.

"You reckon he'll take you up to heaven with him?" said Frank, in no mood for being toyed with as he turned to face the man with the exceptionally poor breath, caused no doubt by several severely rotted teeth that should have been pulled many many months before. "Because if he is coming back, then you would need one hell of a wash friend."

The man called Elmer lifted both eyebrows up high, even tilting back a bit before tilting up the brim of his hat to further express his being so very shocked.

"Shit Elsie. Man's got a mouth on him," he said, before leaning forward again really close to Frank's ear. "Though uh, *friend*. I don't think it's me that needs the wash. Why you're skin's damn near dirtier than any man's in here."

Frank smiled a slow, evil smile.

"Say that again friend. Hard to hear over the crowd. Would you repeat it?"

"Sure," said Elmer, patting Frank hard on the back, beaming just as slow and just as evil a grin as Frank was then. "I said," he said, "you been rolling around in a coal shed mister? Because by God you are one of *the* blackest niggers I have *ever* seen."

Frank laughed then. Laughed long and loud and hard. Elmer laughed too, though wasn't quite sure what at. Then Frank, quicker even than a rattler, picked up a beer tankard and smashed it against the side of Elmer's ignorant head in the same split second. The drunkard dropped to the ground, blood pissing out of the great big gashes up the right side of his face.

"Found it!" Abel bellowed, hoisting his brush up in the air triumphantly. Elmer was grumbling on his knees, carefully picking pieces of shattered glass from his face, though doing a decidedly poor job of it, given how inebriated he was.

"Where they going to Elsie?" said Frank. She just shook her head, appalled – although she had no qualms with black folk – at a black man having assaulted a white one in *her* whorehouse. "Where they going girl?" said Frank, reaching out and grabbing both of her arms. "You tell me! Don't make me ask a third time!"

"She didn't say the town, but it's on the border. It's a brothel she's going to."

"What brothel?" Frank roared, ready to throttle Elsie if he didn't get much further fast with her.

"El Perro Sucio. It's the dirty dog. It's a hole. Not like here. Don't know why she wanted to go there."

"I do," said Frank, before rushing right across the room at Abel and taking the dim-witted Liffey by the hand then hauling him the hell out of there. Abel kept moaning, but the blood was pumping so hard in Frank's ears he couldn't hear him. Abel whinged about being brushed, about how he wanted to find the lady. But Frank just marched Abel right out of the town by the hand.

Once well away from Taughrane Heights, making good progress on the path to the Liffey boys' home the farmhand suddenly dropped down to his knees and began to sob salty tears that dropped into the dust one at a time. Able patted him on the back and asked what was wrong. But Frank just sobbed on. He couldn't hear a thing.

20.

"You're a damn fool Tom Liffey! Letting a good girl like that get away!" Abel boomed, his large voice filling the small space he occupied, in which Tom was sitting swaying in his seat with one eye shut, drunk as a newt.

He'd had no time to secret away the jug sitting on the table, mostly because even if he hadn't have been so damn drunk, he wouldn't have heard Frank and Abel approach, for Frank had ceased his lecturing and lamentations long before the pair had gotten close to the shabby shack.

"You had a good thing," Abel roared, repeating what Frank had said practically verbatim. "You had a good God damn

136

thing and you ruined it. Just like you let this house go to shit. Just like you drink damn near every day. You ain't no better than a bum. If Sarah'd the brains she was born with, she wouldn't have wanted to spend a second with a waste of space like you."

"Alright Abel, that's enough now," said Frank, lightly tapping the verbose Liffey on the back.

Frank felt safe enough, for Tom was indeed inebriated. He was swaying in the way that meant he mightn't remember much of the night before's events when the sun came up again. Frank felt safe, and it was for this very reason that he thought he'd just let Tom have it. Though Frank's knife would not be stabbed as violently as Abel's. Frank's was the slow knife, slipping in between ribs quietly, then and only then starting to twist to make Tom squirm inside. In a moment or two he'd commence, but not before Abel had been gotten rid of.

"Boy you go on now, you hear? You go right on outside and leave me and your brother be. Go on now."

"Why?" said Abel – a fair enough question so far as questions went.

"'Cause I said so. That a good enough reason for you?"

"Yeah I guess." But Abel didn't leave. He still stood staring like a dummy.

"Do I have to repeat myself?" said Frank. "Fuck *off* Abel!"

"Don't you speak to my brother like that. Don't you dare darky," Tom said.

"Oh," said Frank, "so it's darky now? Not Frank. Guess that whiskey's worked wonders on you. Turned you from just a plain old run of the mill son of a bitch into a racist son of a bitch. Boy, I sure got to try some of that. Then maybe I can converse just as ignorantly as you've become."

He then tried to lift the jug, but just as his hand found the little ring near the opening at the top, Tom's hand shot out and grabbed a hold of Frank's wrist.

"Reckon if you want to keep that hand, you'll leave my whiskey be."

Frank tried to stare Tom down, but Tom, being

emboldened by liquor would not blink first.

"Fuck off Abel," Frank told the elder sibling. "Said it twice now. Won't ask so polite the third time."

Abel made a strange gurgling sound as though the words he wanted to say wouldn't come. He scraped a shred of hay with one foot, then did as he was bid and fucked off.

"Who the fuck do you think you are telling my brother what to do? Hah? Who do you think you are?"

"Name's Frank friend, and if my girl's gone off I'll speak however I feel fit to to whatever white man I have the misfortune of addressing."

"*Your* girl?" said Tom. "Hold your hats folks, for we ain't talking about Sarah Herron now, is we?"

"We is," Frank said plainly. "Pretty much mine, given how many times I've been into town to see her. It's been more times I've seen her than you have. Reckon that makes her mine."

"But you're black Frank. What white woman would go with a damn darky? Don't talk foolish Frank. It doesn't suit you."

"Well she suits me. Suits me right down to the ground. Girl's far too good for you, and I don't care if you or her or anyone else is white, that's the damn truth. Don't know what she saw in you. Haven't a notion."

"Now Frank," said Tom, taking his jug from the table and tilting it up so as he could have another healthy slug of whiskey. "You ought to know better than to take after a white man's woman. Why, a white man might become cross. Might get mad, then mean, then *maybe* even take his pistol," Tom said as he removed his Dragoon from its home on his hip and slammed it down hard on the table – so hard Frank was surprised the fucking thing didn't go off – to make his point. "Then he might just about aim it right at the black head who sees fit to make a claim for said woman. We wouldn't want that for you Frank. Abel and I both like you a lot. You're a damn fine hand and an even better help."

Tom then wiped whiskey from his lips with the back of his arm, then, blowing boozy breath straight into Frank's face, continued his sermon on the matter of black men liking white ladies.

"Lots of black folk like white women. Why wouldn't they? Now don't get mad, don't pout so. Sarah's not the girl for you. You fancy marrying a white woman, then we'll get you a white woman. Maybe one with a big ass on her, then you can have the best of both worlds. Big black ass on a skinny white woman. Wouldn't that be nice?"

"I like Sarah," said Frank. "That's…"

"Let me *talk*. What I was about to say is, if you'd let me, is that that's too bad. Because Frank, and I mean this when I say it, so don't argue. That girl is mine. You know what that means? That means mine. Sarah Herron don't belong to you nor any other man, for her heart belongs to me."

"Oh yeah?" said Frank. "Figure that's why she run off with a man to Mexico then, because her heart belongs to you."

"You don't get it Frank. Ladies like that, they need a man of sophistication. A man with panache. You ain't got… Hold on. What'd you say?"

"Said she's gone. Gone down Mexico way. Woman up and left with a fella," Frank said, torn between wanting to grin at Tom because he'd lost his girl and the urge to begin sobbing and commiserating with Tom because he had lost the girl he loved just like his employer. Not knowing which option to decide on, he put his head in his hands and began to count the knots in the wood of the worn-out old table.

"What in the hell's she gonna do in Mexico?" said Tom.

"I don't know," Frank sighed.

"What's she gone there for? Fuck's sake Frank, *Mexico*! Men are dangerous down there. 'Least that's what I've heard. Hell, she might get treated poorly. We gotta do something. We gotta go get her, bring her home. Hell, I ain't letting no Mexican have her. Greasy fuckers don't treat women right."

"Reckon I'll come with you," said Frank. "Reckon she can decide which one of us she wants when we rescue her."

"Oh no," said Tom. "No. No you ain't going. Got other plans for you Frank. Tomorrow morning, we go into town and get them there papers for you. Then you and Abel are going to go

139

across to Georgia on the trains. You'll take *him*, and I'll ride out for *her*. She don't need both of us. Only one man needs to rescue her."

"He's your brother."

"Hah?"

"Said he's your brother, clean out your fucking ears."

"Don't cuss at me Frank. Remember, I'm the one with the pistol here, not you. You speak civil to me, or I'll rearrange your head so as it's filled full of holes and lead balls. Be pretty for Sarah then now, won't you?"

"You try it," said Frank. "Go on ahead."

Tom stared sternly at Frank, feeling the weighty wooden grips under the palm of his hand. He didn't want to shoot Frank. Mostly because he liked him. He didn't like the fact that he was after his woman, but the black man'd been helping him for so long he wouldn't dare try to shoot him. It didn't matter who he fancied. Tom turned the handle of his weapon toward his employee.

"Here Frank. Gun's yours. I'll buy a new one in town tomorrow. You're to take Abel to Georgia on the train and *I'll* go get Sarah. She won't come for you. I think that you know that deep down."

"Don't know nothing of the sort."

"You do," said Tom, taking his jug and getting up from his seat to hide it, though this was a fruitless endeavour, for both Frank and Abel now knew of its existence. Old habits, Tom thought as he hid his precious jug. Just old habits, dying hard.

21.

"This here's the money for the tickets," Tom said, counting several crisp dollars down into Frank's open palm. Pleading was not now Frank's modus operandi. He had a plan. A plan which meant going along with things up to a point. Plenty of dollars in his hand made him feel sure that the scheme could come to fruition, but he had to play the faithful employee a little while longer. "Leaves this for food," said Tom. "You got ammo for that there gun?"

"Yes sir, Mr. Liffey sir. Got it right here."

"Good. Check the loads once you hit Louisiana. Lots of fellas down there'd likely take offence at your color. Could mean trouble. You've got your papers, but it may not be enough. That's what that there's for," said Tom, tapping at the gun housed in the holster on Frank's hip that once belonged to the Liffey boys' father, before his demise due to very harsh, very frosty weather.

"Where we going?" asked Abel. Tom ignored him, as did Frank.

"Find a window seat so as he can look out. He'll be apt to keep quiet if you do. If you don't I reckon he'll talk your ear off until both ears is bleeding," said Tom.

"Yes sir," said Frank.

"Where we *going*?" Abel asked again.

Again Frank and Tom tired to ignore him, not out of impoliteness, but because he'd already been told ten times and neither man felt like repeating themselves again.

"Now I won't be too far behind you. Once I get her, I'm coming straight back up through to Georgia. Don't you worry about that Frank, for I'll be on my way."

"Yes sir," said Frank, before Abel asked yet another the location of their destination.

"*Quiet* Abel!" Frank snapped.

"Damn it," said Tom. "That's the first time I seen you snap at him like that."

"Yeah well, I ain't aiming on listening to him witter once we get on that there stagecoach over yonder. I can cope with him on the farm 'cause I can get away a while. Won't have that luxury riding so close to him in that there stagecoach."

"Where… we… go*ing*!" Abel yelled.

"Shut… the fuck… up!" Tom said, spelling out each syllable so as Abel got the message. But Abel wasn't for abiding. He shoved his brother in the chest. Shoved him really hard. So hard that Tom staggered back, tripped over a sizeable stone and landed right on his coccyx, letting out a hiss in pain that Frank found to be not too far from a sound he'd heard coming from a rattler right under the Liffey boys' front porch.

"Piss on you," Tom said, his one hand on his knee, his other in Frank's hand. Once back to his feet, he spat in the dust, then vowed that if Abel ever did that again it'd mean trouble.

"What kind of trouble?" Abel asked.

"Trouble like you having your brains bashed in by a boulder. There'll be blood all over my hands. They'll hang me, but by God will it be worth it to get you to quit your moaning and whining all day long."

"Shut up," Abel said.

"No you shut up!" said Tom. "You shut up brother. I'm fucking fed up listening to you. Moan, moan, moan is all you ever do. If it's not one thing it's another. Ain't about brushing it's about wondering where you're going. What does it matter? Only thing that matters to you is that there fucker of a brush. You could be anywhere in the world and as long as that there brush was with you, as well as someone to do the brushing, you wouldn't give a fig. You could be freezing your balls off way up in the rockies, or you could be sweating all over in some God forsaken sand box. But as long as you have that there brush then everywhere's just peachy. Makes me sick."

Tom then spat in the dust again, this time it came out green.

"Well you know what makes me sick?"

"No brother. What makes you sick? Aside from worrying about being brushed?"

"What makes me sick as that you're not coming to see mama. Mama did everything for you. She took good care of you."

"No brother, she took good care of *you*. Not me. Me she left alone. It was you she doted on. At least up to a point."

"What's that supposed to mean?"

"Means she couldn't stand to take care of you too long, could she? She did run off, didn't she? Shit. And you pining over her all these years. You wishing you was with her all day, and her not giving a tinker's damn. Does make you wonder."

142

"Wonder what?" Abel said slowly, the syllables oozing out of his mouth, trickling out like poison as the young man poised himself, ready for attack.

"Makes you wonder whether she ever loved us. I'd wager not."

That did it. That was precisely the wrong thing to say, for Abel, upon hearing this remark, ran full speed at Tom, charging him like a herd of very heavy buffalo, sending the younger Liffey staggering back a bit before landing on his butt for the second time that day. But Tom wouldn't let this slide again. He got up like lightning and grabbed a tuft of Abel's hair, hauling his brother's top half down so he was bent over.

"You want your hair brushed brother? Maybe be best if you had no hair *to* brush. Reckon I ought to yank it out for you? Do you a mighty big favour fatso!"

"Fuck *off*!" Abel said as he elbowed his brother hard in the groin, getting a good groan out of Tom as he let go of his hold on Abel's strands of wispy hair then thumping down on the ground cradling his soft bits.

"You see that Frank? Fucker fights dirty," Tom wheezed while massaging himself downstairs.

"Don't you dare pull my hair!" Abel said, stooping to pick up the rock that Tom had first fallen over. He hoisted it high above his head, was ready to let it drop down on Tom's head, when Frank figured now was the time to intervene, seeing as how he didn't think that Abel was as cruel a character to receive a sentence to have himself hung by the neck until dead for murder.

"Come on now boys," he said, lifting the rock out of Abel's hands before he'd had a chance to release it. "That's enough now. Whole town's watching."

"Let them watch," said Tom. "Think I care?"

"You do deep down. Everyone cares what people think somewhere inside. You're just like the rest of us."

"Ah hell!" said Tom, feeling himself a bit to make sure nothing had burst before getting to his feet with Frank's assistance. "You go on to mama," Tom told Abel. "You go on and you get your damn hair brushed. Bet she's sick of you come

Tuesday. Bet she'll have had enough of you again in one week. Then it's goodbye mama. Goodbye to being brushed by your precious mother."

"Maybe you should try getting your hair brushed once in a while. Maybe then you mightn't be so cross," Abel said, his reasoning seeming sound to him, but so silly to Frank and Tom that although Tom wanted to, he didn't smile – Frank did. The thought was funny, as most things were that came out of Abel's mouth.

"Maybe I wouldn't," said Tom. "But maybe I'd be a big dummy like you if I did. And I wouldn't want that. I like having brains me. Means I have the capacity to think, a property you don't possess."

"I don't know what that means. But you're an asshole Tom. You're an asshole and you treat me mean every chance you get. God forgive you, you big lanky prick! Don't you bother coming along. Just you stay here and keep the pigs company. Best chance you have of conversing with someone who understands you. Maybe you could drink as much as you like with me and Frank not around. Maybe you could get drunk all day long. Like that, wouldn't you?"

Tom stared hard, his look filled to the brim with hot hatred. He didn't like that Abel knew he drank. Didn't like him throwing it in his face like this either, for it was a sore point for Tom, for the drinking was something he knew himself he was overfond of.

"Yeah," said Abel. "You'd *love* that. With me and Frank gone you could glug it down all day, every day. Probably poison yourself with it. And you know what!"

"What?" Tom said spitefully.

"When you die," Abel said as he stepped forward so close to Tom the tips of both their noses nearly touched.

"Yeah?" said Tom.

"No one," said Abel. "No one will want to brush your hair."

The thought made Frank feel like laughing, though the look on Tom's face arrested the hiccups he was dying to let out.

144

Tom turned to Frank, held out his hand and said: "Give me that there pistol."

"Please Mr. Liffey. Leave it be. Boy don't mean no harm. He don't. I know him. *You* know him. He just misses his mama, that's all. No harm meant, I'm sure. Ain't that right Abel?"

"Ain't right at all. I mean harm. I mean harm Frank." Then Abel blew a big raspberry into Tom's face, spraying spittle all over the younger Liffey's cheeks. Tom grabbed for the gun on Frank's hip, but Frank swatted his hand away.

"Alright now. That's *enough!*" Frank said firmly. "Now I'm tired of this. Abel, you go on and you get in that there stagecoach. You go to the gunsmith's and be about your business before heading to Mexico. Might be parting on poor terms but you ain't parting with one of you killing the other. Brothers ain't supposed to do that. That ain't right. Now stop the pair of you. You hear? Go on now Abel. What would mama think?"

This changed Abel's tune like someone clicking a fresh cylinder into place on a pistol. Placidity washed over him, followed by a wave of remorse. What *would* mama think? he thought. Then the urge to apologise came. He felt his sorriness start to swell inside like a balloon. Then the tears started to come.

"I'm…" was all he got out before the words caught in his throat, never to be said. Tom just looked at him, hatred flooding his head. And if looks, like pistols could kill, then that nasty face Tom Liffey was pulling would surely have sent Abel to his grave.

"Go on," said Frank. "I won't ask again."

Abel looked into the tired eyes buried deep in the black man's face. Then with one last glance at Tom, turned and marched off towards the stagecoach, fiddling inside his pockets a moment before producing his brush, which he subsequently commenced caressing as he clambered on up inside the wooden wheeled mode of transportation.

"Tell him you're sorry," said Frank. "You write him a letter his mama can read for him once he gets to Georgia. Brothers ain't supposed to fight like that."

"Yeah," said Tom, still watching Abel like a hawk as he

spat into the dust again.

"Ain't fooling," Frank said. "You write him. You hear? You write that there boy because brothers is supposed to love each other. Not hate one another. He's soft that boy. Don't have no grit in him at all."

"You don't know him like I do," said Tom.

"Oh I think I do," said Frank, though that was the last remark he had to make on the matter. "Maybe you should get some sleep before riding off down to Mexico. Might clear your head so as you can think some. Man that took her mightn't be too friendly when you tell him you're there to take who he thinks is his woman."

"Don't have time. Them Mexicans mightn't treat women like some of us gentlemen do. My Sarah's had her time with bad men. I won't stand for anymore ill treatment to come her way. Won't have it Frank."

"Well, whatever you think then," said Frank. Tom nodded.

"Can't say you've the easier job," Tom said. "Seems maybe mine's easier, and mine might mean killing a man."

"Oh he ain't so bad," Frank said, sticking out his large hand for Tom to take.

"He is indeed," Tom said as he took it and shook it. Frank nodded and walked away in the same direction Abel'd gone. "He's every bit as difficult," Tom said, before stuffing his hands in his pockets and walking down the street, seeking out a place to go and get a horse. A horse *and* a gun.

22.

Sarah still wasn't used to being treated so poorly, at least not *that* relentlessly. Being cut up as she had been by that razor-wielding cuss hadn't accustomed her too much to harsh treatment, and she didn't consider taking a slap or two from the occasional cowboy enough to make her feel as though she'd had it hard in life. He, however, was different. He being Juan Lobo. He rode his horses

146

hard and wore out his women even more so, a fact about the man Sarah soon found out.

The buggy carting Sarah to her new place of work was worn, and in very bad need of repair. Riding through the night and on into the next day, the horse he was whipping eventually succumbed to the strain of being pushed to its limit for far too long, lying down in the dust snorting up tornadoes of the stuff and gasping out and in its air in an awful irregular kind of pattern. Sarah felt sorry for the beast and began to stroke its mane after stepping down off the buggy.

"Better shoot it," she told Juan.

"Better not," he said, those beady black eyes of his penetrating Sarah's skull even in the darkness. The moon was lighting the plains well, though the eyes of Juan Lobo sat in his skull like two shining, highly polished marbles. Sarah'd never seen a fellow with eyes as black as he had. He had a hate filled countenance, comprised of a jet-black fringe – creeping down from underneath his big broad sombrero hat – bushy eyebrows that had a hangman's join in the middle – which Sarah thought made the man even uglier looking, if that were possible – as well as swarthy skin stained by too much time spent in the sun. Sarah supposed hers too might turn that color given where she was headed.

"You can't just leave it," she said. "What, you just gonna up and go without putting the poor animal out of his misery? Mister, you better shoot this here horse…"

Then the butt of Juan Lobo's pistol came crashing down on the top of Sarah's skull, splitting it open so that in a moment, hot black blood trickled down her back.

"Be quiet *señorita*. He don't need no bullet, because bullets ain't cheap."

Sarah sat massaging her head. Her hand was so bloody when she looked at it she passed out at the sight, though Juan Lobo was not one for having pity provoked in his broad breast.

"Be better you keep going *señorita*. We get to Hector's soon enough."

Sarah didn't stir. She didn't make a move, except for

147

her breathing, which caused her chest to rise and fall silently.

"You didn't hear me?" said Juan Lobos. He then drew back his boot, then delivered a kick so despicably violent, that if Frank had seen it happen, Juan Lobo would not have very many more minutes to live. He'd take that Dragoon off his hip, cock back the hammer and let the lead ball fly, blowing the belligerent Mexican's brain matter right on out through the back of his beastly skull. Sarah woke with the wind knocked out of her to hear the Mexican laughing.

"You near me now, *si*?" he said, standing looming over her. She gasped and groaned rolling around in the dirt, clutching tightly to her tummy. "I give you thirty seconds," Juan Lobo laughed, lifting his belongings up from the wooden shelf on the back of the buggy. He drank down a healthy amount of water, with some spilling out the sides of his mouth, dribbling down his big black beard before dropping onto his boots, staining both feet with little wet patches.

He corked his canteen, swiped some of the remaining water from his moustache, then told Sarah: "Your time is up. You better be coming along now. No water if you don't obey."

Sarah looked up into his face. It was not harsh, not angry as she'd expected, but smiling so sweetly she thought that any other woman would find him to be companionable. But the eyes. The eyes were evil little things, void of pity and not at all in keeping with the smirk smeared across the rest of his face.

She slowly got to her feet, her guts aching and her head light from the blows.

"You walk ahead," he said. "I follow."

Sarah felt like scratching his eyes out. This wasn't what she was used to at all. Cowboys sometimes gave her a slap, but they never booted her in the belly like that. And they never took to whipping her with the grip of their pistols as Juan Lobo had. He was horrible. He was horrible and she hated him with a passion.

He marched her for three miles before she wanted water. When she asked, he told her to stop and turn around. He then poured a little water into his fingers and flicked some at her

148

face.

"I want a drink you dope!" she said. "A *drink*! Know what that means mister? Means I take it in my mouth."

"You take it in your mouth?" said Juan Lobo. "*Oh, si. Si señorita*. My mistake. I fix for you right away."

The canteen was slung over his shoulder while Sarah watched.

"What you doing?" she said, puzzled by this. Then the Mexican began to make a show of searching for something. He then found what he was looking for in his satchel, produced the pistol and placed it in Sarah's mouth.

"You want something in your mouth then I give you. You going to be quiet *señorita*? Or do I have to put a bullet in your head? It is your choice. I don't mind either way."

The barrel tasted strongly of metal, a taste Sarah'd known from sucking on keys sometimes as a child. Though the memories of tasting metal were welcome, the fact however that this man had put a pistol in her mouth was most certainly not welcome one bit.

"You going to moan?" said Juan Lobo.

Sarah didn't answer. A single tear tumbled down her cheek, which Juan Lobo lifted on the tip of his finger and tasted.

"Don't waste water," he said, savouring the salty solution. "It's no good to waste water way out here. You going to be quiet?"

Sarah nodded, the cylinder inside the pistol rattling with her head's movements.

"Good," said Juan Lobo, removing his pistol and allowing her to taste the air again instead of gun metal. "Move along," he told her, so Sarah did just that.

The threat of her having her head blown off was real. She knew this man was not to be messed with. She marched and marched for many miles and didn't dare ask for another drop of water. While they walked, he whistled the same tune over and over again, which grated on Sarah's nerves immensely. Tom had whistled, though his melodies made her feel fine. Juan Lobo's warbling was something that drilled down into her head, piercing her skull with its song going on and on and on, never letting up. Perhaps she could have listened to him, but her hatred of the man made the whistling what it was – a taunting sound that was like a little victory march making Sarah feel smaller and smaller until she felt just two inches tall.

They kept on going until Sarah saw a building far off in the distance. She stopped and bent over with her hands on her knees, tired out from having walked so much without rest.

"We nearly there *señorita*. We not going to stop yet. You keep going or I give you a bullet for your trouble," said Juan Lobo, lumbering past her and heading onward, that much closer to this little far-off building. "Be best you hurry up," he sang melodically. "Maybe you get some water when we arrive."

Then the whistling started again just where it had left off.

Sarah studied the back of the Mexican's head hidden under his hat. She then surveyed the supply of stones littering the ground upon which they walked. There were some big ones. Ones that would surely do the job. Just lifting it in her hands made her feel better already. He had stolen her. Stolen her like an item in a grocery store and taken her away from her home. From the possibility of seeing Tom traipse in with a hangdog look on his face, fretting for Sarah to come back to him. Of course she *would* come back if he came for her, because he was her man, and that was that. This Juan Lobo was not her man. He wasn't any kind of man. He was a brute, big and ugly and evil. And Sarah Herron considered caving in his big, fat head with the rock in her hands and ridding the world of another fellow who hurts women; who threatens them with guns and promises of murder.

"Maybe I will," she said so softly to herself only the rock could have heard her. Then she started to run. Running faster and faster, not caring if her footfalls made much noise. She hoisted her rock high, ready to be brought down to deliver death to Juan Lobo. Then the Mexican roared with laughter loud enough to fill the whole plain.

"Be better for you if you don't," he said through his chortling. He sounded so full of glee that that alone surprised

150

Sarah more than the fact that he knew she was about to cause her stone to collide with his head. "You don't kill me, and I don't kill you," he laughed. "I make you suffer, but I don't kill you."

Sarah had her rock held high above her head. Standing there panting she thought she must have looked awfully silly. Juan Lobo didn't stop. He spat out in the dust and told her she'd better put the rock down before he got cross.

Sarah felt hopeless as she threw the large rock to the ground with a conclusive thudding sound. She couldn't kill him. And even if she tried, she felt sure he'd follow through on his promise. And Sarah Herron did not wish to suffer.

The building belonged to Hector, or so Sarah supposed. The building was white and had been badly baked by the sun because the painted walls were beginning to peel on the outside. Juan Lobo instructed Sarah to keep her mouth closed in this place, or he would be obliged to close it for her.

"You understand *señorita*?" he asked.

"Yes," she said as quiet as a church mouse, though this too displeased Juan Lobo. He let her have a powerful fistful in her tummy and asked again.

"I said do you understand? I don't need no words. You just nod when I talk. You don't talk. You understand?"

Sarah looked up into his ugly face. She wanted to hurt him, but knew she couldn't, so she just nodded.

"Now we go in," said Juan Lobo, lifting the wooden latch on the gnarled wooden door to the place. "I would say ladies first. But I don't think you're a lady," he said, then laughed at his own wit, which Sarah did not find funny and, she imagined, Elsie wouldn't either if she'd been around to hear it too.

The door swung open and Sarah got a good waft of putrid, stale sweat and even more stagnant whiskey. She gagged though did this quietly so as not to provoke Juan Lobo.

"You better close the door to keep the stink in," came another Mexican voice from inside. "We're used to the smell. Some fresh air might make us sick."

Juan turned to Sarah with the smile still there, though the eyes flashed furiously. He didn't even need to tell her she'd better get into the building quick or there'd be trouble. The look said it all.

"You can keep your hat on for a dollar. If you don't my woman will tell you there is a charge," said a big beefy man standing in a kind of kitchen sitting dead in the centre of the large room.

Along the walls were various items that could be purchased. As well as a couple of tables and a few chairs. There were stairs that led somewhere, though Sarah did not know where to. There was a frying pan filled full of steaming beans cooking behind the man doing the talking, as well as several bottles of liquor lining a stack of shelves situated behind and to the left of this man making remarks on the rules of wearing hats indoors.

"I haven't got a dollar to spare Hector," said Juan Lobo.

"Then you better take your hat off," said Hector, rubbing at his balding head as though there was a phantom hat that sat atop it that only he could feel.

Juan Lobo lifted his hat off and motioned for Sarah to take a seat at one of the tables. Hector saw her and his eyes bulged. Sarah, or so she thought, must have been much more attractive than this Hector fellow's woman, because he looked at her like she had sprouted a second head on her shoulder. Hector rubbed at his chin and moved to pick up his pan of beans in one hand, as well as a bottle of liquor in the other. He took them over to Sarah while Juan Lobo took off his coat and hung it up on the coat rack by the door, along with his sombrero. Hector set the pan down on the table with a grimace, giving Sarah a good look at the sorry state of the man's mouth. The teeth were mostly brown, but some were black. Sarah got another nasty shock when he puffed out a sigh, giving her a sample of the smell that this morbid mouth was capable of producing. Again she felt like gagging, but didn't because he was a strange man and this was a strange place. Her experience with Juan Lobo had already educated her on the capacity for cruelty of Mexican strangers, and this Hector fellow she did not yet know.

Hector raced around the back of the bar, clinked two shot glasses together and brought them back to Sarah.

"What you doing Hector?" said Juan Lobo. "Getting glasses Juan."

"No no. None for her. She wants a drink she can go outside and dunk her head in the donkey's trough. No tequila for her."

Sarah scowled at Juan Lobo, but he just looked back at her. He reached for his pistol, so Sarah looked away. Juan Lobo nodded and grumbled something about a lesson learned. Then he began to scoop spoonfuls of beans up and out of the pan and onto his plate.

"Beans better be better than the last time I came," said Juan Lobo, tasting some, his eyebrows lifting in a pleased sort of way.

"What you think?" asked Hector.

"They are better," said Juan Lobo. "Lots better."

Hector smiled at this remark, then turned to Sarah to get her verdict. But Sarah didn't dare take a single solitary bean without say so from her abductor.

"You want to eat do you?" Juan Lobo laughed, causing Hector too to join in on the fun at her expense. "You eat the beans," he said, sliding the pan over to her. "No need to dirty the plate. Means I have to pay more according to Mrs. Hector. Isn't that so *señor*?"

"That is true," said Hector, before leaning down and whispering in Juan Lobo's left ear. "Though she is asleep at the moment. Maybe we could get away with using the plates."

"How long has she been sleeping?"

"About a half an hour."

Juan Lobo studied for a moment, then nodded.

"Then we use the plates. We use them and you can wash them before she knows any better."

Hector nodded and smiled, clearly gaining some significant measure of satisfaction of getting one over on his lady.

"Let her sleep," he said. "She won't know no better."

Sarah then lifted her spoon and waited for Juan Lobo to allow her to start scooping. He didn't look up from his shovelling of beans into his face, but did nod. Sarah started to scoop and then eat. She'd never felt so hungry in her whole life. Lifting the beans to her face, her dainty ways departed and soon she shovelled them in just as Juan Lobo did. She was parched, but would not yet stoop so low as to go out and dunk her head in a donkey's trough. That was too degrading.

"Don't you want to drink?" Juan Lobo asked as he lifted the tequila bottle and uncorked it.

Sarah nodded, her eyes following the fiery liquid leaving the bottle to greet the glass below.

"Then go ahead and drink. Donkey won't mind," said Juan Lobo as he smiled up at Hector. Hector smiled back, though the smile – or so Sarah thought – looked as though it had been born out of fear, not amusement.

"I'll be alright," said Sarah sourly, though Juan Lobo paid her no mind.

"Many customers you have today *amigo*?" Juan Lobo asked after eating more than his fair share of beans.

"Maybe nine, maybe ten," Hector told him.

"Then business is booming, no?" Juan Lobo boomed.

"Sure *señor*," said Hector. "But maybe you could keep your voice down a bit," he told Juan Lobo. "My wife is a very light sleeper. She will wake if we are too loud."

"She's *your* woman Hector. And you are the man. That means you are in charge, not her."

Sarah scoffed in disgust.

"Don't mind her," Juan Lobo said. "She is just upset because her jaw has been broken."

Sarah's brow furrowed. Then the thought came to her as fast as Juan Lobo's fist. The blow broke her jaw just as Juan Lobo had stated. Sarah screamed in pain, blood pouring out of her mouth from where her molar teeth had bitten down on gum.

"You shouldn't do that to a lady," said Hector. "It's not right to hit a woman like that."

"You can keep your opinion *amigo*," said Juan Lobo. "You can keep your opinion to yourself, or I won't be keeping my bullets in my gun. You can have them if you like," he smiled up at the owner of Hector's place, pistol taken out and set on the table to rest there.

"I was only joking. You do what you want with your woman. Who am I to say?" said Hector.

"Better," said Juan Lobo. "Your manners are improving every minute."

Sarah was still squealing into her bloodied hands when the stairs started to groan with the weight of the woman wakened from her siesta.

"She's up," said Hector. "Look now what you have done!" he scolded Sarah.

Juan Lobo laughed, then started scraping up the remnants of bean juice still clinging to his plate.

"Please," said Hector to his woman. "Go back to bed Maria." But Maria would not listen. She'd spied the girl doing the screaming and had seen Juan Lobo laughing. She knew the man. Knew his cruel nature all too well also. Maria was partial to the company of women, and wouldn't have them treated poorly under her roof, which she expressed immediately.

"You hurt a girl in here and you can go out back with the horses," she said in a lovely Mexican lilt that in her courting days with Hector had sent him into a deep sleep. Her tongue however could be wielded with a jagged sharpness should she wish for it to do so. The lulling kind of lullaby tones would disappear, and the venom appear in full force. Juan Lobo laughed at her remark, which was the incorrect thing to do.

"Do you find me funny?" she said with a smile, her words still soft sounding.

"Find what you *say* funny," Juan Lobo told her.

"Why's that?" she asked.

Juan Lobo looked up at Hector but did not turn to face Maria.

"Because I am not a horse. I may have the cock of a horse, but I am not one."

"You shouldn't speak to her like that," Hector pleaded. "Please don't make her angry. I have to live with her."

"He's alright Hector. He will not be bothering me much longer. You will leave now Juan Lobo, for you are not welcome

155

here. Hector?"

"Yes my darling," said Hector, standing straight to attention like a soldier might.

"Go get this man's things from the hat rack. He will be leaving now."

Hector looked at Juan Lobo, sitting studying Sarah, who was now regarding Maria as though the woman was her very own guardian angel.

Juan Lobo nodded his head for Hector to go get his things. Then Maria went to the counter and reached under to produce a scatter gun. She set it on the bar and folded her arms, thinking that this alone would be enough to deter Juan Lobo from leaving with Sarah.

"She stays," said Maria. "The girl stays with us."

Juan Lobo paid her no mind. Instead, he stood and hooked his hand under the crook of Sarah's arm and hauled her to her feet. Feeling safe, Sarah spat a mouthful of blood in Juan Lobo's face, to which he replied by breaking her nose with his own forehead. Maria picked up the shotgun and pointed it at Juan Lobo, then clicked back both hammers in readiness for the shooting she thought that she was capable of doing. Again Juan Lobo paid her no mind, moving Sarah over to the door where Hector stood with Juan Lobo's coat and hat. Hector held the coat out and Juan Lobo slipped one arm into the sleeve of his coat, then the other. He turned and took his hat from Hector then slapped the chef and owner of Hector's place very lightly on the cheek.

"*Adios* Hector," he said. "We'll be leaving now," he told Hector, to which Maria said that *he* would be leaving, and he alone.

"The girl stays here," she said, both barrels aimed right at the back of Juan Lobo's loathsome head.

He didn't turn, he didn't give her a moment's thought as his hand found the latch, lifted it and swung the door open. He shoved Sarah out through it into the dazzling glare of the sun, then stepped out into it himself. Maria raced round the bar.

"You won't take her," she muttered more to herself than

Hector. He moved aside and let his wife pass, because he knew better than to get in her way. When she stepped out into the sun the pair were nowhere to be seen. Then the sound of a horse whinnying could be heard from around the back of the building. Maria moved like lightning around the walls to get to the stables.

"Stop now and I won't shoot," she said.

Juan Lobo continued saddling a horse, regardless of this woman toting her scattergun. The message hadn't seeped in, so she pointed the weapon up in the air and let the sky have some lead to chew on. Then she resumed pointing it at Juan Lobo with the one barrel still loaded. Juan Lobo helped Sarah onto the horse, who by now knew that to resist this man meant hurt would come her way. He then pulled himself up onto the saddle and sat behind Sarah.

"If you think I won't fire you're wrong," said Maria.

Juan Lobo rode the horse right up to her and drew the reins back so that the beast wouldn't trample her.

"I don't think," he said to the woman. "I know."

He then turned the horse around, gave it two good hard kicks in the belly before the beast burst into a gallop off in the direction of the border. Both barrels of Maria's gun stayed pointed at the riders even as they became nothing more than a speck on the horizon. Maria knew that that man meant trouble for the girl he was with. Maria felt a great swell of pity in her chest for the girl, and by the time Hector felt brave enough to approach her, her cheeks were stained with tears. Gently, as though the slightest sharp movement might shatter his crystalline wife, he took the shotgun from her hands, then led her back inside.

23.

"I reckon I'll need plenty of that there beef jerky. Don't know how much desert I'll have to cross getting down to Mexico, and I sure as shit ain't aiming on eating lizards," Tom told the clerk of the general store.

"Ain't eating lizards," laughed Clarke the clerk. "Why

that sure is a good one if ever I did hear it!" Then Clark shouted a lot louder. "He says he ain't apt to eat no lizards mother! You hear him?"

"Yeah, I heard," Clarke's mother shouted from the back room.

"Right and funny fella don't you think?" Clarke asked, though there was no answer forthcoming. "She's old," Clarke said in hushed tones. "She got the gout and the rheumatism and the arthritis. Her humour ain't as honed as it once was," he told Tom.

Tom just nodded.

"Now mother you just stay there," said Clarke, enunciating every syllable so she could hear. "There's no need for you to get up."

"She deaf too?" Tom asked.

"She pretends not to hear. But if I was to tell her her dinner's ready, she would hear that no problem."

"I can believe that," said Tom, taking his parcel of goods from the clerk and handing him the cash. Clarke let out another horse laugh, loud and large enough to almost make the jars of boiled sweets stacked on the shelves behind him rattle and clink with the vibration.

"You can believe that!" he said slamming his hand down hard on the counter. "Boy you sure is a funny one. Boy's funny ain't he mother?"

But the man's mother did not respond. No doubt due to being sickened by such sycophancy, or so Tom thought anyway. Once out of the shop he said to himself that if he was that man's mother, he wouldn't ever give Clarke a response, given how much of a crawler he was.

Walking down the street he nearly bumped into several people ambling along the boardwalk because his parcel of food was so large. One woman said he was just the rudest man, and that he really ought to watch where he was going. Tom told her he was sorry when really, he wasn't. The way he figured it, it was up to the people coming in his direction to move out of *his* way, not the other way about. When one very posh-sounding man grumbled, "Get out of my way you rude pie!" Tom told him to go fuck himself, to which the man flicked his walking cane against Tom's shins, which although he'd never admit to it, stung like hell.

He was glad to get inside the gunsmiths. Glad to smell gun oil and black powder, but also glad to get out of the road of people perambulating rather rudely right smack into him.

"Say Johnny Black," Tom sang into the store, "you about?"

Tom smiled at the man in the leather chaps standing in front of the glass cabinet with rows upon rows of revolvers of every conceivable kind. The man did not smile back.

"You calling me?" said a thin man who had appeared in the doorway leading to the storage room and gun range.

He was a meek looking man. Looked to Tom as though the fellow had never held a pistol in his life, and yet it was the vocation of the man to hold pistols every damn day God sent his way.

"That I am Johnny Black. Be needing a gun," said Tom. "Reckon you're the man to furnish such a request."

"I am," said Johnny, slamming down a cheap looking percussion revolver right in front of the man in the leather chaps. "Choose whatever weapon you like. I know every price off by heart. Ain't one gun in this whole store I don't know the cost of."

"You got any Colt Dragoons?" Tom asked.

"Do I have a Colt Dragoon?" Johnny said, sounding astounded at the foolishness of Tom Liffey's question. "He asks do I have a Dragoon," he said to the man in the leather chaps, too busy inspecting his rusty old revolver to pay Johnny much mind. "My man, I have several of the pistols you're inquiring after. Several. Some used, some not. All depends which of the two you're after."

"Oh it'd have to be new," Tom told him. "Want one for my very own. Not something used by another's hand. This here's to be my pistol, and mine alone."

"I can understand that. Gun's like a woman. Wouldn't want one that's been with every cowhand comes to town now,

159

would you?"

Tom gulped, thinking of Sarah and the many men she'd taken to bed besides Tom Liffey. Tom nodded and smiled, though there was a sudden sick feeling clutching hold of his guts.

"Got me a brand spanking new pistol here that goes by the name of Colt Dragoon. Damn fine weapon. She'll get the job done alright. Ain't been fired, but I can say with complete confidence she won't let you down. Can damn near guarantee it."

"You can guarantee it?" said Tom.

"I can guarantee it," said Johnny. "Just load her up and you can test her. Hell, I'll even offer to pay for the balls myself."

"And the powder and caps?" said Tom.

"You are a cheeky chap ain't you?" said Johnny.

He pouted his lips a moment then nodded.

"Alright. You can have them gratis. *But*, if you fire it, you're buying it. Once that there pistol's been shot the price of it sort of diminishes. Don't think I could let you give it back once it's been fired."

"Fair enough," Tom said.

Johnny nodded and busied himself collecting balls, powder and caps. Then the leather chap man spoke up.

"You got loads for this here gun or what?" he asked, his voice gruff, rumbling up from pit of his belly before climbing up and out of his throat with a tremendous rumble.

"Right, alright," said Johnny. "Suppose you *was* here first and all."

The gunsmith set down all the ammunition for Tom to take and do with whatever he pleased. Then Johnny Black made the biggest mistake in all his years of commerce and furnished the fellow with the gruff voice and the very dusty leather chaps with the ammunition for the far from pristine pistol he was toying with.

"Why if you want to test it out, we can go right on out back. Be better than taking it out into the street to shoot down Dick or pop Pearl in the head."

The man laughed at this, then muttered in agreement before beginning to load all six cylinders of the percussion

160

revolver. Meanwhile Tom had loaded his and was quite keen to get firing it. He motioned for Johnny to take him out back, but Johnny shook his head and nodded at the other customer.

"Can't," he mouthed but did not say.

Tom mouthed, "Oh right."

Then he asked aloud if he had a holster for the gun, to which Johnny laughed and said of course.

"Silly question don't you think?" he said, handling Tom's soon-to-be holster like as if it were made out of very fragile glass that could shatter should a man take to handling it rough. "Right," Johnny said. "That there's a holster for a Dragoon. You can try it on if you like."

"May I?" said Tom.

"You may," said Johnny. "Just be careful when you're sliding the pistol in and out. Don't do it *too* fast now. You'll destroy the leather with scrapes. If you do that then…"

"Then I got to buy it. Yeah, yeah," said Tom, rolling his eyes at the other customer, who by now had finished loading his pistol.

"Can I go shoot?" he rumbled.

"Of course," said Johnny. "Just this way. You can come too Tom. Try out the Dragoon."

Tom thought that this fellow with the rusted pistol seemed strange. He should have voiced his concern to Johnny but foolishly did not.

"Them's the targets sir. You just point and shoot. It's as easy as that," Johnny told the man.

The man nodded, pointed his pistol, pulled back the hammer and let of a crack causing the wooden target to splinter roughly where the mouth would be.

"By God, didn't I tell you?" said Johnny. "Don't matter how rusted my guns get. They always shoot straight."

"That they do," said the man, before turning to Tom, cocking his gun and pressing the barrel up against Tom's temple. "Take off that there pistol belt friend."

Johnny let out a laugh.

"He's just joking. Mighty fine fun friend. Mighty jest."

The man looked at Johnny in a way that said he was serious, that it was in fact no joke.

"Just take it off and hand it over," said the leather chap man.

"My God," said Tom. "I think you're being robbed Johnny."

"You think!" said Johnny, just about as irritated as you might expect.

Tom handed his weapon over and the stranger removed the pistol from his temple, then pointed both pistols at the gunsmith and his customer and told them to head back into the store.

"I'm only after money," he said. "Ain't after guns. Get the money out slow mister, then put it in whatever tote bag you got."

"You *are*," said Tom, standing stock still in disbelief. "You're being robbed by God."

"Goddamn it stop saying that!" Johnny barked. "Christ! You think I don't know that?" he said, flapping open a bag before walking briskly up to the till to get the money this man wanted from him. "You'll be caught. There's nothing as sure," said Johnny. "Ain't nothing as sure as that."

"That a fact?" said the man.

"It is," said Johnny.

"Just get me my money," said the man before turning to Tom. "*You*!" he said, thrusting the Dragoon pistol Tom wanted to buy a little closer in Tom's direction. "You got money?"

Tom shook his head.

"How you gonna buy this here gun then? What were you going to buy it with? *Air*?"

Tom had his entire remaining sum of money sitting in his pocket. He'd given a good deal to Frank and Abel, bought groceries and a horse and saddle, leaving around a hundred and fifty for further expenses should he need to spend some more.

"Man's a friend of mine," said Tom. "I was going to tell him to put it on my tab. Wasn't aiming to pay for it today."

"*Tab*?" said the man. "My God! I've heard it all now.

162

A tab in a gunsmiths. Boy, you must think I'm about as dumb as a block of wood. Get your money out 'fore I fire off a shot your way. Go on now, hurry it up."

Tom took out twenty dollars and set it on the glass countertop.

"That all?" said the man.

Tom nodded.

"Mmmmm," said the leather chap man. "Reckon there's more."

Johnny Black had finished counting out a considerable sum into the tote bag before he reluctantly set it down on the countertop. The man lifted the money bag, brought it over to where Tom was standing and set it down. He kept one gun pointed at Johnny the whole time, motioning for the gunsmith to move over by Tom.

"Reach into that there fella's pocket. You don't produce a cent, and I'll personally make sure your head gets decorated with a nice red hole for your troubles."

Johnny looked into Tom's face. The Liffey brother's look was one of a beggar. He definitely didn't want robbed. He had to go get Sarah. And he couldn't wait for another wire to come through from his auntie.

"Slow," said the leather chap man. "Nice and easy now. No need for sharp movements mister, alright?"

"Alright," Johnny snarled. "Sorry Tom."

Tom was surprised when Johnny lifted only a little of his money. Maybe it was because he hadn't found it all. Maybe it was because of kindness. Either way a wave of relief washed over Tom. Such a strong wave that he felt like he could kiss Johnny Black.

"That's good," said the stranger. "Put it in the bag with the rest."

Johnny did as he was told, then shoved the bag toward the man.

"Mighty fine," said the man, no doubt delighted with the day's winnings. "Well now gentlemen. It seems that I must be going. Get any ideas about following me and I'll turn right around and kill both of you. Now I mean it. Don't dare come after me. It's my money now. You hear? *Mine*. Meaning not yours."

"You're a son of a bitch," said Johnny. "Just a plain old son of a bitch."

"That may be," said the man. "But now I'm a rich son of a bitch," he said, smiling from ear to ear. "Alright then," he said, pretending to strain lifting the tote bag. "By golly! Sure is heavy!" he said, before bellowing a laugh that sounded like a lion's roar. Then, pistols pointed at the two men, he exited the store and ran off down the street.

"*Bastard*!" said Johnny, before spitting on his own floor.

"Don't spit on the good floors," Tom told him. "Don't do that."

"It's my shop," said Johnny. "Just you don't bother your backside telling me where I ought not to spit. Right?"

"Don't take it out on me Johnny. I didn't rob you!"

"You didn't do nothing to help neither. You might have shot him when you had the Dragoon in your mitts. Might've winged him, then I could have tackled him to the ground God damn it."

He spat again, an even more sizeable sample of saliva this time. Tom couldn't stand it.

"Don't spit on the floor," he said.

"Fuck off," Johnny snapped. "Alright? Just fuck off. My floor ain't it? Why if I was to drop my britches and shit on it it'd be my Goddamn right to do so. So just you don't bother telling me where to *spit*!"

He hawked back another wad of phlegm, ready for firing, when Tom said something that stopped him in his tracks.

"I'll buy a gun," he told the gunsmith. "The most expensive Dragoon you have here in the store. I'll buy it."

Johnny looked at him as he swallowed his spit.

"You don't have to," he said. "You was robbed too."

"But he didn't get all of my money. Now what about it? You go get the best Dragoon in this here store, and whatever price you ask, I'll pay."

Johnny nodded, glad to be back in business.

"Boy you sure are a pal!" he said. "Sure are one swell fella."

"Yeah well," Tom said, not one for being too keen on receiving compliments.

After bidding Johnny Black goodbye, feeling fine for having been given the holster at a discounted price. With his weighty pistol resting on his hip, he stowed his food away in his saddlebags, took hold of his saddle horn and with a grunt got up into the saddle.

"Dee-Cee," he told his horse. "Best be going and getting Sarah now I reckon."

He jabbed his heels a tad too hard into the beast's belly and the animal bolted, with Tom sat in the saddle, trying his very best to hold on for dear life.

"Let's go get her," he said softly, riding harder and harder, faster and faster, leaving the town of Taughrane Heights further and further behind him.

24.

The stagecoach to Galverstone was far too cramped for Frank, though Abel didn't complain. Mostly because Abel was having a wonderful time what with him being the one every other passenger present felt they could complain about. He'd seen a cowboy walk by when he was sat in the stagecoach waiting for it to depart. The cowboy, much to Frank's and everybody else's chagrin, had been whistling while he walked by. Abel had seen this and felt that he too should have a go at this practice.

Poor doesn't do much justice to describe the way in which the elder Liffey attempted and subsequently fumbled his task. He couldn't whistle. That was the fact of the matter. The man couldn't. Though this plain fact didn't stop him from trying.

A peeved woman in a bonnet with some silver hair sprouting out from beneath it was mourning her husband's death. Her daughter was sat opposite her, and looked to be a timid creature who, though she surely didn't take to Abel's attempted whistling with much approval, wouldn't dare say a word to the man for fear of being lambasted with remonstrations from this strange and seemingly simple fellow. Her mother on the other hand had no qualms whatsoever with speaking her mind, and after about five full minutes of attempted whistles – which came out as owl-like hoots in which Abel's vocal cords were put to use to create the sound – she spoke aloud and gave Abel a piece of her mind.

"Excuse *me* sir," she began. "But do you mind! There are other people present and that noise you're making is most irritating."

Abel didn't stop. Not due to defiance or anything like that, but because he didn't imagine that there was even the slightest possibility that the lady was talking to him, for he didn't find his own whistling to be irritating in the least.

Leave him be, was the look the lady's daughter gave her mother. The poor pet didn't want any trouble, though the mother felt differently.

"Do you hear me?" she said. Again Abel persisted, doing a poor imitation of a whistle but a wonderful impression of a barn owl as it swoops through the air in the dead of night.

"Mother *please*," pleaded the daughter. "Don't."

"Don't tell me my business girl. Don't you dare try to impede me in my business. If I feel I've something to say to this imbecile, then I surely will."

Frank now knew why this woman to his right was so very timid. He imagined that had his own mother behaved like that towards him, he might have turned out every bit as nervous as she.

"Sorry mother," she squeaked like a mouse scurrying away from a very large, very hungry cat.

"I should think so," said the mother. "Do *you* hear me!" she roared at Abel, but the young man was not to be deterred. That is until Frank dug his pointy elbow into Abel's ribs, removing the irksome owl in the carriage and replacing it with a bothered simpleton who didn't care much for being elbowed like that.

"*Hey!*" he gurned. "What's the big idea? What you do that for Frank?"

"Lady's looking you," said Frank.

"What lady?" Abel asked.

Frank nodded across the cramped confines of the carriage in the direction of the woman with the supremely sour scowl on a face which was so furious looking it was quite something to behold.

"Boy lady," said Abel. "You look like a kettle that's damn near done boiling!"

The woman made a noise that Abel found funny. It was part squeak, part cough, and Abel laughed long and loud at her when she made it. The woman looked to her daughter, whose small smile was wiped pretty fast when the mother shot the girl a good harsh glance.

"I suppose you think you're funny," she said to Abel, still looking at her daughter to ensure the girl stayed put in her proper place. The mother wouldn't allow her daughter the dignity of having the occasional giggle at her relation. That was out of the question as far as this silver haired hag was concerned.

"Are you talking to me?" Abel asked as he leaned forward to look around Frank at the girl.

"I am," said the woman, turning to him and leaving her daughter be.

"The lady laughs at me," said Abel, referring of course to Sarah.

"That *lady* is my daughter Deborah."

"Nice to meet you Debs," Abel said, reaching round Frank and jutting his hand out for her to take.

Deborah didn't take it though. She looked down into the purse she was clutching on tight to in her lap, then her eyes began to dart from her mother to this young man's hand.

"She does not wish to make your acquaintance," said the woman.

"Well how's about you? You want to make it?"

"I do not," said the woman. Then the daughter, for

167

whatever reason was overcome by a keen sense of wanting to betray her own mother. Maybe because she couldn't stand to see such a friendly fellow suffer at the pointy end of her mother's sharp persona.

"I do too want to make his acquaintance!" Deborah roared at the elderly woman sat opposite her. "Here, take my hand mister. Give it a good shake."

Abel was pleased by this sudden burst of friendliness, so he shook Deborah's hand with fervour. And though he very nearly snapped her hand off at the wrist, it brought a great deal of satisfaction to Deborah.

"And you know what mother? I like his whistling. And I want him to keep on at it. How do you like that!"

"You'll keep a civil tongue with me missus. You'll speak civil to me or else…"

"Or else what? You'll beat me more than you already do? I'm used to it. You can't hurt me anymore. And I'll tell you this, you dare try to strike me I'll strike back. I will, and that's the truth. So maybe you figure out some other way of getting at me, because if you hit me…"

Slap! The crack of palm against cheek flesh filled Abel's ears making him wince. Deborah sat back, not stunned at the actual act of being struck, but by the severity with which the slap was dealt.

"That's the best one yet," said Deborah. "Ought to be proud mother. Very proud indeed. Shall we see how hard I can slap?"

"You slap me and I'll disown you. You'll be cut out of the will and die a pauper. I'll make sure of it."

Deborah thought for a moment, considering the weight of this threat. Then she turned to Abel. He had a look of fear, which only fuelled the fire kindled in Deborah's breast.

"Better not be scaring strangers mother. This man looks frightened. That's your doing."

"Do I look like I give a damn about the feelings of some imbecile? You hush now Deborah and let us ride in silence."

The man sat next to the old woman was reading his

paper. It was at this point that the man flicked a page and found nothing noteworthy on that new page. He then folded it up, laid it in his lap, then looked out the window at the monotonous plains passing them by.

The only sound now was the sound of wooden wheels wheeling along on the earth, intermingled occasionally with the sound of wood colliding with stones of various shapes and sizes. They rode like this for a minute. Then the fight began. Deborah didn't want to put up with her mother any longer. Maybe it was the cramped space of the carriage that caused her blood to boil. Maybe she'd just snapped after so many years of having to deal with the woman's sternness. Either way, that Deborah lady nearly pulled the scalp off her mother's head, yanking thick tufts of hair out in her hands after the bonnet had been removed and discarded out through the carriage window. Deborah might well have killed her, if left to her own devices. But Frank and the man with the paper intervened and separated the two fighting hens.

"Hold on here a minute," said the newspaper man in a deep, rich voice. "There's other folk in this here carriage. If you two can't control yourself then one of you's going to have to ride up top with the driver. It's windy. It'll blow your hair all shapes."

Frank gave him a look like the man was half mad, for both women had already made each other's hair very untidy, sticking out in every conceivable direction. Deborah blew some of it up from her face, still scowling at her mother.

"Be calm," Frank said softly, as if trying to tame a wild mare. "Best be calm now missus. 'Less you want to get up on top with the driver."

Deborah looked at the black man, his big brown eyes pleading like a Labrador.

"You have no right to speak to her darky," said the mother.

"Begging your pardon ma'am," Frank said. "Was just trying to calm things down is all. Didn't mean nothing by it none."

He looked long and hard into the hateful hag's face, eyes fixed firmly and non-wavering.

"You just keep quiet nigger. No need for you to talk to my Deborah. You black bugger you."

Deborah, having thought that the most obvious thing to do to piss off her mother was to kiss this black man, did just that. She forced herself upon his lips with her own, held them there a moment or two, then as she peeled herself off him again, began to howl hysterically.

"Lady's mad as a hatter," Abel said in Frank's ear.

"Coming from you that sure does mean something Mr. Liffey," Frank said.

Abel laughed and said, "Yeah…" in that signature dim-sounding voice of his that he used when something tickled him even though he didn't know exactly why.

"You scoundrel!" said Deborah's mother. "You'll be hung for that! I'll make sure of that! The Sheriff in Galverstone's a good friend of mine. You should have known better than to put your lips on my lovely Deborah."

"Don't talk silly mother," Deborah said. "It was *me* who kissed *him*. You going to see to it that I get hung?"

The mother looked to Deborah, then to Frank, then to her daughter once more.

"Mark me missy. I've had just about enough of your cheek. You've some nerve to take umbrage against your own mother. You've even more nerve to fight me. But planting those lips of yours on a black man's face, well, that I cannot abide. No woman belonging to my family that fancies a darky is going to be bequeathed a dime, let alone a dollar. You're out of the will woman. Whether you like it or not, you're out. So you can pop that in your pipe and smoke it."

"I don't give a damn about that will of yours. You've held that threat over my head for far too long, and I'm sick of it. I don't give a damn… No… I don't give a *shit* about *your will*. Why you could wipe your ass with it for all I care. You can ball it up and hide it in any orifice you see fit. Know why?"

The mother just sat blinking at her daughter.

"Because you're a horrible, hateful old bitch. And I wouldn't want a dollar from you if all I had to do was ask

170

politely."

Deborah then banged on the roof of the carriage.

"*Driver!*" she yelled at the top of her lungs. "Let me out of this carriage."

She then pulled the handle to the door down, though not before blowing a raspberry in her mother's face, which by now had morphed into something beyond indignation.

"I'm through with you. You evil old witch!"

"Well you'll die a pauper!" the old woman shouted out through the window as her daughter clambered up onto the driver's seat.

"Blow it out your ass!" Deborah shouted back, bellowing with laughter as a result of her remark.

Frank shifted over in his seat to replace where Deborah'd been before. He let out a little uncomfortable laugh to try to ease the palpable tension left behind by Deborah, but the old woman was not for lightening up in any way.

"Well," she said, straightening up and combing her hair from her eyes with her hands that looked to Frank as though they must hurt a great deal, due to gout which had made them swell something serious at the tips. "That's that then," she said, trying to recuperate the lost dignity due to fighting and squabbling with her own kin.

"Not very lady like," the man with the paper said, before beginning to roll a cigarette.

"What's it to you?" snapped the old woman. "Hmmm? What's it to you?"

He just smirked and ignored her, then in turn she ignored him.

"Haven't a smidge of manners any the three of you. You've the whistler, you've the remark maker, and worst of all you have the nigger that kisses white women when he knows he ought not to. Well let me tell you this, I'll be glad once we get to Galverstone, because by golly if I don't tell the Sheriff of these goings on then my name isn't Deborah Hamilton Senior. Some company kept on this journey let me tell you."

Then the woman began to fiddle for something in her

handbag.

"Not a nice lady, is she?" Abel said quietly but quite audibly given the close confines of the carriage.

Deborah Sr. gave Abel a good hard glare, then produced a brush from her petit purple handbag.

"*Hey*!" Abel cried. "You gonna brush your hair some?"

"Never you mind. Just you mind your own business, and I'll mind mine," said Deborah Sr.

"Sorry for calling you not nice," Abel said, the young man's motives all too apparent to Frank. "Forgive me?" he asked.

"No!" barked Deborah Sr. "No, I do not."

She then began brushing her hair, though not in the gentle way in which Abel was accustomed to. This woman mauled her head with her brush. She looked to Abel as though she were trying to tug her hair out of her head at the roots.

"Calm down lady," he instructed. "You're supposed to go soft. Here," he said, removing his precious brush from his pocket. "You show her on me Frank. Show her the way you're supposed to brush hair."

Frank didn't feel like giving this lady a lesson in hair-grooming.

"Put the brush away Abel," he said, gently pressing down the brush Abel was sticking in his face.

"For God's sake lady, go easy!" Abel said, ignoring Frank. "You're going to have no hair left!"

"Leave me alone you toad! Why don't you mind your own business. You and your nigger friend. I've had just about enough of you."

"And I've just about had enough of you *too*," Frank snapped.

"Don't you raise your voice to me darky. I'll have you hanging up from the gallows before the sun sets this evening. You mark my words. You just keep it up and you'll see. No nigger'll talk back to a white woman in this country. No *sir*!"

"Shit," Frank said, feeling very much like spitting on this ignorant woman's boots, but refraining from doing so, showing unfathomable restraint. "I don't need this," he said, before lifting his large hand and slamming it against the roof with a handful of heavy bangs.

"By Christ!" yelled the driver. "Do I got to stop every few fucking feet? Somebody got gas in there? There's no need for farting when in the company of ladies."

"Ain't no ladies in here," Frank said as he opened the door and stepped down out of the carriage. "Coming up with you," he informed the driver.

"Well, you're the last is coming up, for it's getting mighty cramped up here."

"Fine," Frank said. But before clambering up, he made sure Deborah Sr. met his eyes as he spat in the dust, saying without words just what he thought of the bigoted old bag.

"Boy," said Abel, "got plenty of room now."

Frank made the carriage rock as he hauled himself up on top.

"We good to go?" said the driver.

Frank muttered that the driver was free to proceed. The air rushed against his cheeks as the stagecoach got going again, cooling the man both in a physical sense as well as his temperament. Half a mile down the road he felt a little less frustrated. A mile down it and he had cooled considerably. When the horses hauled the carriage over the three-mile mark from when he'd gotten up top, he'd forgotten having ever been mad in the first place.

Deborah Jr. had gone quiet again. Frank supposed that that was natural, for it wasn't her custom – or so he reckoned – to be all uppity and rebellious against her mother. She'd shifted back to being a mouse again, which suited Frank fine, for although he was fond of kissing, the lips in this case did not belong to Sarah Herron, no matter how much he might've wished they did.

Abel meanwhile was busy below, tutoring Deborah Sr. in the ways in which one was supposed to brush hair. He'd actually managed to convince her to let him at her head with his brush. The newspaper man could hardly believe his eyes, but it was happening regardless.

"See?" said Abel, presenting the product of his gentle brushing for the man's inspection. "Don't it look much better if you do it gentle?"

Deborah Sr. smiled for the man, though the man was on the verge of giggling – holding it back for fear of another row erupting. He made a grunting noise in agreement, placed his hand in his pocket and begin to dig a pencil into his thigh for something else to focus on so as he didn't laugh in his fellow passengers' faces.

"Fine job," Abel said. "A job well done Deborah."

"Thank you. Might have manners after all young man."

"I've plenty," said Abel. "My mama brought me up right. So the lady says anyway."

"What lady?" Deborah Sr. asked.

"The lady that brushes my hair," Abel answered before looking out the window for a mile, his thoughts of Sarah drifting in and out until he thought it safe to ask again if this woman would brush his. "I did yours," he said, holding his brush for her to take. "Will you do mine?"

The senior Deborah looked at this earnest fellow, feeling deeply sorry for him now, because he was clearly simple.

"You ever kicked in the head when you were young?" she asked. The man with the paper tuned back into the conversation, curious to learn the answer to this question, but nonetheless surprised the lady'd been blunt enough to ask.

"Not as far as I can remember," Abel answered after giving it some thought.

The woman studied him for a moment, then, thinking it improper to brush a stranger's hair, feeling a sudden sense of deep shame that she'd let him at hers, she shook her head.

"No son," she said. "It's not my place."

"Please," Abel said, thrusting the brush at her like a thief might brandish a dagger. "*Please*," he begged. But the woman wouldn't do it. She shook her head and looked out the window and that, as they say, was that.

174

25.

The desert was so dry that Tom had a difficult time imagining how the lizards lived way the hell out here. It was barren country – forsaken by God and Jesus and Mary Magdalene too, or whoever else might be in charge in the great upstairs a long, long time ago. What worried Tom was whether his horse was parched beyond measure or not. The hoof-clops had become slightly sparser, which Tom wouldn't have ordinarily noticed. He only did notice them becoming slower and even fainter because there was no other sound accompanying the horse's hooves, apart from the occasional buzzard or vulture make squealing sounds or a creaking croaking kind of noises.

He didn't like the vultures, nor the buzzards. But what bugged him the most was the dust. It was everywhere. Everywhere imaginable. And he had begun to despise Dee-Cee for kicking up such a storm of the stuff with every clip-clop onward towards their eventual destination. He tried to reassure himself that the horse was just doing his job; that moving on ahead was the task assigned to his poor, dehydrated Dee-Cee.

Dust in the eyes was the worst of it, or so he thought right up until he sneezed very violently, and the mucus came out in a kind of gravelly cement type mixture. The sandy stuff cut his nostrils, making them red raw in an altogether unpleasant way.

He'd never been so uncomfortable in all his life. Longing for the comforts of Taughrane Heights was where his thoughts tended to travel, though he tried everything to keep Sarah situated in the forefront of his mind as much as possible. A man with a woman to chase is a man with purpose. Tom Liffey was just such a man.

The sun-baked sand was inhospitable, though that did not explain the sight he eventually came upon. A buggy, as well as the carcass of a good-looking horse had come to be way out in this scorching hell. Tom did not know why it was there, though decided it best to investigate anyway. As he came closer, a nauseous feeling entered into his stomach, prompted by the pungent odour of rotting horse meat cooking in the sun, as well as the thought that whatever brought about this poor creature's demise could well have brought about his Sarah's as well.

When close enough he noticed that underneath the horse's head a buzzard was busily pecking in its eye hole. Tom took out his gun, cocked his hammer back and let the sky have a speedy lead lunch. The buzzard was not for budging.

"By God," Tom said as he readjusted himself to get comfier in his saddle. "Buzzard's got grit."

He then pointed his pistol in the air just above the horse's head, in the hopes that the buzzard, should it feel the ball whizz by, would then become sufficiently frightened so as to fly off. He let his gun crack like the nastiest whip in the country and the bird flew. Tom nodded and holstered his weapon, satisfied that he could now investigate closely without the interference of the buzzard.

"You stay put now Dee-Cee," he told his horse. "You leave me now and I might just be a goner. We wouldn't want that now, would we?" he said as he rubbed his mute companion along the length of his muzzle. "Mighty fine horse you are Dee-Cee. I'm proud to ride you."

The horse blinked back, but that was all. If he understood Tom, he gave no sign that he had. He took two clops back but that was it. Satisfied that the horse wasn't going to up and bolt, Tom stepped toward the dead horse. Then the smell became quite unbearable.

"*Jesus*!" Tom said, removing his stained handkerchief from his back pocket and holding it to his face. "Fucking hell," he said. "You're lucky you're all the way back there Dee-Cee. Don't bother coming closer, 'less you want to bring up them apples I fed you a while back. *Boy*! How'd you come to be way the hell out here?"

He took three more solid steps forward, then began inching closer and closer, as though the poor beast's body might contain a contagious disease of some kind. Tom knew that that was a foolish thought, but he'd never been too comfortable around rotten meat, or rotten anything for that matter. Mouldy bread even revolted him beyond reason. And this horse was far worse than a bit of blue mould on a loaf.

"Looks like you wasn't shot," he said, supposing that the person who had been driving the buggy didn't have a gun to put the creature out of its misery. "No bullet holes," Tom said softly.

Then a new thought came. Maybe the man or woman that had been driving this buggy *had* bullets, but didn't want to put it out of his misery. Much as it pained him to admit it, this was the likelier of the two options, for no sensible soul would travel way out here without some sort of weapon.

"Could have had a bow and arrow," he mumbled. But then the Indians weren't known for using these kinds of buggies often, as far as Tom knew. "No," he said breathily, still scanning, searching desperately for a bullet hole – he didn't like to think that the animal had suffered, though all the clues led to the conclusion that it had. "Must've been some mean son of a bitch," he said.

Then Sarah flashed into his mind. He worried if the rider had been the one to take his lady love hostage. He got angry then, and looked up at the sun blasting heat down on his head.

"You saw it," he told the fiery ball in the sky. "You know if it was Sarah or not."

He kicked some dust, decided that he'd better keep going, then remounted Dee-Cee.

"Sorry horse," he said. "Sorry for your troubles. If I find the fella that done this to you, I'll make him suffer as you did."

He didn't want to believe that this horse's demise was brought about by the man that stole Sarah, but something inside told him that was the case.

"Come on," he said to Dee-Cee. "Get going now."

Dee-Cee paid his deceased kin no mind at all. Just trotted by as though the thing weren't there. The smell soon went, but Tom wouldn't forget the pong for many miles yet.

"You just keep going," he told Dee-Cee. "Soon as we see an outpost, we'll get you water."

It was a good few miles more when Tom and Dee-Cee saw Hector's place. The sight was welcome to Tom, and had his horse had the gumption to know water was near, he just might have trotted up to it that much faster. There were two horses hitched out the front of the building, but seeing as Tom supposed he had no quarrels with whomever had travelled all the way out to this place, he kicked his horse onward and hitched him right beside the other two.

"I'll get you water," he told Dee-Cee. "I'll get you water now. You just wait there, and I'll go get some. Alright?"

Dee-Cee didn't blink. He just stared at Tom with a vacant look that brought a smile to Tom's face.

"Alright," he said, patting Dee-Cee on the neck, "no need to huff. I'll go get you some."

Tom then ambled over to the door to this outpost, tried to open it, but found that the door wouldn't budge. He gave it a shove. Still it didn't move.

"Give it a kick!" came a voice from the other side.

"Hah?" said Tom.

"You've got to kick it," said the Mexican sounding man.

Tom took two steps back then brought his boot against the door so hard the thing flew open, swinging inward and smacking into the wall inside.

"See?" said the Mexican man that Tom couldn't see because of the glare from the sun. "That's how you do it *amigo*."

Tom took a few steps in. It was an alright looking place, though not one Tom wanted to stay in for very long, as it was grubby, and God knew what was happening to Sarah while he was busy trying to get to her.

"Horse needs water mister," he told the man behind the bar. "You the one that has it?"

"*Si señor*. I got the water. One moment please. *Maria*! Man wants some water."

"Well go get it for him," came a voice from upstairs.

"*You* get it," the man shouted back.

Then the sound of short, sharp steps trotting across the

178

bottom floor's ceiling sounded out, with the Mexican man beaming a smile at Tom as if to say everything was alright, when his eyes said he was now in some serious trouble. The woman who appeared was very tanned, and looked a little tired to Tom. She began to speak Spanish very angrily at the Mexican man, who after she'd finished her ranting, turned to Tom and apologised.

"I am so sorry *señor*. My name is Hector. And this is Maria."

He turned to his wife who was standing arms akimbo, eyes shooting daggers at Hector.

"Happy now?"

"Are we still married?" she asked.

"*Si*," said Hector.

"Then no, I am not happy. Go get the water while I feed the man."

Hector then threw the wash rag he'd been polishing the glasses with down on the floor and exited through the back door muttering Spanish sounds as he went.

"We have beans," said Maria. "We have plenty. You go and sit down, and I bring them over to you right away."

"Mighty kind of you," Tom smiled.

"They are not for free," she said. "You will have to pay."

"I can pay," Tom said.

"Then you're welcome to a plate. Sit, *sit*. You are tired no doubt, *si*?"

"Suppose I am," Tom told her, before turning to go find a table. "On the hunt for someone," he said. And as the words left his lips, he noticed two fellas sitting in the darkest corner of the place, perched there like the black vultures that had been Tom's constant companions through this deserted desert.

"Don't suppose a man that talks to his horse has many friends," one fellow said, prompting an explosion of a horse laugh from the other man at the table.

"Talking to horses," said the second man, slapping at his knee, just about having the time of his life hearing these few

179

words alone.

"Am I right?" said the first fellow.

Tom just ignored them. He wasn't much interested in being drawn into a verbal joust. Just wanted some beans and his horse watered and rested a while, then he'd be on his way.

"You hear me?" said the first fellow. "I'm talking to you dude. You answer me when I talk to you."

"Got nothing to say," said Tom, wishing with everything he had that Maria would hurry up with those damn beans.

"Got plenty to say to your horse," said the man, getting another good guffaw from his easily amused associate.

"Yeah, that's a real knee-slapper alright," Tom said as Maria set a tin plate down on the table in front of him.

"What was that?" said the man. "You being cheeky?"

"Just speaking my mind is all," Tom told him.

"That so?" said the man. "Well, what if I was to tell you I don't like you. I don't like a man talks to his horse like he's human. Don't like people being cheeky. And I sure as shit don't like people speaking their mind to me."

"Then you don't like me," said Tom. "You can just sit there and not like me all you like, for I ain't aiming on staying too long."

"You won't be staying any. Maria?"

"*Si?*" said Maria.

"You aim on keeping this place tidy then you don't dare feed him one single bean. I mean it. Don't need no lip from no stranger, and if I get some, he ain't eating in my company."

"Come on," said Tom. "Leave me be. I ain't done nothing. Ain't done nothing at all. What's your problem anyway?"

"What's my problem?" said the man. "Boy you got some set of stones on you asking a man that."

"Yeah well, what is the problem? Only thing I done was walk in here. Didn't do nothing else to warrant you taking to disliking me."

"Maybe it's his face," said the second man. "Mighty

180

ugly face on him, don't you think Red?"

"Quiet Cletus. Just you stay hushed now."

"Sorry Red."

"Maybe I don't like your face. Figure it's an ugly one alright, and I just so happen to have taken a disliking to it. That and the fact that you talk to your horse, that makes me hate you even more."

"Listen, just fuck off," Tom told him. "I'm tired as hell. And hungrier than that. I don't want to fight, and I'd just as soon be left alone. Alright?"

"By God, got a mouth on him ain't he Maria?"

"You best be leaving it alone," she said, lifting the pan with the sloppy pile of beans sitting steaming in it and brought it over to Tom's plate.

"You give him one bean," said Red. "One bean and we will tear this place apart. That ain't a lie. That there's a promise."

"You do that," she said, scraping some beans onto Tom's plate. "Go ahead and try it. I'll take my scattergun and open you up so this here fella can see the beans I fed you ten minutes ago."

"Ain't too hospitable is you hostess?" said Red.

"Maybe I'm not," she said, winking at Tom, who had begun shovelling beans into his face at an alarming rate. "Slow *down*!" Maria suggested. "You'll get gut ache *señor*."

"Suppose I will," Tom smiled through a mouthful of mushed up beans. "Better than being famished," he told her, to which she tutted and brought her panful of beans back around the other side of the bar. Beans went everywhere when the shot went off. Tom's tin plate flew several feet to his right, the beans spilling all over the floor Maria'd taken so much time to sweep with her broom every time a new man sauntered in through the door.

"Don't do that!" Maria yelled.

Cletus was whooping and hollering hysterically.

"Hell, you gonna get it now boy! How you like them beans boy?"

"*Quiet* Cletus!" Red snapped. "Said he ain't getting no beans and I meant it Maria. Now I'm telling you dude, *you* can

181

be the one to fuck off. Best be doing it right and sharpish, 'less you fancy me furnishing your head with a nice new hole in it."

Maria then reached down below the bar, lifted her scattergun, and in one slick motion had cocked both hammers back and aimed both long, blued barrels directly at Red's head.

"You leave now you cockroach. This boy didn't do no trouble. You leave now or I open up your head, then your friend's."

"Fucking wouldn't dare," said Red, ready to fire a fatal shot into Tom's startled head.

"It's alright Maria. I'll go," Tom said, standing from his table to leave.

"*He* leaves," said Maria. "Not you. You stay in your seat son."

Tom didn't know what to do. He'd never been in such a situation in his life. He couldn't just die in this God forsaken hole, not just because it'd mean losing his life, but because it would leave Sarah to whatever fate she'd been dealt, disastrous or otherwise – Tom did not know.

"No," said Tom, "it's fine."

"Sit *down*!" Maria instructed in a way that made Tom feel scared she might very well use that shotgun on him just as quick as Cletus and Red. Tom took his seat slowly, not too happy to do so, but feeling there was no other choice. "You two get out," Maria instructed the two. "*Now*!"

Red still had his pistol pointed at Tom.

"When I fire," he told Cletus. "You go for your gun and cut that bitch down, you hear?"

"Hell," said Cletus, sounding worried for the first time since the whole business had begun. "I can't shoot for shit."

"So what?" said Red. "She ain't far from you."

Tom's hand meanwhile had found its way to the handle of his Dragoon, and though he didn't desire to shoot it, he supposed now that that was inevitable. Red raised his gun a little higher, cocked his hammer, which rotated the cylinder into place, ready for firing and, perhaps, taking Tom Liffey's life.

"Let me be," were the last words Tom's mouth sounded

before the shooting commenced.

The pistol in Red's hand was the first to go off. The noise was awful, a little like a whip cracking, made all the noisier by the closeness of the cramped setting for the shootout. The ball that was fired did not obliterate Tom's head, as the assassin had desired it to do. Instead, the little ball, moving at an alarming speed, tore through the flesh in Tom's shoulder, stopping and settling neatly in the man's collarbone, but causing a considerable pang of pain. Tom drew his gun before Red could cock his piece again, but that didn't matter much, for Maria, ready for firing, had already blasted Red in the head, making mush of skull, bone, cartilage and whatever the hell else heads are made of. The now practically decapitated corpse collapsed to the floor, when Cletus attempted and fumbled his gun, dropping the thing to the ground.

"Go for it and I'll shoot," Tom warned him.

Cletus looked up at Tom, then at Maria, who had one barrel remaining, ready for firing. Cletus didn't want to lose his head. He didn't want to end up like Red, but he knew that he'd more than likely be hung now for causing the trouble with his companion. That's when Hector came through the door, causing Maria to move the business end of her barrels to the door, giving Cletus the time to stoop, gather up his gun and point it as he called Maria a "Silly bitch!"

But Tom was ready. He fired and hit Cletus in the throat, causing the man to drop his gun to the floor – though the weapon did not discharge – and make an awful gurgling sound as the blood climbed up out of his throat, out through the man's mouth as Cletus clutched his throat in a feeble attempt to stop the bleeding. But it was no use. In a matter of moment's his body, like Red's collapsed to the ground, and the gurgling sound came to a stop.

26.

"It was swell meeting you," Abel told Deborah Sr. as the old woman helped her daughter down off the front seat of the stagecoach, with Deborah Jr. not quite forgiven, but not doomed to suffer some more of the brunt of Deborah Sr.'s being frustrated just yet. "You have lovely hair," he told her. "Very soft."

But the woman wouldn't pay him any mind. She'd allowed a stranger to do something as intimate as touch her head, and with her being a woman of good standing she felt she'd let both her sex and social class down immensely. To Deborah Sr. it was an improper thing to do, and though she enjoyed it while it had happened, she'd never, *ever* admit to that out loud. And so, the only sensible thing she could think of as to how best to proceed was to pretend that Abel didn't even exist.

"Say," said Abel once Frank was by his side. "I gave her a good brush and now she won't even look at me. I do something wrong?"

"You brushed that there lady's hair?" said Frank, his face ashen with the dust that had been kicked up by the four horses doing the hauling.

"Uh-huh," Abel nodded. "And I thought I did it good too. I was real gentle. *Real* gentle."

"Jesus," Frank said with a smile. "If that don't beat all."

"She should be thanking me," Abel said. "I ought to give her a piece of my mind."

"Maybe best not to," said Frank. "Might be best to let sleeping dogs lie."

Abel didn't know what this phrase meant, but agreed heartily nevertheless.

"No," he told Frank. "I suppose you're right. Best to let cats that *are* awake purr," he said, trying but failing to wink, blinking both eyes instead. This caused Frank to laugh longer and louder than Abel had ever heard him do so. So amused was Frank that it tickled Abel's funny bone, getting both men clutching at their bellies, both doubled over laughing down at the ground beneath their feet.

"By God," Frank said, tears streaming down his dusty cheeks, leaving little damp trails in the dirt. "I ain't ever heard the like of it in all my living life."

"Me neither," said Abel, getting Frank going again.

After a little while, once the last few traces of giggles had been giggled, Frank took Abel by the arm and the two men went in search of the train station.

Taughrane Heights, Abel thought, could never be as busy as this place was. Not in a million years, he thought. He was so sure of this fact that he voiced it to Frank.

"Reckon you is right Mr. Liffey sir. Sure seems busy now, don't it?" Frank replied.

"It *does*!" said Abel, almost bewildered by the bustling throng of people busying about tending to their daily chores and errands. Abel couldn't decide if he liked it or not. He liked to see so many people. He liked the aliveness of it. But then he decided that he missed the quiet of home too much. That maybe this wasn't the proper place for a fellow like him. "It's almost too busy," he said after almost bumping into several souls that sped by him.

"Hell," said Frank, "you're right there Mr. Liffey. Too busy indeed."

But the pair persisted and marched on and on down the street until they came to a grand structure with a sign bolted to the roof with beautiful gold lettering on it that Abel couldn't read but Frank could.

"This is it," said Frank. "Galverstone Station," he declared. "Don't think I've ever seen a train in person," Frank told Abel.

"*Really*?" said Abel. "But you've seen my toy trains back home."

Frank smiled a little at this.

"These trains ain't no toys Mr. Liffey sir. These here is bigger than them toys I reckon."

"You think?" Abel asked.

Frank nodded.

"They'd have to be," he said. "How else would they get the people in them if they was as small as your toys?"

The thought tickled Abel, making him giggle quietly, though the young man was extremely nervous about greeting his first ever train. He was right to, as he soon found out.

The doors to the station were painted a deep, dark brown, verging almost on black, with wonderfully ornate golden handles to be handled by oh so many, many people who wished to travel out of the state of Texas. Taking the handle in his hand, Frank felt the coolness of the metal as he opened the door to another ample amount of potential passengers chittering amongst themselves in the various queues for tickets. As well as the people queuing there were people littering the benches, beside which they'd rested suitcases of a great number of differing sizes. Abel noted one man with a trunk sitting beside him and smiled. The man was almost as wide as the trunk.

He pulled Frank close and whispered, "Reckon that there fella'd take two seats all to himself."

Frank looked in the direction that Abel was nodding, noticed the fat fellow and shook his head in disagreement.

"Don't reckon that's true," he said soberly, making Abel suddenly serious. Then the black man's face broke into a wicked smile as he said, "Think he'd need three."

This got Abel going so loud and so hard that he made almost every man, woman and child turn to face him, with some smiling, though for the most part scowling in disapproval.

"Don't laugh so loud," Frank whispered.

"But it's funny!" said Abel. "That man's so... so damn *big*!" he said, pointing to the large man then doubling over, his belly beginning to ache from the strain. "Three seats," he shrieked. "Maybe he might even need four Frank!"

He yipped and hiccupped hysterically, watching as the fat man tried to get to his feet.

Frank was busy studying the timetable, leaving Abel a moment while he did so. Abel was transfixed beyond measure, for watching this man move – or try to – was quite the sight. First of all, he spread his feet far apart, then pressed his upper body back against the bench. Then, with visible frustration, his face strained as he tried to push his upper body forward, almost as though he were attempting to launch himself up. But he failed miserably. Again he tried, and again he failed. He began to puff, peeved that this young man several feet from him wouldn't stop

186

gawking with a slack jawed gaze.

"Goddamn it Frank," Abel said to the man who was no longer by his side. "I'm gonna go and help him."

Frank did not respond, for Frank was not there. The man was over in the queue now, occasionally turning to check to see if Abel was alright. He hadn't noticed Abel had moved from where he left him when the young man made to go for this great big fat man. Maybe if he had seen he'd have stopped him.

"Need any help?" Abel asked as he approached the man making the awful grunting sounds.

"Not from you anyway," he said, before blowing out a big blast of air that smelled of spitting tobacco to Abel.

"Why not?" said Abel. "You look like you need it. You can't get up."

"That's a very rude thing to say young man. Manners cost nothing you know."

"Well, why *don't* you want my help?"

"Why because you were laughing at me."

"I wasn't."

"You were. I saw you pointing."

"Okay. So I was laughing. But even you got to admit mister, it's always funny watching a fat fella that can't move try to move when he can't. Come on, I'll help you up."

Abel then tried to hook his arm under the grotesquely goodly man's armpit, but the fellow threw him off in a fussy, flustered sort of way.

"I don't need your help! Excuse me?" he called out to one of the railway porters racing about the station, seeming as though they were busy, but in actuality not very busy at all.

The fat fellow clicked his fingers, which looked like ginormous pink pork sausages to Abel. A strange thought came into Abel's head – that thought being: what would they taste like if fried up in a pan? – then vanished again just as quickly as it had materialised.

"Yes sir?" said a railway porter with about as much fat on him as a schoolboy's pencil.

"Would you mind helping me up?" said the fat man.

187

"Certainly sir," said the chap that Abel thought belonged in a pencil case, instead of racing round a railway station. "One moment sir," he said, before removing his handkerchief from a pocket in the seat of his pressed black pants, covering his face with it, then coughing very violently into the piece of linen.

"Lunger?" asked the fat man.

"I'm afraid so sir," said the pencil.

"No," said the fat man, shaking his head and flapping his meaty mitts in a shooing sort of way. "No. No you get away from me. Get someone else."

The pencil man looked despondent, though not supremely so. Abel thought that he looked as though he was used to this kind of treatment – Tom had told him what a lunger was, and although Abel had always wondered about them, he wasn't especially keen on meeting a fellow who had tuberculosis. Now that he *had* met a so called lunger, he didn't think it was all that bad. He didn't want to catch it, and though Tom told him you couldn't catch it like a common cold, Abel still tried to cover his mouth and nose in a way he thought discrete, though the pencil man did not.

"No problem sir," said the pencil man. "I'll find you a *clean* porter then, shall I?"

"I didn't mean it like that," said the fat man. "There's no need to take offence."

"No no," said the pencil. "None taken of course. I'll get you a proper, *clean* porter right away." And with that the pencil of a porter penetrated the crowd and dissolved into it like table salt in water.

"What are you still doing here?" said the fat man to Abel. "Go on. Get away from me."

"I don't reckon that there fella's gonna get someone else."

"*No*!" said the fat man. "You don't say."

"Here let me help," Abel insisted, not finding this man funny any longer, but rather pitiable instead.

"Get *away*!" flapped the man. "When I say I don't need

188

your help, I mean it!"

He then rolled his upper body forward and collapsed his left leg down so that the knee nearly touched the highly polished tiles of the train station's floor. Abel didn't know just what he hoped to accomplish by doing this, but stood there, dumbstruck and captivated nonetheless. The fat man then slid his huge behind forward off the bench, then with one hand on his right knee, attempted to lever himself up with a great grunt Abel had heard the pigs make out in their back yard many, many times. But he was stuck. He stayed there like that looking awfully silly, though Abel didn't laugh *or* smile. He just sighed and decided that the man was going to get his help whether he liked it or not.

"Look," he said. "Let me help and I'll leave you alone. Alright? You can't get up mister. Come on."

Abel then slung the fat man's right arm over his shoulder, then, straining and grunting himself, eventually got him to his delicate looking little feet. The fat man staggered forward for a moment, then came to a halt, his breast heaving up and down in exasperation at the spectacle he felt sure he'd made of himself.

"There," said Abel, "looking good."

"Is that sarcasm?" said the fat man, adjusting the blazer that wouldn't button across his broad belly.

Abel shrugged.

"Don't know," he said. "Don't know that word."

"What are you, an imbecile?" snarled the fat man.

"Maybe," Abel said plainly, offended a little, for though he didn't know that word either, from the way the man said it to him he knew it was an insult. So he fired one straight back at the big man for him to try on for size.

"Might be one of those. Might be a imbecile. But at least I'm not a great big pig."

He then rubbed some more salt in the wound and made a noise he thought to be a splendid imitation of a pig. The fat man then slapped him hard in the face, so hard the slap surprised Abel a lot, and even brought tears to the young man's eyes.

"That's not nice," he said, ready to cry. "I didn't hit *you*."

189

"You didn't," said the man. "But if you're going to throw your words around as recklessly as that you should be prepared to take a blow every so often. Good day sir," he said.

Then the man began to strain once again, trying to get his trunk moving, sliding it along the ground like a big brown slug off in the direction of one of the platforms.

Abel didn't feel like helping the fat man with his trunk. In fact he'd developed such a strong aversion to this man, he swore at him under his breath – something Abel had only done once or twice before, usually when Tom got really, *really* mad at him and struck him.

Abel stood there, the tears threatening to flow when Frank came back with one ticket held in his hand.

"Here," he said, thrusting the little cardboard coupon into Abel's hand. "You take that, and you don't lose it. You lose it and you ain't gonna get to see your mama none, you understand? I'm giving it to you now, and you don't go losing it. You hear Mr. Liffey? That's your ticket to mama."

"This is my ticket to mama," Abel nodded, wiping the wet from his eyes in case Frank asked why he was crying. He figured Frank wouldn't take to hearing he'd been smacked by the fat man, and didn't want Frank to start any trouble. "Where's yours?" Abel asked in a perceptive way Frank didn't appreciate at that precise moment.

"In my pocket," Frank said. "Go on now. Head over through them doors. Don't dawdle now."

"Okay," said Abel, as Frank gently prodded him from behind in the correct direction.

The two men stood on the platform for fifteen minutes waiting on the train. When Frank saw the steam trailing through the sky on the horizon he pressed a wad of dollars deep down into Abel's pocket.

"You is gonna need that," he told him when Abel swung round surprised. "That there's for stagecoaches once you get to Georgia. There's a bit of paper that's got your mama's address on it. You get lost and you show that to someone."

"Why do I have to? Why can't you?" Abel asked,

190

though Frank didn't answer.

Abel screwed up his face, waiting and watching as the train gradually got bigger and bigger until eventually it was upon them. The locomotive snorted steam like a great beastly bull, or so Abel thought. A bull was the closest thing he had to compare this colossal steel creature to, and like a bull, the thing frightened him a great deal. So much so, he started to weep for fear of it. Snivelling, he told Frank he didn't want to get on it. Frank said he had to, and poked him in the ribs to make him move towards it. The thing let out another blast of steam and Abel shrieked. This thing wasn't like his toys. This thing was mean, and shot out clouds that hissed like snakes. He felt it was dangerous – didn't want anything to do with it, and was almost made sick from being so scared of it.

"Go on now," Frank insisted. "It won't hurt you none."

"It will," Abel protested. "I don't wanna get on it!" he whined.

"Well if you wanna see your mama then you're gonna just have to," Frank said, starting to grow frustrated from having to worry about both Sarah *and* Abel. He didn't like the notion of sending Abel away on his own. He doubted he'd make it to his mama, though he tried to push those thoughts from his mind as hard and as fast as he could. Maybe he will, he thought. Yeah, maybe he'll find his mama and be happy. That'd be just swell. Some fat chance, however, was the thought that followed thereafter.

But between a life with Sarah and a life in Georgia, where white folks treated black folks lower than the dirt on their boots, there was but one option for Frank, and that was very clear.

Abel, prodded by Frank, found himself up the steps that led to a carriage.

"Get a move on nigger," came a voice from behind Frank and Abel. "Want to get on the train today, not tomorrow."

Frank did not turn to try to reprimand the bigot, but instead pushed Abel onward so that the young man and himself would be out of the way of this racist fool behind.

Abel stood stock still once onboard, afraid all of a

sudden that the train might consume him, gobbling him up like a troll from the stories his mama used to read to get him to sleep so very long ago. Frank shoved him to a seat and pushed him down into it by the shoulders.

"There now," he said. "That wasn't so hard now was it?"

"I don't like it here," said Abel. "I don't like it."

"I know. But it's only for a short while," Frank lied. "Once you get going, you'll be fine. You got your ticket still, haven't you?"

"Yes," Abel nodded, sick to his stomach with worry. The train let out a whistle.

"What was that?" Abel asked.

"Just the whistle," Frank answered. "You got your money Mr. Liffey?"

Abel checked his pocket, felt the dollar bills and nodded.

"That's good," said Frank. "You get off in *Georgia*," he told Abel, saying the name of the state slowly so as Abel got it in his mind. "Say it back. *Georgia*."

"*Georgia*," Abel said slowly like Frank had.

"Good. That's good," said Frank, looking over his shoulders nervously, knowing he was going to have to leave Abel any second now. "Now I'm gonna go speak to a porter," he lied again. "I'll be back in a minute," he lied for the last time.

As he tried to leave Abel stood to follow.

"No, you stay," Frank said. "You stay there. Alright?"

Abel nodded and took his seat. Then Frank disappeared through the door to the cabin just as the train let out another of those shrill whistles. Abel looked out the window, wishing to God Frank would hurry back. But then Abel saw him. He was hurrying through the crowd, shoving his way through all the people, pushing them gently out of his road.

"Frank!" Abel roared at the glass. "Goddamn it!" he said, feeling fear like he'd never felt before in his whole life. "*Frank*!" he said, slapping his hand against the glass window.

Then the train began to move. Abel stood so fast his

192

head got light, though that didn't slow him any. He raced right through the length of the carriage, flung open the door and stepped outside.

The train was still moving slowly, so he could jump off without any trouble. But where was Frank? He called out his name, hoping, dying to hear him answer. He shoved through the crowd as he called out.

"Frank!" he yelled. "*Frank*, where *are* you?"

He went through the doors to the station, swinging all about him wildly, searching for Frank with worried, weary eyes. Again he called out, and again there was no answer, nor would there ever be, for Frank, unfortunately, was gone.

27.

Tom helped Hector drag both bodies outside, though it caused him considerable pain to do so what with that ball stuck in his collarbone. He didn't groan, he didn't grumble, though Hector could see he was hurting, as did Maria once they re-entered Hector's place.

"Sit down," Maria instructed. "Sit down and let me see that wound."

"Didn't go all the way through," Hector said as he inspected the back of Tom's grubby shirt. He said something then in Spanish to Maria, who nodded before going back to the bar, bending down and lifting a bottle of clear liquid from one of the hidden shelves.

"This is moonshine," she told Tom. "You know this?"

"Yes," Tom answered. "But I ain't drinking it. Heard tell it can make a man go blind, and I ain't aiming on going blind any time soon. So you'd best go get me some regular whiskey. I'll pay for it. Don't worry about that none."

"No good," said Maria. "Need something stronger than whiskey. Need this."

Then she thrust the bottle into Tom's breast, but the young man couldn't be told. He set the thing down on the table then pushed it away from himself.

"Go get me whiskey. I won't take shine. I won't have a drop. You ain't gonna get me whiskey, well then I'll do without."

"We have no whiskey *señor*. Only tequila. Take the moonshine," Hector implored of him. "It's only for the pain. Tequila's no good. You need something stronger."

Tom's gaze didn't leave Maria, who was glaring just as stubbornly back.

"Take the ball out," he said. "I'll do without, for God's sake."

Maria muttered something in Spanish, then told her husband Hector to hold the fool down in his seat. She then sauntered slowly over to the bar once more, bent, then came back up with a tin box from which she took a pair of tweezers. She brought them over to Tom, poured some moonshine over them, then went about digging with them in Tom's tender flesh.

"*Fuck*!" he shouted, before beginning to hiss in and out through gritted teeth. The pain was extraordinary. It was as though someone were lighting a book of matches just beneath the surface of his skin, singeing him from within. Hector had a hard job keeping him still, but the owner of the establishment did his damnedest regardless of the young lad's struggling and violent cussing. "Come *on*!" Tom yelled after Maria'd been digging for what felt to him like several hours. "What are you doing!" he bellowed.

Maria then withdrew the tweezers and threw them on the table.

"I can't get it. It's too deep."

"So what?" said Tom. "You just gonna leave it in there? The lead'll poison me."

"What do you want me to do? I've tried," Maria said. "I'm not a doctor."

"Here, let me have a go," said Hector. "Hold him still," he instructed his wife.

She was far firmer than Hector, her big meaty hands holding Tom down in a way which restricted his movement considerably despite his attempted wriggling.

194

"Right," Hector said once the tweezers were in. "Now then."

He then dug around in a way which Tom found to be excruciating. He screamed as the Mexican made the wound way wider than it already was, scraping bone with the miniature metal implement.

"Hurry the fuck up!" Tom yelled.

"You hold on *amigo*," said Hector. "I am doing my best."

But Tom had had enough. He'd decided he'd take his chances and try to find a doctor down the trail. He shoved poor Hector off him, who tripped over a chair and landed on his behind in a very painful way which made Maria smile.

"What you smiling at?" Hector asked her.

"You!" she boomed. "Who else?"

Hector got up rubbing at his rump, reeling off a series of Spanish words which made Maria mad, with the woman roaring in Spanish back at him. Tom meanwhile was buttoning back up his shirt.

"Shit," he said, looking at the dark red stain where the blood had bled out of him. "Shirt sure is in a sorry state now," he said, though he supposed that the shirt was the least of his problems. Poisoning from lead was something he'd only heard tell of from conversations with cowboys in Elsie's. He didn't know how long it took to take hold, but he knew it was nasty, and plenty painful. He took his gun out of his holster and went about reloading it slowly and meticulously, making sure the thing was done right.

"You're welcome to stay until a doctor comes along," Hector told him.

"When will that be?" Tom asked.

"I don't know *señor*. Hard to say. Could be a day. Could be a week, we don't know."

"No," said Maria. "It's best he goes on. My husband is a fool to think that a doctor will come along."

Again she spoke Spanish, though this time it sounded as though she were muttering to herself. Hector lifted the stool he'd fallen over, pulled it into the table and plonked down heavily on it. Tom was still reloading, and didn't much fancy conversation, trying as he was to focus on getting his gun loaded correctly.

"Does it hurt now?" said Hector. "You know, now that we leave it alone?"

"Hurts some. Not as much though," Tom answered abruptly, giving the signal that he didn't want to talk, which Hector received loud and clear.

The Mexican began to study his boots, making Tom feel bad for being so blunt. The young man puffed out a sigh and spoke on, supposing Hector had little-to-no conversation which wasn't with his wife. He suspected too that the talk from wife wasn't welcome anyway, sour as she seemed to be towards her husband.

"Reckon it's fine," he told the man. "Reckon it ain't so bad. But I sure wouldn't want you *or* her going and digging around again. Hurt like a son of a gun."

"*Si?*" said Hector.

"*Si,*" said Tom. "Mucho."

This made Hector smile. He said a string of Spanish syllables, but Tom shook his head to say he hadn't understood a word. Hector grumbled.

"You don't know no Spanish. Just a little," he said.

"That's the truth," Tom told him, holstering his heavy weapon on his hip, then drumming his fingers on the table. "Don't suppose I could have another plate of beans?" he called out to Maria, who was busy scrubbing some of the blood staining her good hardwood floor. She took the sponge, soaked it in the pale of water, then went back to wiping without a word said.

"I'll get it," Hector said as he gave Tom's arm a squeeze. "She not in the mood now I think."

"Thanks a lot," Tom said, meaning it with all his heart.

He could in truth have stayed sat there and eaten beans for the rest of his years. He just might have done too had he not Sarah Herron to think of.

Hector brought him his beans, this time supplying a

196

beautifully baked loaf of white bread, which Tom scoffed down greedily, using the crust to scrape up beans with every bit of bread torn off.

He belched loudly once, then when Maria moaned about how rude he was to do so, belched a second time into the back of his hand discretely. He caught Hector beaming at him, beamed back for a moment or two, then slapped his thighs and stood up from his seat.

"Much I owe you?" he asked Hector.

"On the house," was the reply. "You no need to pay for the beans. You have had enough trouble without having to pay too."

"No," Tom said. "I won't walk out of here without paying. Them there fellas caused you trouble, and it likely wouldn't have happened had it not been for me. Here," he said, holding up three dollars. "That there's for your trouble," he said, lifting up the plate and placing the dollar bills beneath it. "The beans were exceptional. So was her shooting," he winked at Hector, who shot Maria a glance, though the woman didn't seem to be listening.

"*Gracias amigo*," said Hector, coming round from behind the bar to retrieve the cash before his wife saw him do so. Whispering to Tom he said, "Be better in my pocket than hers. She no let me spend it on whatever I like."

Tom shook his head and smiled.

"Women," he said. "Can't live with them, can't live without."

Hector nodded and smiled too. Tom then thought that he'd wasted too much time. That wherever Sarah was she more than likely would not have a smile on her face. Thinking of this made him mad, and quite keen to get back on the trail to get after her. He bid farewell to Maria, who didn't answer as Hector guided Tom to the door.

"Don't suppose you'll be leaving them there fellas to rot by the door," Tom said, feeling like giving the meaner one of two a boot, but refraining from doing so out of respect for the dead, despite what they were when alive.

197

"*Si*," said Hector. "We bury them right away."

"Might have some money on them," Tom told him.

"*Si*," said Hector, patting his waistcoat pocket. "I have already take," he smiled.

"That's good. Got no use for it now none, now that them boys is dead. Don't expect it belongs in their pockets."

"No," said Hector, spitting on the knee of the mean man's corpse, staining the cloth with saliva. Tom thought it bad taste to do so but shrugged the thought off – the man was a dung beetle, so what did it matter if Hector spat on him. "Horse is watered," said Hector. "He drink a lot of it. I had to go get three buckets before he stop drinking."

"That's good," Tom said, rubbing Dee-Cee's silky-smooth neck.

"Nice horse," Hector said. "He no bite like some," he said, rubbing at his elbow where he'd been bitten before by a stranger's animal. Sometimes it still hurt, even with it having healed many months ago.

"Yeah, he's a good one," Tom agreed.

The two men stood in silence a moment, looking at the corpses sitting lying limp up against the white wall of Hector's place. The flies had begun to feast. The bluebottles buzzed all around the wounds, though the carcasses had yet to rot.

"Best be getting them underground," Tom said as he clambered up back into the saddle. "Sun'll make them rot right and fast I reckon."

"*Si*," said Hector, already hating the notion of the back breaking work before him. He didn't want to dig one grave, let alone two. He didn't dare ask his wife for help either, for that would no doubt cause a massive argument to erupt. "I bury now," he told Tom, but Tom was already riding away.

He had to go to Sarah. Standing lamenting Hector's task wouldn't get him any closer to the girl.

Hector stood watching Tom and the animal he rode on gallop off farther and farther into the distance, until both horse and rider were nothing more than a dot on the horizon. When he could no longer discern where Tom was, he turned to those corpses and spat in the dirt, deciding that they were probably laughing in hell at the horrid task he had before him. The sun *was* scorching. It was no weather for such labour, though loathsome as it was, Hector had to do it. He moseyed around the back of the building and searched lazily for a shovel. Then, after a full fifteen minutes, finally having to look in the place he knew that it was – for there were no other places *to* look by then – he threw the thing down on the ground and went around the front of the building to collect the men's corpses. He mumbled and grumbled about how heavy they were while he dragged.

"Damn bastards," he said to himself before letting the second man's body drop to the ground. He then picked up his shovel, arched his back so that he could look his deadly enemy the sun square in the face.

"*Coño*," he muttered, before digging down into the scorched earth, the steel spade parting the dirt, the start of the hole being dug having begun.

28.

El Perro Sucio lived up to its name and then some, for it was very, very dirty. Tom had never set foot in as filthy an establishment as it was. Not in all his years of living. The floor was caked with mud and bits of rotten hay and, for some strange reason that Tom could not comprehend, huge hunks of horse manure, just sitting there on the floor.

"Fuck me," Tom said once in through the swinging doors.

"Do you want fucked baby boy?" said a swarthy skinned girl who looked far too pretty for a place called the dirty dog.

"Don't I'm afraid," Tom said. "Sorry."

"Why you waste my time? Huh? You got a problem *señor*? I go get Pablo. Pablo pistol whip you when you waste my time. He hurt like hell. You pay me, maybe I won't tell."

"Take a hike," Tom told her then shoved her out of his

road, getting a "*Hey!*" from the woman in protest.

"*Bastardo!*" she called from behind his back, but he wasn't listening, and even if he had been he probably wouldn't have heard her over the noise in the place. It was packed, though Tom couldn't see how it could be so damn popular, what with the pong.

Prostitutes littered the floor like flies on shit. Those that weren't standing were on men's knees, waiting until they'd gotten them drunk enough so that the men might take them upstairs and show the women a very mediocre time. The men had clearly come in after cattle drives for the most part, or so Tom thought going by the smell. It reeked of stale sweat which had been built up on the cowboys' bodies over time. Tom reckoned it would take several soaks in a tub to get rid of some of the smell. Three washes might only just scratch the surface.

Feeling sick, he decided that he didn't much care for the place, and wanted to just go get Sarah quickly and gallop off back to Georgia with her, her arms clinging tight to his body from behind.

"Boy," he said softly to himself. "If ever there was a place that Sarah didn't belong, then by Christ this sure is it."

"You want a drink?" came a voice to Tom's left.

Tom turned to find a bartender looking at him, his eyebrows raised expectantly for Tom to answer him.

Tom just looked at the man, wondering if it was he who had stolen Sarah and taken her to this hellhole.

"You want a drink?" the bartender enunciated.

When Tom still stood staring, the bartender made an "Aah!" noise, flapped his hand dismissively and went to move along down the bar.

"Wait!" Tom said. "Hold your horses. Yeah, I'll take a drink. Make mine a double whiskey," he said, making the bartender shrug and begin gathering this customer his glass and bottle.

"We charge by the bottle," said the barman. "Not the glass."

"Reckon you can rip people off better that way," Tom

lamented, looking all around the room for any sign of Sarah. She was nowhere to be seen, which worried Tom terribly. He wanted to ask the bartender if he'd seen her, and if so where would a man looking her go to to get a good galloping off her. But this bartender looked like he might be the Pablo fellow that the whore at the door had spoken of, so Tom decided that this man was not the way to finding Sarah. Tom knew Sarah never normally liked to leave her room at Elsie's, and supposed that this custom carried over to this her new place of employment.

He took his bottle, poured himself a very healthy measure of whiskey, then poured it down his neck, letting it linger with a welcome burning sensation, first in his throat, then a moment later on down in his belly.

"*Gracias*," Tom told the bartender. "How much I owe you?"

"Two dollars," the bartender told him.

Tom fished for the funds in his pocket, which were beginning to dwindle down to nearly nothing. If she wasn't in this hellhole, Tom would have a tough time paying for a trip elsewhere, which made his stomach twist into a knot, though the whiskey would help him with that problem, as it always had done before.

He brought both bottle and glass over to a table in the far corner to assess the situation better. So far as he could tell there was one way in, and that that was the very same way out. There was a door down at the end of the bar that Tom supposed might lead to a room in the back, where he imagined he might find an enormous stash of whiskeys and beers galore. This was not where Sarah was, and Tom knew that.

The girls in here were prettier than at Elsie's, which perplexed Tom as he sat trying to puzzle why a girl might think this a suitable place in which to work. Then the thought came sudden and clear. They weren't here because they wanted to be. They'd been forced. Tom looked again at that Pablo person, shooting him a hateful glance that the barman did not notice.

"Hmmm," Tom rumbled, before helping himself to another generous helping of his whiskey. "Well," he mumbled, then gulped down his glassful.

The fiery liquid was working wonders on his anger levels. He was getting meaner and meaner with every drop drank, though whether this was appropriate for the situation he found himself in was another matter entirely.

He had a third drink, then pushed the glass just beyond his reach, as though that might stop him from imbibing any further.

"For fuck's *sake*!" he seethed, slamming his open palm down hard on the table, causing his hand to sting he'd done it that forcefully. "Fuck me," he said, removing a splinter from the heel of his hand, holding it up to his face with one eye shut, then flicking away the little wooden soldier that had the audacity to assault the hand of one Tom Liffey. "Leave it be," he said to himself, now pushing the whiskey bottle farther out of reach. "Right," he said, head swimming. "Let's go get her Dee-Cee," he told the horse that wasn't there.

Right at that moment Dee-Cee blinked a fly from his face, lifted his tail, then promptly squeezed out a healthy helping of horse dung that fell to the floor of the earth with a satisfying splat.

"Darn fool horse," Tom laughed to himself, for though he didn't imagine Dee-Cee had shit upon his talking to him, he did see the beast blinking at him in his mind, making Tom laugh a little more and shake his head at how silly that dumb animal was.

Walking was proving difficult. Downing the whiskey was to blame, but Tom would sooner blame the bottle than take accountability for his own actions, as alcoholics tend to do when in the throes of the condition.

Maybe he'd give it up. Maybe once he'd got Sarah he'd start to straighten up and lead a good, Christian life. Having a lady on his arm whom he doted upon seemed to Tom the perfect solution for ridding him of his plight, or affliction with the liquid he longed for practically every minute of the day.

Drinking was fun, but the mornings after were where the real cost was calculated and administered, as the suffering soon began upon wakening.

"Watch yourself!" barked a man sat at the next table, when Tom stumbled slightly and had to rest on his shoulder lest he fall face down towards the deck.

"Don't know if I can do that," said Tom. "Ain't got no mirror."

"*What*?" said the man, puzzled by this stranger's remark.

"You," Tom began, pointing at the man first then himself second. "*You*, told *me* to watch myself."

"Yeah?"

"Well how on earth do you expect me to do so," Tom told the man, while doing an awful amount of flapping with his hands. "Without first obtaining… a mirror!"

"Go on away," grumbled the man.

"With pleasure," Tom said, staggering backwards and falling into the seat he'd stood from mere moments before. "No good," he slurred. "Say," he said to his companion the bottle. "Be you the bottle belonging to *me*?" he asked it, whilst simultaneously pulling the cork out with his teeth then titling the bottle up and letting the lovely brown liquid fall into the glass with a splash, the bottle making gurgling sounds as it was slowly drained of some more whiskey. "Why hell," Tom said. "I don't mind if I do *Señor* Bottle."

Then the fool lifted the glass to his lips and downed another measure. "Maybe she ain't here. *Hell*!" he roared all of a sudden. "*No*!" he declared defiantly. "*NO*!" he barked before slamming his hand on the table. "She is here! I know it. I know it. I'll give up this life of debauchery. Got me a good woman waiting for me. Don't need no drink. I'm a man, not a mouse. Only mice need drink and I ain't no mouse. Mighty man," he said before tipping the bottle up and disposing of his remaining whiskey by letting it flow from the lip of the bottle onto the floor – an act he assumed the bartender would not take umbrage with, due to the sorry state the place's floors found themselves in already. "Alright," he said, setting the bottle down with a thunk. "That's it. I'm coming," he said matter-of-factly. "I'm coming for you…"

But then the sick feeling began deep down inside. He didn't know how fast it was going to come up, but he knew he'd better hurry, because he couldn't get kicked out of this place. Not if he wanted Sarah back, which he most certainly did.

He bolted for the doors, shoving his way through the throng of protesting prostitutes and curmudgeonly clientele who didn't take to being pushed too kindly. He made it outside then brought up plenty of whiskey and plenty of beans. He barfed and barfed until he felt hollowed out. He looked up at Dee-Cee who met his gaze with that glazed vacancy that the man had become accustomed to receiving from the animal.

"Alright," Tom told his horse. "Alright I know. We're here to get Sarah. Sober now, ain't I? I got it up."

But if the truth be told, Tom was still a touch inebriated, and though the man didn't think that he'd need to be as sober as a priest come Sunday mornings, he knew somewhere inside that he shouldn't have gotten so damn drunk.

The sick stank, though not nearly as bad as the sweat did inside the dirty dog. Tom sat for a moment longer, looking at the few people passing by in the streets of the town. There was a Sheriff's office, a bank, a hotel and then another bar then a handful of houses. Further out of town there were more houses, though Tom couldn't spot them from where he was resting.

"Right," he said, slapping his thighs and trying awkwardly to get back to his feet. "First thing's first Dee-Cee," he said once erect again. "If there's gonna be a fight, then this thing," he said as he removed his pistol from its holster, "had better be loaded. Ain't that right?"

The horse blinked, then took two small steps backward, as though the very mention of a weapon made the beast a little uneasy.

"It's alright Dee-Cee. Don't worry. If things go the way I reckon they will, then I won't need it none. Take it easy now horsey. Dunk your head in that there trough and take a drink," he said pointing to the trough, then after glancing at the murkiness of the water inside, instructed Dee-Cee to forget he'd said that.

That the horse could get a drink at Hector's place on the way back. "Wouldn't want you poisoned none Dee-Cee. Be awful sad if you was to die. So don't," he said rubbing his horse's muzzle.

Then, after running his fingers through the horse's mane a time or two, he inspected his gun. Satisfied that the thing was in working order, he holstered it, readjusted his groin and got going back into the horrid whorehouse.

This time there was no woman to greet him, which was just fine. Tom wasn't sure what the plan was, though an admittedly flimsy scheme came to mind, which would have to do, for there was no other option. Again Tom approached the bar, then stood waiting while the bartender busily tended to other customers before eventually coming down to ask Tom just what he wanted now.

"Looking a white woman," said Tom. "Don't want no Mexican mister. Want a white woman."

"We got two," the barman told him. "They both upstairs *señor*, but you no pay me. You pay them. That is the way it works."

"Which rooms?" Tom asked.

The bartender pointed.

"There and there," he said. "You must have a appetite for women which is very large. If you are to please the both of them."

"Oh I aim to," Tom lied. "Been on the trail too long," he said, the fibs flowing from him like fine wine.

"I understand. You go up there and you pay them first. They be pleased to meet you," said the bartender.

But Tom was already walking away. He had neither the time nor the patience for this man, for although he didn't reckon he was the abductor, he didn't imagine the man was too courteous toward his Sarah.

Stepping up the stairs took time, for Tom was still not in the best shape what with the dregs of the drink still sitting in him. He wondered whether he should have gone outside again and got up some more of the stuff, but then he heard a man laughing loudly from behind the first door the barman had indicated.

Tom briskly took the last few stairs two at a time, stumbling on the last one and landing flat on his face on the floor.

"Fucking stairs. Damn them," he said, before getting up again.

He walked over to the door, his hand on the grip of his pistol. He didn't want to use it. He didn't want there to be a gunfight, for though he could shoot quite competently, if there *was* trouble in this place, it might mean every single Mexican man and woman inside the building would just as soon take him out to hang as look at him.

He'd have to get her away quietly. Discretion was the name of the game.

He took his hand from his pistol, then with his knuckle, rapped lightly on the first door. The laughing stopped suddenly, though there was no one calling out to Tom from within. Whatever, or rather, whomever had been making the noise had suddenly ceased their fun to listen for the intruder on this their special private time.

Tom was just about to reach for the handle when the door opened slightly. There was a man's face in the crack in the door.

"*Si?*" he said.

"I'm looking for a white woman," Tom said, not knowing what else to say.

"She no here *amigo*," said the man. Then a woman's voice sounded, which wasn't Sarah's by any stretch of the imagination.

"You wanna come back to bed or you wanna fuck that there fella instead?" drawled the uncouth whore.

"You go now," said the man. "Maybe you go now, I don't shoot you."

"No problem friend," Tom said. "You have yourself a nice evening now."

"*Si*," croaked the stranger before closing the door with a click.

This was it. The next door Tom stepped up to, he hoped,

had Sarah sitting inside, a veritable princess waiting with longing for her loving prince to rescue her from the tower, taking her far, far away to a much more pleasant land.

Well, maybe it wasn't so pleasant. It had the stench of pig shit stinking up the place, and there was a good deal of dust on the floors. But it wasn't a whorehouse. And it didn't stink like this place. And she wouldn't ever have to lie down on her back and get poked by men that had garnered a smell far worse than even the dirtiest pig could collect as an accolade all for its very own. She'll come home, or else to Georgia, Tom thought. There's no doubt. What would she want staying in a place like this? This is no place for a lady like her.

His hand found the handle. There was no noise from within, which made him feel like retching again, though he didn't, for this wasn't the time.

"Time to be a man," Tom Liffey whispered to himself, before he twisted the doorknob around and gently pressed on the wood, pushing the door open.

29.

Abel felt sick with worry. He didn't know what to do, for Frank had abandoned him to fend for himself – a state of being Abel was not accustomed to, and therefore badly frightened of. But then he thought, Heck, I've been with a woman! That makes me a man.

The thought swiftly evaporated as he exited the train station only to find that there was still no sign of Frank. He had his brush. He hadn't lost that, though what help the object offered he did not know. He clung to it, desperately dying to see Tom again, even if he was cussing and giving off to him for having lost Frank.

"Maybe he'll come back," he said to himself, before beginning to hum a nondescript hymn he'd heard coming from the church once back in Taughrane Heights.

He stood staring into the public walking this way and

that, though there was still no sign of Frank.

Then – and the rarity of such a thing cannot be overstated enough – Abel had himself a bright idea. He wouldn't go to Georgia, because the thought of sitting on that horrid train made him feel even worse than he already did. But he could go home. He could get the stagecoach.

He knew he could handle a stagecoach journey because he'd done it before, and had even found it to be a bit of good fun. But which one? There were so many stagecoaches hurrying in and out of town. How was he to know which one was for him? He could only ask, and so he did just that.

The first two said they'd never even heard of a town called Taughrane Heights, with both drivers telling him to get lost once Abel had said he could point it out to them – which wasn't true at all; he just wanted to get home and get away from Galverstone and that God awful train lurking somewhere behind the station building.

But he persisted, and on the fifth try, though a little exhausted from all this rushing around trying to find the appropriate stagecoach, the driver told Abel that that was just where he was headed.

"My goodness," Abel beamed at the driver. "You have no idea how glad I am to hear that."

Then he went to clamber on up into the carriage when the driver stopped him with a "Woah, woah, woah! Where you going slick?"

"Home," Abel said.

"Not without paying you ain't. Ain't a free service I is running mister. Money is required if you're wishing to get home."

"Oh yes," Abel said. "Dim of me. How much is it to Taughrane Heights?"

The driver rubbed at his chin a moment, making a kind of strained groaning noise.

"Well now, let me see," said the driver. "How much you got?"

"Thirty dollars," Abel told the man.

"My God!" said the driver. "Boy are you in luck!"

"Why?" Abel asked.

"*Why?*" said the driver. "Why because that's the exact amount it takes to get to Taughrane Heights."

"Gee," said Abel. "That sure is swell."

"Ain't it?" said the driver. "You just hand the dough on over and then you can clamber on up inside. Kept the windows open so that when we get moving the wind'll keep my passengers cool. Don't do to have folks sweating buckets right next to each other."

"No sir," said Abel. "It does not."

He then took his wad of cash from his pocket, strained to reach it up to the driver, who bent down to meet him before snatching the cash, counting it out, then popping it in his own pocket where it would stay until Taughrane Heights, whereupon he would spend, spend, spend on whiskey galore until good and drunk. Driving was a tedious business, and a touch stressful when going through bandit country. The driver didn't have much of a reprieve save turning to a bottle, so that was just what he was so inclined to do.

Frank was watching when Abel got in the stagecoach. He hadn't left him alone when he heard him calling for him in the station. He wasn't sure when he departed company from the young man if he'd have the stones to stay onboard the train, though Abel quickly confirmed Frank's suspicion that he didn't.

He watched him like a hawk, making sure to hide himself from view save one eye. He couldn't leave Abel be. The young man might have had good intentions. He might have longed for his mama, but the brains weren't there. And in a city like Galverstone there were far too many folks that'd just as soon take advantage of poor Abel as look at him.

So Frank watched and waited. Once Abel was on the stagecoach Frank still waited, and didn't move until the stagecoach was full of people and had then set off.

Frank felt fine knowing Abel would be going home. He didn't like the notion of him going home to his mama, because whether Abel realised it or not, she was the woman who had run off and left the Liffey boys behind.

She didn't care, Frank thought. That woman wouldn't care for her son if he showed up, and she certainly wouldn't brush his hair. This thought angered Frank a little, but he turned to the stagecoach and thought of Abel being rocked about a bit by the carriage's movements and that made him feel alright again.

Frank needed a horse. He needed one fast, for he had to get to Sarah. He wasn't sure exactly what he'd say when he saw her, though he suspected he might just tell her he loved her. That he had done from the very first time he laid eyes on her. He might get shot down. He knew his skin colour didn't help him any, but by God was he going to try. But first a horse.

He went to the Galverstone livery and knocked on the door of the office adjacent as he removed his hat.

"Come in!" came a voice from the other side of the door.

Frank opened the door and then the little man with the crop of white hair combed over the bald bit on top told Frank without looking up to shut the damn door to keep the dust out of his office.

The man was portly, and sat in an ill-fitting suit stretched across his shoulders. His shirt collar was far too tight, and Frank wondered whether the man could breathe properly with such a restricting garment. The man clutched tightly to a pencil, and with one eye closed sat etching out lettering and figures in his beautiful leather-bound ledger resting atop his desk.

"Do you need a horse?" asked the man.

"Yes sir," said Frank.

"I suspected as much," said the man. "For horses is what we sell."

"Yes sir," said Frank again.

"My name is Potter. Cornelius Potter. You may have a seat if you like, though if you are prepared to stand you'd be sparing me the cleaning of dust from the seat after your departure from my company."

"Yes sir," said Frank again. "I think I'll stand. If it's all the same to you."

"It is," said Cornelius. "I have several horses in the

stables. Have you looked them over yet or do you require my stable hand to show them to you?"

"No sir," said Frank. "I ain't seen them. To tell the truth I don't need to see them. All I need is whatever horse you got to spare. I got good money to pay for it. I'll pay whatever you ask, just so long as you're quick about it."

"You're in a hurry then," said Cornelius Potter, putting his pencil down and lifting his head for the first time. His eyes bulged in his skull. "No," he said plainly. "No. Can't you read?" he said, pointing to a sign that hung on the back of the door that read NO DOGS, NO NIGGERS, MEXICANS WELCOME.

"No sir," Frank said, suddenly feel very bitter indeed. "I did not."

"Don't sell to no niggers son. Sorry. There are other liveries in other towns, though this one won't sell you a one-legged foal that's opposed to even trying to walk," Cornelius said, a small smile playing on his twitching lips. "You may leave now," he said, waving his hand toward the door, then picking up his pencil again before beginning to etch out some more markings in his ledger.

"Yes sir," Frank said, placing his hat on his head again. "Thank you sir."

Then he left the livery office and its bigoted, balding owner. But he did not leave the livery itself. Instead, he ducked down below the windows, crawling up the side of the office so that the balding man wouldn't see him. He creaked open the stable door a little, then stepped inside. There were four horses in total. Frank inspected each and decided in the end on a big American stud that was a sort of sandy colour with a white patch on his muzzle.

"You'll do," Frank whispered.

"What you doing in here?" said the stable hand, who had been shovelling manure down at the opposite end of the stable.

"Cornelius sent me," Frank lied. "Bought this horse here just a moment ago," he said.

"You didn't buy no horse from no Cornelius," said the

211

stable hand. "Hates niggers does Mr. Potter. And you boy sure is a nigger."

"Now don't test me," said Frank, drawing his pistol and pointing it at this racist bastard. "You just get this here horse saddled up and maybe I won't shoot you none. You understand?"

The stable hand stared at Frank, then spat out on the hay covered ground.

"Supposing I don't?" he said, taking a step or two toward Frank.

"If you fancy a bullet in your head then I'd be happy to put it there for you. Won't even charge you for it," Frank told the man. Frank then cocked his piece and stepped swiftly up close to the hand. "You try me motherfucker. Go on ahead and try me. I got a woman was taken by a bad man, and I aim on going and getting her back, and there ain't *nothing*, and I mean nothing, is gonna get in my way. Not you. Not Cornelius Potter. Not nobody. Now you either saddle up that there stud or I let this pistol go off and send you up and into God's good kingdom. So, you tell me, what's it gonna be? Huh?"

The stable hand spat again.

"Sorry mister," he said. "I'll saddle it for you right now."

True to his word, the man did just that. He didn't holler. He didn't complain. He saddled it for Frank and Frank even handed him a five-dollar bill for the trouble.

The man looked at the money in his hand in disbelief, then watched Frank climb up into the saddle.

The black man tipped his hat pulled the reins round and rode off out of the livery, leaving the town of Galverstone behind him as the stable hand watched, spat, then promptly returned to shovel shit without saying a single word.

30.

Sarah was weak with weeping. She lay on her bed curled up in a big ball beneath the sheets like a hedgehog that was scared. The pillow beneath her head was soaked with salty tears, and though she thought that if she stayed lying there in the damp, she might get a cold, she couldn't have cared less even if she did. She figured it might make the men leave her alone for an hour or two, if she were sneezing and her nose running and her eyes red raw.

She was still snivelling when the door opened and Tom Liffey entered the room. Sarah Herron didn't look up. Instead she lay listening to the man's boots step towards her across the floorboards of this horrid whorehouse where the men treated women like animals, with most deriving a great deal of pleasure in providing pain for the women they'd paid for a time with.

"What you reckon?" Tom said once he'd stopped in front of her face. He then knelt down and set his hand very gently on hers, which was covering a badly blackened eye from some brute's beating a half hour earlier.

He lifted her hand away from her face and spoke so gently, as though the words might cause this precious vase before him to crack and possibly even shatter should the sound hit it too hard.

"You reckon you wanna come home?" he asked. The word 'home' made Sarah open her eyes, and though she felt like screaming for joy at the sight of her Tom come to rescue her, she knew far better than to make much of a ruckus. After all, Juan Lobo was in the adjacent room.

Sarah looked at Tom, and though she didn't smile – because they weren't away home yet – her eyes showed him that she was enormously pleased to see him. She took her hand back and extended her index finger, then pressed it to her lovely lips, making a shushing sound simultaneously.

"You alright?" Tom whispered so softly and so close to her face that although she could smell the whiskey and vomit on him, she didn't mind at all.

She nodded.

"Now I see your silly face," she whispered back almost inaudibly.

Tom brushed the black eye with his thumb, and though he didn't mean to, and though it hurt her, she didn't dare wince.

She had her Tom now, and that meant more to her than anything had ever mattered before. But they *still* weren't out of the building.

Tom didn't seem to realise the seriousness of the situation, going by that gormless grin plastered across his face. He's just happy to see me, Sarah thought. That's all. He don't know we're in such a bad place. Not yet anyways.

"I'm sorry I was so mean back home," he told her. "I never meant to hurt you none. Honest I didn't. And I swear…"

She then put her finger to *his* lips.

"Leave it be," she said. "That don't matter none. You're here now. That's all that matters."

"Can you get dressed?" he asked her, to which she nodded that yes she could. When she got up out of the bed her eyes nearly popped right out of her skull, for foolish Tom had left the door wide open behind him. She flew like a flash to the door and shut it with an accidental bang, making the first big error of the evening.

"*Shit!*" she whispered.

"Why? What's wrong?" Tom whispered to his woman. "What's the matter?"

Sarah just shook her head.

"Don't matter," she said. "Help me get dressed," she said, making the second blunder that night. She only thought later on that it might have been best she left in her nightie. That had she just strolled out of that horrible hellhole of a whorehouse in her night clothes, tragedy would not have befallen the two of them. Though she didn't think, and *did* decide to get dressed.

Tom was helping her on with her dress when there came a knocking at the door.

"Don't come in!" Sarah shouted. "I'm with a client," she said, swatting Tom's tummy so that he knew to play the part of the customer.

He put on a gruff voice and said, "Who the hell's that? Interrupting me in my business?"

There was a pause, during which Sarah felt sure Juan Lobo would open the door and step inside regardless of whether

214

a customer was present or not. But he didn't.

"Don't bang the door," he said, then all was still again, save the tinkling of the piano and the general hubbub floating upwards from the bottom floor.

"Fucker," Sarah whispered.

"Who?" said Tom. "*Me*?"

"Not you," she said. "Don't be so silly. It's him. The man that took me away. He stays next door with his woman."

"He's the one took you away?" Tom said, studying the door, his hand involuntarily finding its way to his pistol grip, unguided by consciousness.

"Now no trouble. He's mean," Sarah said, lifting his hand from his pistol and planting a kiss on the backs of his knuckles. "Leave him be. You can't kill him. He's meaner than you Tom. Far meaner. You ain't a killer. *He* is."

"Don't mean I ain't mean. Man takes my woman and he'll not live to know not to. Why I ought to kill him right now."

"No Tom," she said. "You leave him be. That's coming from me, and I've more reason to want him dead than you do. So stop! Okay?"

"He do that to your face?" Tom asked her.

"No," she said. "He did not."

Tom looked at her like he didn't believe her.

"Alright yes," she hissed. "He did. What you gonna do? Murder him for giving a bitch a black eye? They'll hang you for it. They'll hang you, and I'll stay stuck here forever. That what you want? 'Cause boy let me tell you, this here place ain't no Elsie's. Ain't no pleasure palace. Them boys that come to see me here's horrid bastards. They don't treat women kind. They like to hurt us. That what you want? You strung up, me *here*?"

She started to cry then, so Tom took her in his arms and squeezed awfully tight.

"There," he said, patting the back of her mousy brown hair. "There now. That ain't gonna happen. I ain't gonna kill nobody. You just get dressed, alright? You just get dressed and I'll take you far from this place."

She nodded into his shoulder, then, when he released

her, she busily dressed herself while Tom took a seat on the bed.

"Mattress ain't too comfy," he said, bouncing gently on the thing. "Ain't no kind of man'd make love lying on this."

"You're telling me," Sarah said. "I had to sleep on the thing."

They both smiled then. She looked at the back of his head, thinking that she'd never been so happy to see a certain soul ever before. But they still weren't away, so there was no time to spend lingering long on how much either one of them doted upon the other.

"Alright," she said once dressed. "That's me."

"Right," Tom said. "Let's go."

He went first, while she held his hand. He opened the door ever so slightly, just enough to peek out and see if this fellow was standing guard. Much to Tom's delight, he was not.

"Coast's clear," he told Sarah, who though she didn't say anything, gave his hand a good hard squeeze that said, "Okay, get going then."

The two then took their first few steps out onto the landing. The door to Juan Lobo's lair was closed shut.

"That him in there?" Tom nodded toward the door.

Sarah nodded. Tom took out his pistol and almost reached for the handle. Sarah quickly grabbed Tom's gun hand and shoved it down to his side. She shook her head and told him, "No!" So Tom did as bid and holstered his gun again, before taking three more steps toward the top of the stairs. He had his foot down one step when Juan Lobo opened the door. Sarah heard him. She let go of Tom's hand and told him to go, but Tom wouldn't dare do such a thing, choosing instead to spin around as well.

"Where you going?" Juan Lobo said to Sarah. "You thinking of leaving?"

"No," she said. "Just going to get a drink."

"That so?" said Juan Lobo, looking at Tom, who with his fists balled up so hard his knuckles had turned white with rage. "That what you doing *amigo*? Going to get a drink?"

Tom took two steps forward, shoving Sarah behind him

so he could square up to this man that had taken his woman away from him.

"Ain't going to get a drink at all," Tom told him.

Sarah put her hands on Tom's shoulders and tried to pull him back.

"Don't Tom," she said in his ear.

"It's alright," Tom told her. "It's alright. I'm just telling this here fella that you're leaving. That alright with you mister?" he said, staring into Juan Lobo's black, evil eyes.

"She going nowhere *pendejo*. She staying here," Juan Lobo told Tom.

"That a fact?" Tom said, his finger feeling his gun's trigger, his thumb on the hammer.

"*Si*," growled Juan Lobo, his own hand feeling his gun's grip as well.

"Well," said Tom, "you'll have to go through me mister. If you want her that is."

"Not a problem," said Juan Lobo, lifting his gun out of its holster. Tom, too quick and filled full of hatred for this evil Mexican man had his gun up first. He cocked his hammer back, brought the business end of the barrel up under Juan Lobo's chin, and pulled the trigger. But Mr. Samuel Colt and his Dragoon decided to forget to let that lead ball fly, leaving Tom embarrassed and susceptible to whatever punishment Juan Lobo fancied dishing out.

The Mexican grinned an awful grin, pointed his own pistol into Tom's belly, then firing, the noise of the gun going off causing the crowd below to cease conversing and the piano player to stop his tinkling. Tom collapsed to the ground writhing in pain, his pistol dropping to the floor with a pathetic thud. Then, not prepared to miss the opportunity, Sarah threw herself at the ground, picked up the pistol, pointed it at Juan Lobo's toes and this time fired the thing successfully.

The shape it left Juan Lobo's foot in was not good. The Mexican cried out in pain, shouting the odds at Sarah.

"*Tu perra!*" he roared. "*Tu perra!*"

She knocked the gun from his hand and the thing fell

down to the bottom floor, crashing into a table where several fellows had been playing poker.

One disgruntled man moaned that the gun had destroyed his chances of acquiring the pot, which he exclaimed was a sizeable sum, and that he'd shoot any man that contested his taking the money gathered in the table.

Another man did contest, and very soon thereafter a row had erupted, and blows began to be struck. This distraction allowed Sarah to cock Tom's pistol again as Juan Lobo hopped around like a cricket, complaining in Spanish about the shape of his foot.

"Forget your foot," Sarah said, pointing the Colt Dragoon up under Juan Lobo's chin as Tom had done moments before. "Your foot ain't all you've got to worry about," Sarah said. Juan Lobo went to speak, but swiftly expired as Sarah squeezed the trigger, causing the matter that once resided inside his skull to relocate to its new place of residence, coating the upstairs walls of the whorehouse.

His body dropped down to the ground as the girl inside his room joined Sarah and Tom on the balcony.

"Bastard!" she said before kicking his head – or rather, where his head had been before – then spitting on his chest and thanking Sarah wholeheartedly.

"He'll not bother you no more," she told the woman, who nodded at this then disappeared back into the room, presumably to pack up her things and make good her escape.

Tom meanwhile, was doing his best not to groan, even though the pain he felt in his gut was excruciating.

"Let's go," he told Sarah, who helped him to his feet, clutching her man in one hand and the gun in the other. "Give me that," he instructed her gently, taking the gun from her and holding it in his hand, ready for firing at any man who happened to come between himself and Sarah and the door to this establishment. "Go on and get the horse ready girl. I can make it on my own."

"I'm not leaving you," Sarah said, not just out of stubbornness, but because she honestly believed that if she

218

weren't there to prop Tom up, he'd collapse and not make it out of the whorehouse.

He wrapped his arm around her tighter and told her to march the pair of them out the door. No man stepped in their way, because for the most part everyone's attention went towards the brawl that had erupted between the gamblers.

"*Gah!*" Tom sighed when Sarah set him down once out through the doors. "Goddamn it all to hell," he groaned, hitching his breath in slowly so as there was the minimum amount of movement made by his torso. Taking breaths became harder and harder, and the blood being lost made Tom wonder whether he'd die way the hell down here on the doorstep of a whorehouse close to the border.

He thought of Abel and his darn brush, then set to wishing he'd never left Taughrane Heights at all. It was only when he looked at the splendour of Sarah that he was reminded why he had to leave him, why he had to come to this awful place. She was his woman. Whatever trouble came his way, that fact was concrete.

"Can you mount?" Sarah asked him once she'd taken the reins from the hitching post.

"Maybe," Tom said, trying to stand. "Might need your help," he said once he'd collapsed to the ground again.

Standing hurt him.

"You sore?" Sarah said, not knowing anything sensible to say other than that.

"Sore?" said Tom. "Nah, just tickles is all," he smiled, making Sarah smile back.

"Boy you never quit, do you?" she said.

"Made you smile though, didn't it?" he said as she lifted him painfully to his feet. He let out a few expletives as he did so, but he made it up onto the horse and even took the reins.

"You'll have to ride in front of me," he told Sarah. "Don't think I could face you holding onto my belly from behind. Be too painful, even though the ride with you at my back would be so sweet. Now clamber up before that there fight concludes and someone notices you're gone."

Sarah didn't need to be told twice. She clambered up and sat in front of her man, who once ready, dug his heels into the beast below's belly and the horse got going out of town.

The night was quiet, save for the chirping of grasshoppers, which was welcome to Tom. His belly ached the whole way to Hector's place, and dismounting the horse had been twice as painful as the mounting of the animal outside the dirty dog.

Tom didn't know when he approached Hector's who was waiting inside. It was a pleasant surprise when he stepped through the door and collapsed to the ground – his head light from blood loss – watching as Frank emerged from the shadowy corner.

"Hell Mr. Liffey sir," said the black man who had appeared. "I sure am glad to see you," he said.

Tom smiled, his teeth stained with a sticky mixture of blood and spittle.

"Glad to see you too," he told his employee, before closing his eyes and promptly passing out.

31.

"Rode like hell Miss Sarah," said Frank, removing his hat once he saw her walk through the door.

"Frank!" she said, rushing into his arms and hugging him tight. Then she remembered Tom in a hurry and released Frank, who, if he were being honest with her, could have held her like that the rest of his days and still wouldn't have complained.

"Come and help me," she said, kneeling down by Tom, whose eyes were closed and his face vacant of any emotion.

"He shot Miss Sarah?" said Frank, setting his hat on a table and bending down to tend to Tom too.

"In the belly," said Sarah. "But he didn't grumble much while we rode," she said, brushing his fringe back from his face while she spoke. "He was so brave. You should have seen him Frank. He saved me from a beast."

Frank felt a surge of envy, for it was he who wanted with all his heart to do the saving. Then the farmhand though that had he been the one to do the saving, then it would surely be that he would be the one lying with a hole bore right through the middle of him, not Tom.

"Ain't got much hope having a hole in the belly," he said to Sarah as he studied that porcelain white neck of hers, unburdened by blemish or markings or moles of any kind. Kissing her on the neck now would not be at all appropriate, though that didn't put a halt to his desires to do so. "Might be best we put him in bed," Frank suggested. "Might be more comfortable Miss Sarah."

Sarah just nodded.

Hector, who had been out at the outhouse performing his necessaries, walked in then, thinking the man on the floor to be dead already. His first subsequent thought was a selfish one. He didn't want his place to garner the reputation of an establishment where men went to die. He didn't want any potential customers that passed by to become spooked by the notions of ghosts lingering long after this boy's body'd been buried.

"You want we can bury him right away," he suggested, picking up his wash rag and slinging it over one shoulder.

"He's not dead," said Sarah. "So you'd better come help him into this bed before I take his gun and give you something that might make you dead."

Hector just stood blinking at her when his wife's voice sounded from over in the direction of the stairs.

"Help them!" she roared, startling the man, making him almost jump out of his skin but accomplishing the task of getting him going. "I'll go get some water," said Maria. "Might not cure him, but it will help to cool him down."

Hector helped Frank lift Tom into bed, bringing the blankets up round Tom's chin. Sarah pulled them down again.

"Don't do that!" she barked. "He's hot enough."

Frank, feeling as though the pity and feeling was wasted on a man like Tom, took his seat again in the corner, biding his time for the Liffey boy to die, thereafter allowing him to swoop in and steal Sarah for his very own. His thoughts weren't without guilt however. Frank knew he was being selfish. He knew he was not being righteous, but he just couldn't help himself. Sarah Herron had bewitched him, and the girl was all he wanted in the whole wide world. He would let his boss die. He'd allow the girl to grieve. But that didn't mean that he wouldn't try to win her heart as soon as the appropriate moment came along to do so.

Sitting there, watching Tom take his last few breaths, Frank thought to himself that he should show his master the respect he owed him, and try to seem as though he wanted to do right by him. He thought that this might make him shine like a new penny in Sarah's eyes.

"There was a buggy back along the trail," he said as he stood.

"What of it?" said Sarah.

Frank took two tiny steps forward.

"If it alright with you miss, maybe I'll go get it. Mr. Liffey might want to die in his hometown. No offence Mr. Hector sir."

"None taken," said Hector, watching as his wife came in with a bucket filled to the brim with water.

She sloshed some all over his floor, which vexed him, though he knew now was not the time to complain. He studied the blood stain on the floor near the door, supposing that sooner or later his wife would notice, and he'd get the brunt of her being irritated by the stain. So Hector went and got himself his own bucket, as well as a mop. Then the man moseyed on out the back to the well to start cleaning the stain, thereby saving him the aggravation his wife would dish out quite readily.

"Right," said Maria. "This will sting," she said, dunking a clean looking rag into her bucket. She then handed the soaked cloth to Sarah and told her to place it upon the young man's forehead, which Sarah did very carefully so as not to wake her man. Maria, as though able to read minds, told her that he would wake once she did this. Then the wife of Hector dunked a second rag into the bucket, brought it to the bloody hole in Tom's belly and pressed ever so gently.

Tom did waken. Woke with such a start that Sarah jumped. The noise he made was a harrowing kind of howl that chilled Sarah to the bone. She'd heard men make all sorts of noises. Never one like this though. Tom's teeth clacked together, and he began to shiver. Sarah swabbed his sweaty forehead with her rag and Maria dunked hers again.

"I'm so sorry," Sarah said before leaning down to kiss Tom's head. He hissed in through his teeth as Maria pressed down upon his wound once more. Then Tom noticed Sarah's face and for a split second forgot his pain.

"It's…" he said weakly. "It's fine. No need to be *so-horry*!" he then cried out.

"Will you *stop*!" Sarah boomed at Maria. "You're hurting him for no reason."

"I can try to take the bullet out," she suggested. "It will be sore."

"Do you want her to try Tom?" Sarah said to her man.

"No," said Tom. "No don't bother. I'll die once the bullet's been taken out, and I sure as shit ain't aiming on dying in more pain than I need to."

"Leave him," Sarah told Maria, so the Mexican woman did just that and stood up from where she'd been sat on the bed.

"You want me to go get the buggy?" Frank asked the girl tending to Tom's sweaty head.

"I don't *care*!" Sarah cried. "Does it look like I give a shit?"

Frank nodded as Sarah began to cry, then headed for the door. Maria rushed over to him and lead the black man outside.

"She doesn't mean it," she told him, his face with an awful hang dog look to it. "You like that lady?" she asked.

Frank looked away, the pain of the question too strong, the hurt of the answer too great.

223

"Go get the buggy," Maria said. "Be better he dies at home. The girl will remember that you did this for him. Go quickly now," she said, her heart breaking from that sad stare of Frank's.

The farmhand mounted his horse while Maria watched him go. She shook her head then turned and went back inside, thankful to God that she had her Hector.

32.

"Don't die yet Mr. Liffey sir," Frank said while he whipped his horse so severely the poor animal couldn't help but cry out in pain. He was pushing it hard, but he had to get Tom home. He had to show Sarah the sort of man he was, this being the best way of doing it. "We almost there now!" he sang cheerfully. "He still breathing Miss Sarah?"

"Just barely," she answered, before whispering in the wind into Tom's ears that they were nearly home, that he should hold on just a little while longer.

The air was cooling to Tom. He was barely awake, the blood loss too great to sustain normal bodily function. Though the sky was beautiful, the night having passed and the sun just beginning to peek out over the horizon to the east. The clouds were coloured a blazing red. Tom actually pointed once at one of them, mumbling the word "Horse," though Sarah didn't understand.

Her man was dying. He was no longer her Tom, though he was not yet gone.

The plains all around them hummed with the morning's life. Lots of coyotes called out as if clearing the path for Tom's return to home. The crickets had ceased their sounds, and the rabbits that ran from the horse and buggy, disappearing down into their burrows did not make much noise as they did so. The rattle of the buggy frightened every rattlesnake out of the road as it moved across the desert, barren for the most part of any shrubbery save a few thorny weeds.

"We nearly there now sir," said Frank whipping one last time before the Liffey boys' home came into view. "Mr. Abel be waiting on you!" Frank told his employer. "That boy'll want to see you 'fore you go," he said, tipping the brim of his hat up out of his eyes as he scanned the house for signs of life.

The roar of the buggy was what woke Abel from his nap, who, having no money with which to purchase food in Taughrane Heights, was immensely hungry. He felt like moaning to himself, but then thought he'd be better going outside to see what that awful racket was.

When he stepped out, Frank saw him and shouted for the elder Liffey boy to come closer.

"You wanna see your brother alive again, you best be hurrying on over here!" Frank yelled.

Sarah didn't approve of his bluntness, but then she knew one had to be blunt with Abel, or else he was apt not to obey.

Abel, feeling the seriousness of Frank's statement, started running towards the wagon, brush to hand as always. When he saw Sarah, he smiled. When he saw the look on her face his smile soon disappeared.

"Woah now!" Frank said as he drew rein. "Easy up now," he told his horse, then took off his hat as Abel approached. "He in the back Mr. Liffey sir. But don't ask him to brush you none, for he ain't in no shape to do so."

Abel, who had been feeling the handle of his brush, slackened his grip of the object slightly and walked around the side of the wagon. Sarah's face was well warranted such a look, for the state of Abel's brother horrified Abel as well. He didn't know what to do. He hadn't been there when his pa had passed, and so far as he knew his mama was still out there somewhere. But here was his brother, breathing his last few breaths in and out through a belly with a hole shot right through the middle of it.

"You alright?" Abel asked as he clambered up.

Tom's eyelids parted. When he saw his brother's large head looming above him the eyes widened further.

225

"I'll be damned," Tom said. "What you doing way out here?"

Abel looked to Sarah, who shook her head, with Abel getting the picture maybe for the first time ever in his life.

"Thought I'd come and see you brother," Abel said. Then, not knowing what else to do, he held out his brush. "Brought you this," he said, the words almost catching in his throat. "Thought you might want your head brushed," he said, then went about the brushing.

Tom took a look at his brother, then his Sarah.

"See Sarah," he told his woman. "Brother's brains to burn," he said, making Abel laugh as a tear rolled down the simple soul's cheek.

"You alright?" Abel asked again.

Though the answer was apparent to all.

Frank was stood at the foot of the wagon when Tom asked where he was.

"Why I is here," Frank told him. "I is right here Mr. Liffey sir."

Tom lifted his head and Sarah supported him. He even laughed when he saw those sad eyes of his employee.

"There you are Frank," he said softly. "Think I'm dying sir," he said. "Think I'm just about done."

"Don't matter sir. I'm staying put," Frank said, not knowing what else he could say.

"You do me a favour Frank," Tom instructed.

"Yes sir Mr. Liffey sir. What you want me to do?"

"You take care of her," Tom said. "You take damn good care of her."

Sarah turned to Frank, who stood with tears streaming down his face, unable to lift his head to look at Sarah for fear that the love he had for her wouldn't show in her face too.

Tom took Sarah by the hand, pulled her close and whispered something into her ear that neither Abel nor Frank could hear. Sarah nodded, laying his head gently down on the boards of the buggy.

"Be going now Mr. Abel," Tom told his brother.

"Reckon I…"

But that was all Tom could manage.

The youngest Liffey boy breathed his last, closed his eyes and was no more.

Abel didn't know what to do, so he just kept on brushing. Sarah pulled the blanket Hector and Maria had gifted them, and covered Tom up to the neck with it. She then carefully removed the brush from Abel's hand and covered the rest of Tom up. Abel just looked down at the body, blinking and blinking and blinking.

Sarah turned to Frank then, who helped her clamber down off the wagon.

"Well then," she smiled into the black man's face. "Reckon we ought to go get Mr. Abel here some burnt bacon," she said, before sauntering off in the direction of the house.

Frank followed her soon thereafter, though Abel didn't leave his brother's side. He looked down at the lifeless corpse before him and leant down close to Tom's ear. Knowing that his brother couldn't hear him, but wishing with all his heart that he still did, he supposed aloud that he might just ask that lady to brush his hair for him. When Tom didn't answer, Abel slowly clambered down off the buggy, the object groaning with relief to be unburdened with the weight of him. Abel watched Sarah disappear into the house, holding his brush. He thought then that he could do with being brushed. And though the lady sure wasn't mama, she would just have to do.

Printed in Great Britain
by Amazon

prune and walking in further into the post office, letting go his hold on the door, causing it to slam against the granny's elbow.

"That hurt young man!" she said. Then, telling him he was the rudest man she'd ever met, receiving a kiss blown by Tom, she at last exited and stomped off down the street.

"Say Pat," said Tom to the man behind the counter. "Any post for me?"

"Is indeed as it happens. Came for you this very morning."

"You know I never get mail," said Tom, "but I thought that there might be something for me today."

"There is. Came through this morning. Think I have it here somewhere. Might be in the bag in the back still. Hold on a second and I'll go look."

"No problem," said Tom, eyeing the vase of flowers sitting on the counter.

By the time Pat O'Grady returned clutching Tom Liffey's letter the flowers in the vase could no longer be seen and there was a flower-shaped lump underneath the front of Tom's overalls.

"Much obliged Pat," said Tom, taking the letter. "Mighty fine day don't you think?" he said, sauntering over in the door's direction.

"Beautiful day," Pat agreed. "Though Tom?"

"Yes Pat?" said Tom.

"The flowers is free this time. Take 'em again without asking and I'll call for the Sheriff."

Tom removed the flowers from beneath his overalls and held them out for Pat to take back.

"Take 'em," said Pat. "Take 'em just this once. But I'm telling you here and now, you take 'em again without asking me, and I'll not be so kindly."

"They're for a girl," said Tom.

"Then that's alright," said Pat O'Grady, watching Tom scurry out the door, closing it gently behind him. Then, just as gently as Tom had closed the door, Pat spoke so gently to himself the words: "Girl's as good a reason as any. Good a reason as any I suppose."

8.

Tom didn't know if the flowers had worked or not, for Sarah hadn't even been gracious enough to open the door to him. Elsie shouted up at him to cut that banging out, once he'd started hammering at that door.

"Don't you keep on at that!" she barked from below. "You break my door then you'd better be able to pay for it son. Seeing as how you ain't got no money for no poke, I'm betting you ain't got the funds for fixing doors none neither."

"No," Tom said to himself. "You're right there."

He laid the flowers down and made to exit the whorehouse, with Elsie swatting at him with her broom as he went.

"We don't need troublemakers son, go on now, out, *out*!"

"I'm going! Alright? I'm fucking *going*!" Tom shouted so loud it startled Elsie, who wasn't used to being spoken to by men like that, at least not in recent years. When she was just starting out some men might shout, some men might even smack her around a little, but it had been a long time since one had spun on her with as much anger as Tom had done then. It thrilled her a little to get such a reaction out of a man. Making a man's blood boil brought a kind of enjoyment to a whore, and as much as Elsie didn't want to admit it to herself any longer, the woman was still just a whore. A businesswoman yes, but a whore nonetheless.

Tom walked the whole way home with a sick feeling that grew and grew with every step. He felt as though that was the last he'd ever see of Sarah, and the thought didn't sit comfortably inside. By the time he reached his home, he had developed a case of the skitters so bad he'd had to burst into a gallop to get back to the outhouse before he soiled his britches.

"*Brother*?" came that voice that made Tom's life a misery, once the younger sibling'd sat down on the commode. "Brother? You back home?"

Tom was nearly doubled over on the commode, with the world and the sun and the moon and the stars streaming out of his rear, firing fast and loudly, like a fanfare of trumpets sounding out its nasty notes.

"Go on away Abel. I'm at my business."

"But I'm hungry," Abel whined.

"I don't care if you're hungry, I'm at my business. Best you just leave me to it and I'll fix you something to eat soon. Now on you…" He then grunted and groaned to try and get a good bit of the rusty water inside out of him. "*GOOO*!" he strained.

"Where were you all day? Didn't tell me where you was going none."

"Went to town," said Tom, kicking on the outhouse door. "Don't keep on aggravating me. Go on now 'fore I get mad."

There was silence then. Tom thought that he was past being bothered.

"*Brother*?" came the whining once again. That did it. Tom didn't even bother wiping his ass. He stood so fast it made his head light, lifted his overalls up to his waist and waddled out to try and hurt his brother. But the elder brother'd backed up already, and Tom tripped, falling face first into the earth. He got up, gritting and baring his teeth, as cross as a grizzly bear.

"Be best you stay still brother. For I intend on whupping you now."

"No!" Abel shouted. "You just leave me be. I was only trying to ask a question."

"You was interrupting me in my business brother. That there's a hanging crime." He got up, pulled the straps of his dungarees up over his shoulders and pounced on poor Abel.

"Don't hurt me! *Don't hurt me*!" Abel squealed like a pig.

"I'll hurt you if I like. You'll know now won't you?

39

You'll know to leave a man be when he's tending to his business. Understand?"

Tom didn't give Abel time to answer. He scooped handfuls of earth up and smeared it in his brother's face. Then he stood up from where he'd held his brother down and began booting the life out of him.

"Get off!" squealed Abel. "I won't bother you none no more."

"Like hell you won't! Why you wouldn't leave me be if someone was to pay you to. Could give you a million dollars and you, Abel *fucking* Liffey'd leave me be just about the same as a moth would a fucking flame. Now I'm sick and tired of tending to you. I'm done with not being able to do my business without being bothered."

Tom delivered one last kick that knocked the wind right out of Abel.

"And I'll tell you this just the once. When it comes time for you to go to sleep, you'll do your own damn brushing at your hair, for I ain't intending on doing it no more. You hear? Speak up now. I can't hear you through your grunting."

"I'll tell mama," said Abel, as helpless as a rabbit caught in a snare trap. "Tell her you done hurt me real bad. Then you'll get in trouble. Real bad trouble too."

Tom hissed in through his teeth, then stooped to grab Abel by his shirt, hauling the helpless brother up onto his feet.

"Fucking listen close now Abel. And I mean it when I tell you I'm done repeating this. Our mama's gone. Gone long ago, and not likely to come back. Matter of fact I'd say the chances of her coming back's about the same as you growing a brain in that there skull of yours. You understand this now, once and for all. Our mama left us. And she ain't ever fixing on coming home."

"You don't know that!" Abel bellowed. "You don't know for sure!"

"Shit! I fucking *do* damn it! I know it ain't never gonna happen. And if you'd get that fact through your fucking head, then maybe we could get along. Maybe we could have some sort

40

of life, where I don't despise you, and you could try and look after yourself some, instead of *waiting* for your mama to come along and wipe the snot from your nose. Now I'm gonna conclude my business because my stomach's hurting. You go on about whatever it was was occupying your mind meanwhile. Then I'll fix us some supper and maybe we could have us a nice evening. Maybe if the pair of us was to sit out on the porch, you, me and Frank, watching the sun go down together. Alright?"

"Alright brother," Abel nodded. "That sounds good."

"Good. Get going now. Shit's running right out of me. My stomach's bad because I had a bad day in town. Maybe tell you about it some once I've sorted myself out."

"I'd like that," Abel smiled.

Tom smiled back and patted his brother on the shoulder, then cupped his brother's rosy cheek.

"Ain't so bad brother," Tom said before backing up towards the outhouse again. As soon as the door latched shut, Abel had forgotten all about what was said, and in a moment or two he was wanting his mama again, convinced that the woman would one day return. Ragging on Tom about it would recommence shortly, just as soon as he'd concluded his business with the commode.

"Come on out brother," Abel said through the door once he'd heard his brother stop splattering out what was inside of him. "Why mama won't want to hear you at your business when she comes."

"Yeah," Tom said, disappointed now more than angry. He knew his brother wasn't right in the head, but he was getting worse by the day. Tom didn't know for how much longer he *could* cope, but he suspected it wasn't a great deal of time. "Take yourself off and go get Frank," he said through the door. "Tell him he'd better get the stove lit now if we're to eat this evening. Can you handle that?"

"Yeah," answered Abel. "Yeah I can handle that."

"Then go and do it," said Tom, beginning to wipe his rear. Once he was done, he stood, stiff from sitting for so long hunched over. Sometimes he got a bit of peace in the commode, so he normally took too much time sat there on his throne. The joints and bones became stiff from the tense position, clicking and cracking once made to move again. A groan and a stretch with a few brittle bony snaps got him out of the outhouse, blinking into a blinding sun.

His guts felt better, being bereft of any and all contents therein. Though the trouble for that day was still to continue. When he stepped in through the back door, Frank was sat at the kitchen table tutting.

"What's the matter with you? Wait. Don't tell me. Abel."

"Ain't Abel Mr. Liffey sir. It's them there pigs. Took my boots off and left them at the back porch and look. Animals has chewed right through the both of them."

Tom laughed.

"Hell Frank, you ought to know better. Why a boot's a banquet for them there pigs. Why they'll chew through anything, boot leather included. Reckon it's your own damn fault."

"Yes sir. Reckon maybe you're right.

"Ain't no reckoning about it," Tom said, taking his seat beside Frank. "That's the fact of the matter. Them there boots is mighty tasty to my pigs. Bastards'll chew through whatever they find. Frank, tell me this. You ever had much luck with women?"

"Why you asking sir? Woman giving you trouble?"

"Sadly yes. Girl in town I got the hots for is fucking with my head. Had a row likes. Left on bad terms, even after I damn near thumped that bedroom door of hers right in. Left it sour so to speak. Was wondering if you have any advice? On the subject of women I mean."

"Women are like flowers sir. Flowers Mr. Liffey sir."

"How do you mean?"

"Well, being kind to 'em's like planting them in fertile soil. Watering them is when you keep 'em happy with kind conversation, good company and food and shelter. Only there's the shade. Shouldn't keep a woman in the shade none."

"What's the shade?"

"Shouting and such. Barking orders and getting into

42

rows regular like. Woman won't flourish under the hand of an angry man. But if you let them be most of the time, treat 'em kindly all the rest of the time, chances are they'll look after you good. Good life with a woman that's treated kindly. 'Least that's what I reckon."

"Why I reckon you're right."

"You been putting your woman in the shade then?"

"That I have Frank. That I have."

"Should take her flowers," Frank suggested.

"Did just that. Didn't work none. Left them outside her door," said Tom, taking the letter out of his back pocket. "Wouldn't open up for me so I said to myself I'll just leave them for her. Maybe calm her down later."

"Maybe," Frank agreed, though his mind elsewhere as he sat staring at the pigs poking their noses around in the muck outside.

Tom studied the letter carefully, a look of horror washing over his countenance. Frank turned eventually to look at his employer, only to find him shaking like a leaf, the letter paper vibrating in his hands.

"You alright?" he asked his boss.

"I don't… it's my…"

"What's the matter Mr. Liffey? Look like you seen you a ghost."

"It's my mama," said Tom. "She's dying Frank. Woman's living, though not for much longer so it seems."

Tom hadn't noticed, but Abel had been standing in the doorway, his jaw hanging down.

"Mama's alive?" he said, startling both Tom and Tom's guts into another bad bout of the skitters. He didn't excuse himself before bolting out of the house, barely making it to the tall wooden outhouse.

9.

"You give me that!" Abel demanded.

"Don't *do* that!" Tom ordered, as Abel's hand latched onto his younger brother's face, fingers finding their way up inside his nostrils.

"Leave each other alone will you!" Frank begged. But the brothers had begun to become entangled up in each other, with the elder brother now exhibiting a strength that for the majority of the time remained quite dormant. Doting on mama however roused this strength from its slumber, as did a letter likewise – especially one concerning his beloved mama.

"My mama wrote to me, didn't she?" he gurned.

"Get off me right now you damn fool. Fuck off and I'll tell you what the letter says. Let go of me first you idiot."

"Fucking give it to me," Abel said, spraying a fine mist of spittle all over his brother's face. Tom wiped it off with the back of his hand.

"Don't spit on me! *Get off*!"

He then shoved with an almighty force even he didn't know he possessed, propelling poor Abel across the kitchen, crashing through the kitchen table, splintering the piece of furniture in two.

"See what you've done now! Damn good table's busted," Tom panted.

"Please give me the letter," Abel began blubbering. "She's my mama too brother."

"You can't read Abel. Tell him Frank for fuck's sake. Tell him this here letter might as well be handed to a blind beggar in town, for all the good it would do him."

"He's right Mr. Abel sir. No sense in giving that there sheet of paper to you. You can't read none. Mr. Tom can sir, so maybe you'd be best leaving the reading up to him."

The elder brother began to gather himself, though the fight hadn't finished. He stepped back, resting on his right foot with the left foot forward. He looked like a mighty mean bull to

Tom, and a bull that was just about ready to snort and charge.

Abel was quick. He thundered across the room and tackled Tom around the middle, shifting the brother out through the back door and on out into the yard. The younger brother hit the dirt at such a speed, and with such a force, that he thought for a moment the elder brother, or the bull he'd transformed into, had broken his back.

He lay groaning on the ground, not daring to move for fear of snapping something out of place irreparably, all while Abel delicately took the piece of parchment and began giggling as he scanned the inky etchings to see if there was anything he could make of them. There wasn't, though this letter had something to do with his mama, which was enough to warrant such diligent coveting of the item in question.

"You've busted my back you bastard," Tom said, still recumbent and reluctant to twitch his spine should something snap. He could wiggle his toes, which he did for a moment. Then he dared to operate his knees and, after establishing that they were in operation, Tom Liffey sat up only to be greeted by Frank's weathered hand held out for him to take and get the younger sibling back up on his feet once more.

"Mighty strong Mr. Tom sir. Mighty strong brother you got there, if you don't mind me saying sir."

"Strong indeed," Tom said quietly as he swatted the dust off the seat of his dungarees. "Don't expect he'll know what that letter says," Tom told Frank. Then much louder, for Abel's benefit, he declared, "Yeah, I reckon I'll just about keep what that there letter said about mama to myself. No need to tell anyone what mama wants or how she is. Ain't no need." Then Tom said very quietly to Frank, "How much you wanna bet he'll be begging in the next minute?"

"Hell," said Frank with a grin, "Got to take all of ten seconds, never mind a minute sir."

Tom clapped Frank on the back and directed his hard-working employee and, if he was being honest, friend into the kitchen.

"Look at the mess he's made," Tom said, surveying the

wreck of a table that once was but was now no more. "Damn good table."

"Fine table Mr. Liffey sir. Fine item for a home to have."

"Yeah," Tom said, rubbing at his stubbly chin which was long overdue the scrape of a razor. "Reckon you'd be able to fix it?"

"I can try, but I ain't gonna promise you none sir. Split right down the middle. Might be able to get two planks. Might be able to nail 'em to it on the underside. Yes sir," Frank said with growing optimism as he planned out the repairing of the table. "Hell, I think that just might do it Mr. Liffey sir. Reckon I ought to at least try. Can't hurt none can it?"

"Can't hurt at all Frank. Fucking back's aching all up and down now. Nincompoop busted something in me."

"Maybe you ought to go see the doctor. In town like."

"Like hell I will. We ain't got the money. Fixing on marrying Sarah soon, and I'll need a ring if I'm gonna do that. The doctor's out of the question. Out of the question Frank. Maybe get me some…"

But Tom stopped suddenly, before he gave away that he had whiskey stashed somewhere in the house. Though it didn't matter much what he said then, for Frank wasn't listening. Any mention of Sarah and Frank clammed up, his train of thought thundering down any track that Sarah wasn't a station on. Frank fretted at the mere mention of her name, and made it his sole ambition to remove any signs of sweetness that might show up on his face for Sarah.

Frank was sweet on her too. And though the loyal employee was a hard worker, and very grateful to Tom for taking him in and giving him a job, his heart still sat in the lap of that lovely whore Sarah Herron. He knew that someday the penny might drop, though that didn't mean he wasn't going to do everything in his power to keep that day from coming any time soon.

As Frank started to examine the splintered table, Tom nudged him and whispered, "Here he comes," in the man's ear.

46

"*Brother?*" Abel whined in that nasally way that went right through Tom. "What does this here letter say?"

It was almost as if nothing had transpired between the two. That there had been no fight and all was forgiven, at least as far as Abel was concerned.

"Sorry brother," said Tom, screwing up his face so hard it looked as though someone had tied a knot with it. "Can't hear you none. What'd you say?"

"What's this here letter say? I can't read none."

"What'd you say? Couldn't hear the magic word."

"What word?" Abel said, cocking his head like a sparrow would at a very large grinning cat.

"Can't hear your request when you ain't said the magic word."

"But I don't know the magic word," Abel said, actually pouting his lips like a little girl that hasn't got the kiss from the boy she fancies.

"Forget it then. You just hold onto that there sheet of paper. You can have it like you wanted. Won't hear about mama though, that's for damn sure," Tom said, thinking about drinking with such fervour he had to show some amount of personal restraint to keep from clambering up and retrieving his jug from atop the cupboard – the jug was laughing down at him, or so Tom thought; chuckling away at the brother's bad back that only the jug and its fiery contents could soothe.

"What's the word?" Abel gurned. "Goddamn tell me. Goddamn tell me right now or I'll thump you."

"Yeah, you just try it. I'll take this here gun out of the holster and hammer your head with it. Then, even if you drop dead from the blow, I'll still go to bed and sleep like a darn baby. Be snoring in five minutes flat once my head hits that pillow. And I mean that. I ain't fooling none. No sir."

"Say sorry," Frank whispered to Abel as he went out to the shed to fetch the two planks he planned to use to sort the table.

"I'm sorry," said Abel. "Alright? I'm sorry. I didn't mean it none."

"You're just saying that 'cause Frank told you to say it.

Don't mean nothing if you've to be told to say it. It's just words when someone else tells you. You ain't sorry none at all. And I ain't telling you shit about what's in that there letter."

Tom didn't want to tell Abel, not because he'd broken the table, *or* indeed damaged his spine some. He didn't want to tell Abel what was in that letter because it meant moaning would start and never cease once Abel had heard what it said, and that the elder brother'd bother his kin until he set off on the journey that Tom didn't want to make.

He looked at his brother. Looked into his sad eyes wet with tears for his mama. Then the thought came to him. It was a wonderful notion and, yes, it certainly would mean making a significant journey, but it might mean being able to get rid of Abel for good. He could put his brother into the care of other relatives, meaning he would be free. Tom was smiling when Frank returned, lumbering in with the lumber.

"You made up then Mr. Tom sir. Hell I am glad to see it. Yes sir I surely am. Ain't nice at all to see two brothers fighting."

"Fix the table Frank," Tom said, still smiling. "You fix the table and I'll fix us all something to eat."

"What about the letter?" Abel asked. "I want to know what's in that goddamn letter!"

"And you will brother. You will. We'll eat us a good solid meal. Then we'll all three sit down and I'll tell you both what was in the letter. That fair enough?"

"Yes sir Mr. Tom. That'd be fine," Frank said, starting to busy himself by turning the table so that the legs were pointing up at the ceiling. He put a couple of nails in his mouth and set about his hammering.

Tom looked to Abel.

"That suit you brother?"

Abel squinted at his brother soberly, before bursting into a radiant smile.

"Suits me just fine," he grinned a gormless grin.

"Good," said Tom. "That's what I like to hear."